UNDEFEATED

BLOOD BOND SAGA: VOLUME FIVE
PARTS 13 - 14 - 15

HELEN HARDT

UNDEFEATED

BLOOD BOND SAGA: VOLUME FIVE
PARTS 13 - 14 - 15

HELEN HARDT

WATERHOUSE PRESS

TABLE OF CONTENTS

To those who challenge what they perceive.

BLOOD BOND SAGA

PART 13

PROLOGUE

DANTE

Anger coursed through me, a black rage that curtained my mind. Blood thrummed in my ears, and I clenched my hands into fists.

Control. I needed my control. Needed Erin.

But Erin wasn't here.

I snarled again, my teeth descending farther.

"That's it. Show yourself, Dante. Show your *true* self."

I'd already unleashed the darkness. I'd needed it to find this place, to return to hell. But now it whirled through me, overtaking my logic, my light, like a gray cloud consuming a sunny day with a raging storm.

I was the raging storm.

A click. A door opening. All the while red noise penetrated my ears.

She stood before me, waiting, her arms outstretched.

Go forward, the cloud urged. *Go and be who you're meant to be.*

I grabbed fistfuls of my hair. *Must fight. Must fight. Must fight.*

Dante!

I jerked, looking backward toward the sound of a voice I knew. A voice I recognized.

A voice that meant something to me. A voice that exuded light.

Light...

But the black cloud edged out the light.

I squinted.

Three images. Two men, one woman. A daze swept over me. I squinted but could not see them clearly.

Control, son.

Another voice I knew, but it wasn't connected to anything.

My gaze was drawn back to *her.*

Dr. Bonneville! I knew it!

The feminine voice again. I blinked. Two men, one woman. I knew these people.

Knew these people...

Or maybe I didn't.

A duel of swords clashed within me, between light and dark. Pain. Searing pain lanced my organs. I growled, letting my fangs sharpen to their most lethal points. I snarled toward the three images. I recognized them, as if I'd encountered them in a dream. Or a dream within a dream.

Or a nightmare.

Dante!

Be strong, son.

Remember that part inside you, the part no one can touch.

Remember...

Remember...

Remember...

Re...mem...

Re...

The voices became high-pitched buzzing, and the images...
They blurred into nothingness.

Nothingness...

Then I turned toward the blond woman, whose image was so clear, as if she were outlined by fine black ink.

I dropped to my knees.

"I have returned, my queen."

ONE

Erin

"N*o!*"

I tried to race forward, but Jay grabbed my arm, pulling me back against him abruptly.

"No, Sis. It's not safe."

I pulled, desperate to disentangle myself from my brother. "Let me go! He needs me!"

"Erin," River said solemnly, "he doesn't even know you right now."

"Dr. Bonneville!" I yelled. "Let him go! Let him go!"

"You three need to leave before she decides to take you."

I looked upward toward the sound of Julian's voice. Nothing. He didn't materialize.

"I will not leave his side," he continued. "I promise you."

"I'm not leaving." I pulled once more against my brother's strength, trying to free myself from his grip. No one was going to keep me from Dante. "I can get through to him. I know I can!"

Dr. Bonneville was ignoring us, as if we were nothing more

than three flies on the wall.

To her, perhaps, we were.

She was a vampire. Dr. Bonneville. I'd had my hunches, but to be confronted with it, to know the truth, finally...

She couldn't smell River because he was also a vampire. Jay and I were wearing the basil and calendula potion that protected us from most vampires, but would it protect us from her? She was clearly very powerful to hold Dante in thrall.

Rage bubbled within me. I didn't care if my scent made her crazy. I wasn't going anywhere. Not without Dante.

"Get her out of here," Julian said.

Did he mean me? Oh, no. I was not leaving.

Jay forced me outside the room and back into the dark tunnel anyway.

"Can you find your way back outside?" River asked Jay.

"Yeah. I think so."

"Good. Take her home. Keep her safe."

"What about you?" my brother asked.

"I'm staying."

My mouth dropped open. "Stop deciding what I'm going to do. We're *all* staying. That's why we came here."

"No." He stuffed his fingers into his pockets. "I didn't expect Dante to get... He was glamoured. Glamoured. I never would have believed it. She has some kind of glamour over him."

"But you said vampires can't get glamoured!" Jay's tone seemed almost accusatory.

"Apparently they can. Or she has him under some other kind of spell." River turned to me. "So that's your Dr. Bonneville. She's the one. You were right."

"I didn't want to be right." I looked down at my thigh

covered in black spandex leggings. Dr. Bonneville had been feeding from me. Who else could it have been?

And she had fed from Dante. Icicles chilled my veins.

"Get her out of here, partner."

Jay met River's gaze. "No. We're staying. We're not leaving you here alone. My unborn child is in there. Remember?"

"Are you nuts? She'll glamour the two of you, and you won't be any help to Dante or anyone else."

"What makes you think she won't glamour you? Clearly she's able to control Dante."

"It's a chance I have to take. My father's in there somewhere. Lucy's in there. Em is in there. I'm going to—" He drew in a deep breath. "I'm going to use myself as bait."

"You've lost your mind," Jay said.

"Have I? She's got my father and my cousins. I'm from the same stock."

"If she wanted you, she would have come for you by now," Jay said. "No offense. I'm sure you're great stock."

The two of them went back and forth like a couple of bullies on the playground, quarreling over who was tougher. *You're going. No, I'm staying. No, you're going. Hell, no. I'm staying.* The words became muffled in my ears, as if a pillow were over my head, or as if I were hearing them from underwater.

Soon they were completely unintelligible.

Invisible cellophane suffocated my skin, even as goose bumps rose all over me. My heart pounded wildly, and bile clawed up my throat.

Dante was in there. With *her*.

Fear boiled within me, but if she thought I'd back down and let her have him, she thought wrong. He was mine. I would not give him up.

Somehow, I'd get through to him.

If I couldn't?

I'd take care of *her*. I *knew* this woman. I'd worked with her for years. I knew the ins and outs of her narcissistic personality. Plus, I had one more reason I couldn't leave—a damned good one.

Dante needed me. Sooner or later, he'd require sustenance. He would *not* feed from her. Not as long as my heart was pumping blood.

River and Jay were still arguing back and forth. About what? I didn't know at this point. I didn't care.

I knew only one thing.

I wasn't going anywhere.

TWO

DANTE

"I've missed you, Dante." The woman touched me under my chin. "Remarkable. You've become even more handsome. More majestic."

"Thank you, my queen."

"I know I was hard on you while you were here before. You bore it well." She fingered my cheek.

A chill rushed through me. Not a good chill. The torture. The electrocution. *She* had been the mastermind behind all of it.

"Why? You dare to ask me why?"

I lay limp, knives of pain lancing through my body, my flesh buzzing from the electricity the goons had sent surging through me.

"Why?" I whispered once more.

Why do you take my blood? Why do you force me to drink

yours? Why do you have me tortured? Why do you make me fight? Why do you reward me with human blood that I can't resist? Why, after rewarding me, do you torture me again?

All those questions, but all that came out was another weak, "Why?"

⚜

Now here I stood, before her. She looked upon me with admiration in her icy-blue eyes.

You dare to ask me why?

For once, she would answer for her crimes upon my body and mind. I met her cold gaze. "Why?"

She waved away my question with a flick of her hand. "You'll know everything before long."

"Where's my sister? What have you done with her?"

"Your sister is part of a higher purpose, just as you are. Just as everyone here is, Dante."

"I don't understand."

"You will. When you're ready." She touched my arm.

Her touch burned like someone had ground a lit cigarette into my skin. I yanked my arm away.

My queen. I called her my queen. That's not right. Why did I do that?

I bared my fangs with a growl.

"Put those away. I'll let you know when I want you to feed." She touched me again.

And again, the burn.

"Now, come."

She opened the door, and light flooded into a hallway. Had I been here before? I recalled only darkness. Never light.

Light. I knew light. Light was something—some*one*—in my life.

Love and light.

Someone had shown me...

Scattered jigsaw pieces scrambled together in my mind. A body. A face. Full pink lips. Piercing peridot eyes. No sweeter blood.

Erin. Her name was Erin.

A heavy fog lifted from my brain as I forced the dark energy out.

Erin. My perfect love. She'd come here, and I'd turned my back on her.

How could she ever forgive me?

I clenched my hands into fists, ready to overpower this horrible and evil woman—

"Your sister and the others are safe," she said.

My hands unclenched.

"They are vitally important to my research."

I forced myself to calm. As much as I'd have liked to take *her* out, I needed to stay aware of the big picture. I was here now. I'd penetrated her lair. Now I had to find Emilia and the others and free them.

I'd last fed about twelve hours ago. I could go a week without blood if I had to... But the bond. Could I go that long without Erin's blood?

I inhaled.

No specific human scents. Apparently I could still smell only Erin. That wouldn't help me in finding Lucy and the other human females who'd disappeared.

"Where are we going, my queen?"

Those last two words were bitter on my tongue, but better

for her to think I was still under her spell, that I hadn't chased the darkness away.

Darkness rising.

The darkness.

The darkness had helped me find this place. If I could learn to control it, I could use it.

"I'm taking you back. Back to your dungeon, Dante."

Oh, hell, no. I bared my teeth at her. Rage bristled inside me, and energy pulsed through my veins. I clenched my hands into fists. I was bigger and stronger. I would *not* go back there.

"You returned to me," she said. "Did you think I wouldn't keep you this time?"

"Think again." The darkness. The darkness that was her would now be her undoing. My fangs sharpened.

"You have more to learn."

"Why did you let me go, then?" I growled. "Why did you unchain me, let me escape?"

"You had things to learn that you could only learn in the world. You learned a lot, Dante. Most of all, you learned how powerful you are, and what you can become. But you're not ready yet. You require more training."

"Training? Is that what you call it? Forced captivity? Torture? Fighting to the death?"

She turned and met my gaze, her cuspids descending into sharp points. "You are magnificent, Dante, but don't overestimate your importance just yet. You still have more to prove."

"Your teeth don't scare me. They've been embedded in my flesh, remember?"

"Oh, you *are* formidable." She snarled, a sound almost like a groan of gratification that seemed to shake the walls. "So perfect in nearly every way. Stronger than your own father and his twin brother. But you are not indispensable. If you fail me, there is one more."

Though shudders threatened to rack my body, I tamped them down.

River.

She could only be talking about River. He was also the son of one of the Gabriel twins.

"You leave him alone," I gritted out.

"He has his own purpose to serve," she said nonchalantly, but then she narrowed her eyes. "You were chosen over him for good reason, but he is just as perfect. It's always prudent to have a spare in place. Just in case."

"I'm here, son. She cannot hear me."

Thank God! My father was back.

"I was always here. I never left your side. You left *me* for a little while."

I couldn't reply. I couldn't even nod and take the chance that *she* might detect a difference in my demeanor.

"It's okay. Do not move. Do not make any indication that I'm here."

Did I need to let him know I could hear him? I didn't dare.

"Listen well, Dante. She doesn't know I'm here. She's a woman of science. From what I can surmise, she doesn't concern herself with anything other than the science of the earthly plane. As far as she is concerned, when my body died, I no longer existed."

I remained silent.

"As you are developing new powers, it seems I am too. After I knocked my father off his feet, I conferred with a few others in the ghostly realm. Apparently, most ghosts cannot move things on the earthly plane no matter how hard they try."

I inhaled harshly at his words, but then exhaled slowly so as not to give myself away. She continued speaking, but I concentrated on my father.

"It's possible something was done to me while I was held captive—something that changed the energy that is me. I don't know. Something was done to both of us. I have no idea whether my blood was tampered with as yours was, and there's no way to tell now, as my body has been cremated. But I'm certain experimentation is being done here. Experimentation that I fear you and I were a part of."

"You *will* listen to me!"

I jerked. I'd been much more interested in my father's words.

"Pretend," my father said. "Show her she still has control over you. Then ask to see your sister. I will not leave your side, but I'll stay quiet for now."

I swallowed the nausea creeping up my throat. "I apologize, my queen."

"Yes, that's better."

"Why am I here, my queen? How big is this place?"

"That's none of your concern for now."

"Then it will be my concern sometime in the future?"

"Perhaps. If you prove yourself worthy."

"How do I do that, my queen? I want more than anything to be worthy of you." I nearly retched at my own words.

"Please, Dante," she said with an eye roll. "I wasn't born yesterday. In fact, I was born long ago, and I have you—among others—to thank for my long life."

THREE

Erin

"Would the two of you please shut the fuck up?"

River and Jay turned to me, their gazes both burning.

At least they'd stopped bickering.

"I'm not leaving." I set my hands on my hips, hoping I looked stronger and more indignant than I actually felt. "I have the most at stake here. If what Bill told us about the blood bond is true, I will die if I don't feed Dante. So there. Top that one."

"Erin—" Jay began.

"Don't. I need to be here."

"You'll be glamoured," River said.

"I have to believe"—I paused a moment, inhaling deeply—"that I will find Dante, or that he will find me when he needs to feed. Our connection is so strong, and our need for each other too great. We will find each other and keep each other from death. We *will*."

"But—"

I stopped River with a hand on his arm. "The bond is

strong. It will resist a glamour. I have to believe that. Even if I *am* glamoured, Dante will be able to find me and take what he needs. But I have to *be* here for that to happen."

"You'd let him feed from you while you're glamoured?" Jay asked. "Isn't that kind of like...rape?"

Jay was ever the older brother, always trying to protect me. "It's not like that, Jay. We have a bond. There is always consent between us for a feeding. There always has been."

River started to speak again, and again I stopped him.

"Please. I know neither of you understand because you don't share a bond like this with anyone. I can't describe it, other than to say that we are meant to be in every way. We will have children someday, and our first child will be—"

I stopped abruptly.

The vision I'd had during an orgasm came hurtling back into my mind in vivid color. The beautiful baby boy, our son, who I handed to Dante.

He was vampire.

Dante said he'd had the same vision.

"What is it?" River asked.

I rubbed my forehead, thinking. "Levi Gaston thought he could produce a vampire child with his human wife, but he wasn't successful."

"Of course he wasn't successful," River said. "It's impossible."

"But what if it's not?" My mind raced. "What if there's a way to tamper with genetics? To produce a vampire child through mating a human and a vampire? Oh my God. We've got to get back in there. We've got to find Emilia."

"Are you saying that my child could be a vampire?" Jay asked.

"I don't know," I said. "But they took Emilia for some reason, and they wanted to make sure she was pregnant. They made her take a pregnancy test before they took her. And they took the others, all with B positive blood..."

I flashed back quickly to my dream. The baby crying. And the blood bank full of nothing but B positive units.

"Something about the blood type and the positive Rh factor must be the key."

"The key to what?" Jay asked.

"The key to producing a vampire baby from a human and vampire."

"I think you're stretching here, Erin," River said.

"Bonneville wanted me pregnant. Why else would she have replaced my pills with placebos?"

"We still don't know she's the one who did it," Jay reminded me.

"Who else could it have been? She came to my home to tell me she was going on vacation. Why? This isn't a woman who fraternizes with the hospital staff. So why would she come to my home just to tell me something when she could have called or texted? Why, except to have access to my home and my pills?"

"You don't think—"

"She let Dante go," I said, ignoring my brother. "She let him escape so he could find me. Get me pregnant."

"Erin," River said, "you and the others have B positive blood, true. But if a B positive human can mate with a vampire and produce a vampire child, we'd have figured it out by now. There would also be a lot more vampires. We'd still be a minority, but we'd be numbering in the millions."

"Not necessarily," I said. "B is the second-least common of all the types."

"That makes it the third-most common," my smartass brother said.

"Thanks for that," I snapped. Then I sighed. "You're right. Just by random selection there would be a lot more vampires in the world if mating a vampire with a B positive human produced one. I'm a nurse. What was I thinking?"

"You were thinking you want an answer," Jay said. "Nothing wrong with that. We know B positive blood has something to do with all of this. We just don't know what."

"I hate to interrupt this scientific discussion—"

I glared at River. "Don't even *think* about rolling your eyes."

"Hey"—he held up his hands in mock surrender—"I'd never."

"Right."

"Whatever. We've got to get back to basics here. We need a plan. If I'm going to be bait—"

"Sorry, partner," Jay interrupted. "We've already determined that Erin and I are staying, so scrap that idea."

"Why? It's a good idea."

"To put yourself in harm's way?" Jay shook his head. "Do you think your father would want that?"

"He has a point, River," I agreed.

"You're right. But we've got to do something. Maybe we can go talk to Bea. See if she can help."

"How would we get to her?" Jay asked. "By the time we did, someone could cut off this entrance."

"I doubt it," River said. "Bonneville has a way to get in and out. So do the Claiborne vamps. If this isn't the only entrance, there has to be another one."

"Yeah," Jay said, "but do we want to have to go to the

trouble to find that one? We already know where this one is."

"Another good point, River," I said.

"I'm beginning to feel ganged up on here." River rubbed his forehead. "We have only a little food and water with us. It won't last more than a couple days."

"Then we'll just have to find the women, your dad, and Dante, and free them in a few days. Simple as that." I dug into my backpack and pulled out my mother's book. Still glued shut. "Damn."

"We could sure use the wisdom of the book right now," Jay said. "Maybe it's not shielded after all. Maybe it's just glued shut."

"Bea assured me it was shielded," I said, though I was feeling pretty skeptical myself at this point.

"Then, apparently, if what Mom says is true, we don't need the book yet," Jay said.

"We sure as hell need something." River shoved his hands into the pockets of his black jeans. "If you two are bound and determined to stay here, I won't try anymore to talk you out of it. But there won't be anything I can do for you if you get glamoured."

"Don't worry about that," Jay said. "If it happens, you get your sister and the others out of here. That's what we came here to do, and that's what we should each, individually, concentrate on, no matter what happens to any of us."

I swallowed the acidic fear in my throat. My brother was right. We had one goal here—to free those being held captive against their will. Once that was done, we needed to get the hell out of this place. We could study the *Texts* and figure out what was happening to Dante once we were back home.

If we made it home.

FOUR

DANTE

Had I gone too far?

"Easy, son," my father said.

Yes. Clearly, in my father's eyes, I had gone too far. What had I been thinking? Baring my fangs at her and then suddenly wanting more than anything to be worthy of her?

Might as well go for broke at this point.

"I want to see my sister."

"I assure you she is safe."

"Fine. She's safe. She's also my sister, and I want to see her."

"You doubt my word?" Her eyes turned an even icier light blue.

"I heard her scream when I was coming down here," I said, willing myself not to lose my temper. "I know her voice. If she's safe, why was she screaming?"

"You must be mistaken, Dante."

"I'm not mistaken. I heard a baby cry, and I heard two different women scream. The second scream was my sister."

"Perhaps you were hearing things," she said.

I paused a moment to see if my father had any advice.

He remained silent.

Damn!

I inhaled. Best to stay focused.

"I want to see my sister," I said again.

"I assure you she is safe."

Big *déjà vu*. Were we going to repeat the entire previous conversation?

"Try a different angle, Dante. Thank her, and then ask again."

Thank her? For kidnapping my sister? I exhaled, gathering my nerves.

"Thank you for keeping her safe," I said, forcing the words out. "I'd still like to see her. She's pregnant, and I want to make sure she's all right."

"She's fine. Her baby is fine."

"Thank you, my queen. May I please see her anyway? It would mean a lot to me."

She sighed. "If I let you see her, you must then go straight back to your dungeon. Is that clear?"

"Tell her yes, son."

Was he crazy? As much as I wanted to see Emilia and assure her I was here to protect her, no way could I go back to that horrible place.

I remained silent.

"Tell her yes. I'll find a way to get you out of it. I've tried moving through this underground compound without you, but most of it is shielded. I have not yet seen your sister."

My father had never let me down. But what if he couldn't keep me from being taken back to the dungeon? Back to true hell?

Trust, Dante.

The words came from within me. From the light within me. From Erin.

"Yes, my queen. If you allow me to see and speak to my sister, I will go back to my dungeon."

I'd almost said "willingly" but thought better of it. This way, if my father couldn't change anything, I could fight her and not break my word.

"Very well. You've been through a lot, and you made your way back to me. I suppose you deserve a small reward."

She led me to another door, a double door this time, made of stainless steel. She inserted a key into the lock—

One of the disgusting human goons walked in. "It's your lucky day, shithead. The queen has something to teach you." He unbound my leather restraints and put a black mask over my head.

I inhaled through my mouth so I didn't have to smell his unbearable stench. I said nothing. Didn't matter anyway. If I asked questions, he either wouldn't respond or he'd lie to me. I'd eventually find out where I was going.

He led me to another room, this one with more light. Harsh fluorescent light. Sitting at a table was a masked vampire. He had no scent.

"Sit down," the vampire said gruffly.

I stood.

"You hard of hearing? I said sit down. I'm not here to hurt you. I'm here to teach you something."

On the table before him sat several different kinds of locks.

A padlock. A combination lock. A deadbolt like one used on a front door.

I sat. The vampire could very well be lying, but what the hell else was there to do?

"Ever pick a lock before?" he asked.

I shook my head.

"You will today. It's a skill that'll come in handy when you're out of here."

I stayed silent. Why would picking a lock come in handy? I was no thief.

"Why do I need to learn to pick a lock?" I asked.

"Don't have the foggiest. I do what I'm told, and today I was told to teach you how to pick locks." He leaned forward, and something sparkled on the lapel of his jacket.

A gold pin...with an odd-looking fleur-de-lis engraved on it. I squinted to make it out. The two downward petals were pointed, like fangs. I was intrigued. Should I ask about it? He'd probably lie.

No. I wouldn't ask about the strange symbol. But I did have another question.

"Why do you do what she tells you?"

His dark-blue eyes burned as he met my gaze. "You think you're the only one around here who gets tortured? I like to avoid it as much as possible. Now let's get to work."

⚜

Dark-blue eyes. The symbol. Decker? Had Decker taught me how to pick locks? I'd been able to pick the lock at Em's apartment. Was that the reason *she* taught me how to pick locks? So I could get into Em's apartment?

No. First, it couldn't have been Decker. He would have recognized me when we fought that day in the alley. I touched my face. No. I'd been masked. The goon had given me a mask. If Decker had been my instructor, he wouldn't have recognized me when we fought.

Giles had recognized me, or at least recognized something in me. He'd said, "It's him. The one she talks about."

Em's apartment. Had everything so far been preordained? Orchestrated by *her*? All to bring me to this point? And if so, what about Erin? What about our blood bond? Had *she* orchestrated *that* as well?

She was the female boss they worked for. That part I'd figured out a while ago, but now it all made more sense. She was dealing not only in certain drugs but also in B positive blood.

She opened the stainless-steel door, and I followed her into—

"Oh my God," I said. "This is a hospital."

"Fully equipped and staffed," she said. "Took me decades to get it built." She nodded to nurses and orderlies as we walked.

None of them seemed to take any notice of me, even when I met their eyes directly. I inhaled. Again, no unique human scents, but I did smell the iron and oxygen combination that was blood.

There was a blood bank here. My bet was that it was full of B positive.

"What do you do here?" I asked.

"All questions will be answered in good time."

"Why not now? I've been asking question after question since I left, and you've answered with riddles and metaphors. Why did you go to all the trouble to build a secret hospital under New Orleans?"

"Easy, son."

Thank God! My father was still here.

Wait! She'd said it had taken her decades to get it built. She couldn't be more than forty or so.

"This place is amazing," I said. "It truly took decades to build?"

"It did. But I was determined."

"How many decades?"

"Why does that matter?"

Because you're not very old. Though she'd said earlier that she was older than I knew, and that she had me to thank. "I suppose it doesn't. What do you do here?"

"Research, mostly."

"You don't perform operations on people?"

"Of course I do. In the name of research."

I swallowed the lump in my throat. "Are you a surgeon, then?"

"I'm a hematologist and an emergency medicine physician. I'm perfectly capable of minor surgeries, but I bring in actual surgeons for the more difficult cases."

Logan Crown. I didn't dare mention his name. I didn't want her to know what I was thinking, but I had the eerie feeling she already knew exactly where I'd been and what had happened to me every minute since I'd been gone.

She'd been in my head, whether by her doing or my own. Now I was convinced she'd been watching my every move as well.

We finally turned down a hallway. "Here's where the patients stay."

"Patients?"

"Of course, patients. I'm a doctor. I took an oath to cause no harm."

I resisted the urge to scoff. Her definition of "causing no harm" clearly didn't include kidnapping, torture, and false imprisonment.

We walked to a closed door, and she opened it. "Emilia, I have someone here who wants to see you."

FIVE

Erin

"Does something seem off to you?" River asked Jay.

"Partner, this whole thing is off, wouldn't you say?"

"I mean, we were able to get right in. The door wasn't locked. No one was guarding it."

"Yeah, the thought had occurred to me."

"For God's sake!" I interrupted. "Lucy is in there! And Bea as good as said they were going to kill her. We have to get to her before that happens!"

River stiffened. His distress was clear. "Are you sure that's what she said?"

"It's difficult to decipher Bea's quotes sometimes, but I'd rather err on the side of caution. We've got to find her."

"She's not killing people," Jay said. "She returned two of them unharmed."

"So what? Are you willing to take a chance with Lucy's life?"

"No," River said adamantly. "No, I'm not."

"Neither am I. So we go back in there, and we find Lucy. If we find her, we'll find the others. I just hope we're not too late." Shivers coursed through me. The thought of Lucy not being alive—I couldn't even wrap my head around the idea. We had to find her and get her to safety.

"We still need to be cautious," Jay warned. "The fact that we were able to get right in could signal a trap."

"You want to look for a back door?" River asked.

"Are you guys kidding me? We go in the way we know!"

"Erin," River said, "I care just as much about Lucy as you do. But they know we're here now. They expect us to go back in. I think your brother has a point."

"Fuck both of you, then." I stalked forward toward the wooden door and opened it. Again I shielded my eyes against the fluorescent light.

Jay pulled me backward until I *oofed* when my back hit his hard chest. "Are you nuts? That woman inside is dangerous, and she already knows we're here."

"Dante will protect us," I said.

"Sis, Dante didn't even know you. He was under some kind of spell."

"No." I disentangled myself from my brother, only to have his partner grab me instead. "Let go of me!"

"Quiet," River admonished.

"Why? You've already said they know we're here. If they know anything about any of us, they know we won't stop until we free our friends. Your father is in there somewhere too, River. Julian says he doesn't have much time left."

"What?" River froze.

"I'm sorry. I shouldn't have blurted it out like that, but that's what Julian told me. He said our first priority is Emilia,

Lucy, and the others, but then we have to find Braedon. Julian feels strongly that his time is running out."

"Fuck." River shoved his hands through his hair, which was growing longer.

"Still want to look for that back door?" I said to my brother.

"No, Sis. You win. We're going in. You with me, Riv?"

River nodded, his eyes glazed over. "I was going in anyway. I tried to get you two to leave. My place is here, with my cousins, my father, and with Lucy. I have nothing on the surface right now. Everything I care about is here."

"Everything I care about is here too," I said. "Except my parents, of course. But Dante and Lucy are in there. And I care deeply about Emilia and the others as well."

"My child is in there," Jay said solemnly. "My place is here also."

"Erin, you stay between us like before." River grabbed his gun out of his holster. "I'm going in armed, Jay."

"Right behind you." Jay removed his gun as well.

River eased open the wooden door, and we all blinked against the harsh lighting. The room was oblong and now empty. The door where Dr. Bonneville had stood—where Dante had knelt before her—sat in the distance, seemingly farther away than I remembered.

I blinked. Something was wrong with my perspective.

River led the way, and as we walked, the door seemed to be getting farther and farther away. I blinked again. This room was an illusion. Everything was an illusion.

Until the door appeared abruptly in front of me.

River turned the knob slowly.

SIX

DANTE

"**G**et away from me!"

My sister's voice.

"Em," I said softly. "It's me."

She lay in a hospital bed, her abdomen hooked up to what I assumed was a fetal monitor. A rapid heartbeat echoed from a screen that also showed an ultrasound image of Em's baby. At least I assumed it was the baby. It looked like a bunch of squiggles to me. Her dark hair was stringy around her shoulders, and her complexion—well, it was better than when I'd last seen her. Maybe they *were* taking care of her here.

"Dante?"

"Yeah, it's me."

"I'm here also, Emilia." My father's voice. "Do not let anyone know you hear me. I'm audible only to you and Dante."

"It's good to see you. Can you get me out of here?"

I turned to *her*. "Why is she here?"

"She requires special treatment. The baby she carries has a positive Rh factor, and you know how difficult pregnancy and childbirth are for our women. We're going to make sure both she and this baby survive."

I regarded *her*. Though physically young and beautiful, she exuded ugliness. And evil. Yet was *she* truly doing good here, helping Em carry her baby to term? Em's fair pallor had returned, replacing the green.

"Why are you telling me this?"

"Why shouldn't I? You won't be leaving here, so there's no one you could tell."

"Are you feeling okay, Em?" my father asked. "Blink if you are."

Em blinked.

Good. She was okay. For now, at least. If she was telling the truth, Em would be fine...at least until the baby was born. We'd have her out of here way before then, if I had anything to say about it.

"Is there a woman named Lucy here?" my father asked. "Blond hair, blue eyes?"

Em blinked.

"Is she okay?"

Emilia widened her eyes slightly.

Shit. What did that mean?

"You don't know?" my father said.

This time Em blinked again.

"Dante," my father said, "I need to leave you."

My heart fluttered, but I made no reaction.

"I need to see Bea. I need her to break the shield surrounding this place so I can enter all areas. She should be able to use my ashes."

No! Don't leave us, Dad!

But the words never left my vocal cords, nor did the

expression change on my face.

I couldn't let it.

Inside me, fear was churning. I needed my father. Needed his presence and his wisdom. Needed whatever new power he was developing. Needed his energy.

All this I had to keep harnessed up inside me.

How could he leave me? Leave Em?

My fangs elongated, but I kept my mouth closed and the growl lodged in my throat. The darkness swirled within me, threatening to consume me as it had earlier.

Control, son.

Damn his words!

My sister lay before me, unable to speak of our father. "Em," I said, willing my voice not to shake with rage, "everything will be all right."

The words I longed to say to her I could not.

I'll get you out of here. I'll free you and the others. I'll do whatever it takes.

"Your sister needs her rest, Dante," *she* said. "We need to leave now. You made a promise to me."

Damn my father! He'd promised to find a way to keep me from going back to the dungeon. Now, he'd forsaken me, forsaken Em, forsaken his twin brother. All for what? To get a nutty voodoo priestess to somehow get him access to the shielded parts of this place?

I suppressed a growl.

"I want to see Lucy," I said to her.

"The deal was that you'd see your sister, and then you'd go back in chains."

I showed my teeth. "New deal, my *queen*. I see Lucy, or I go nowhere."

"Who do you think you are, giving *me* orders?" She bared her fangs at me.

I laughed. Mine were twice as long.

"You'll come with me. Now."

"Not until I see Lucy."

"Lucy hasn't been cooperative," she said. "We've had to take...measures."

"What kind of measures?"

"That's not your concern."

Bea had quoted something about a wolf. I couldn't remember the words, but Erin had thought they meant that Lucy was going to be killed.

Not on my watch.

"Is she alive?"

"She is. For now."

"What do you mean for now?"

"I don't mince words, Dante. I say *exactly* what I mean."

"The priestess was right," I said, more to myself than to her. "You're going to kill her."

"I'm not a killer...though in her case, it has crossed my mind."

"What about your oath as a physician, as a healer? You made a big deal of it minutes ago."

"The little wolf is a danger to what I'm trying to accomplish here. I brought her here for her value in research, but she refuses to cooperate. Drugging her does no good. Something in her physiology has made her immune to all the sedatives I've tried."

"That's not possible," I said. "She just had surgery for a stab wound. She must have been sedated for that."

"They must have knocked her out with a mallet.

Unfortunately, no one here knows much about wolf physiology. Tying her down does no good. She forces the change and escapes. So I've done the only thing I could."

"Which is?" Rage oozed out of me.

"She is in training. Then she'll go into the arena."

Fight or die in the arena.

I seethed. "Against whom?"

"Against whomever I see fit." She smiled. "Perhaps against *you.*"

SEVEN

Erin

"Emilia is alive."

I jolted at the words. "Julian?"

"I'm here but not visible. Em and her baby are being closely monitored."

"And the baby is okay too?" Jay asked.

"From what I can tell, yes," Julian's disembodied voice said.

"What about Lucy?" River asked.

"I don't know yet. Dante is asking to see her."

"Why aren't you with him?" I demanded. "Is he all right?"

"He is, for now. He let the darkness overtake him for a few minutes, and I'm sorry you had to witness that, but he's back in his right mind now."

"That's why he didn't seem to see or hear us?" I said.

"Correct. He feels terrible about it."

"Not terrible enough," River said. "If he'd been in his right mind, we could have overtaken his queen right then and there."

"Don't underestimate her. There's something strange about her. Something I haven't been able to put my finger on yet. She's not what she seems. You were right about your Dr. Bonneville, Erin."

"She's not *my* Dr. Bonneville. I can't stand the sight of her. And if she's responsible for what Dante has been through—" I curled my hands into fists. "I wish I could take her out myself."

"She's got a whole hospital built underneath here," Julian continued. "I can't get to any of the other facilities. They're all heavily shielded. I'm going above ground to get Bea to force me through the shield with my ashes."

I gulped. "Bea says breaking a shield takes dark magic. I asked her to break the shield on my book, and she refused."

"She won't refuse me," Julian said. "Besides, all I need is for her to let my energy pass through the shield. She should be able to do that with my ashes."

"But Dante!"

"Dante is not happy that I've left, and I hated to leave him, but my hands are tied. I can't do anything for him at the moment, and he'll understand when I can get through to find out where my brother and the others are."

"Don't be long," River said. "We need you down here."

"I won't be. I'll let you know when I return."

"No," I said. "Don't worry about us. Stay with Dante." Was I the only one concerned about Dante? I was beginning to feel like it. I itched to get to him, to be with him, to protect him in any way I could.

"Dante would want me making sure the three of you are okay. I will see you, and then I'll see him. Be careful. Please. And good luck."

"Wait! Why aren't there—"

"Too late, Erin," River said. "He's gone."

I sighed. "I wanted to know why the door isn't locked. Why there aren't any guards or anything. If this is a top-secret hospital, shouldn't it be harder to get into?"

"Yeah," River said. "It doesn't take detective training to know they want us here. They're letting us get in."

"Too easy. They'll know we're armed, too," Jay said.

"What do we have that will surprise them?" I asked. "How can we not walk into a trap?"

"We outsmart them, Sis." Jay turned to River. "You're a vampire. Help us think like vampires."

"I'm not sure we have to," River said thoughtfully, scratching his temple. "Now that I think about it, I don't believe anyone in there will harm us. Well, relatively speaking. I don't think they'll kill us."

"How can you be sure?" I asked.

"If your hypothesis is correct, Erin, and they're trying to find a way to produce vampire offspring from mating vampires and humans, we're all very valuable to them. I'm a full-blooded vampire, and the two of you are quarter-bloods. One of you is bonded to a vampire, and the other is father to a vampire's baby. They're not luring us in so they can get rid of us. They're luring us in so they can study us."

"This is all a setup. Is that what you're saying?" Jay rubbed his forehead. "It does make a certain amount of sense. Why else would they leave this placed unlocked?"

"So Dante could come back," I said. "He got here before us, remember? She was luring him back."

"That's a good point too," River agreed. "This could all be circumstance. The entrance was open for Dante, and we simply followed him."

"And remember what Lucien's note said," I reminded them. "It said we'd find what we *need* between the doors of perception. There's something here that we need."

"Simple enough," Jay said. "We *need* to find the missing women, and they are most certainly here. We know for sure that Emilia is, and that means the others are probably here too."

"It also means that this Lucien Crown fellow knows what's going on here," River said. "How else would he have known about the doors of perception?"

"True," I agreed. "He was also into research, and he lost his medical license because of it. He was onto something. Something the vampire council didn't want him researching. Something to do with pregnancy and childbirth in vampire women. But why? Why wouldn't the council want him to find a way to make childbirth easier for vampire women?"

"You got me," River said. "My mother and my aunt might be alive today if Crown could have continued his research."

"Our grandmother too," Jay said. "This whole thing stinks like shit, if you ask me."

"If my dumbass grandfather hadn't tried to poison himself—"

"He poisoned himself to get us away from Lucien Crown," I said. "But why? Why wouldn't Bill want to make pregnancy and childbirth easier for women of his kind? I don't understand."

"And he certainly won't tell us," Jay said.

"His poisoning came at another opportune time." River rolled his eyes. "He never got around to telling Uncle Jules what he'd read in the *Texts*. The old coot planned all of this. Mark my words."

"But why?" I said again. "Why wouldn't he want pregnancy and childbirth to be easier for his people? I'll never understand."

"Unless..." River stroked his chin, as if rubbing an invisible goatee.

"Unless what, partner?"

"This is going to sound pretty out there."

"This whole thing is out there, Riv," Jay said. "Lay it on us."

"What if making childbirth easier for vampire women leads to some other problem? Something Bill knows about?"

"What kind of problem could it lead to?" I asked. "Other than having more vampires in the world. Why would that be an issue?"

"It wouldn't be. Not for any of us, at least. Humans would still vastly outnumber us, and for the most part, vampires have been living side by side with humans for millennia without the latter any wiser. We've adapted to live on stored animal blood, and although our skin remains sensitive, we've also adapted to the sunlight."

"So again," I said, "how could making childbirth easier for vampires have any unwanted side effects?"

"I haven't got a clue," River said, shoving his fingers through his hair. "But we're sure as hell going to find out."

EIGHT

DANTE

"You want me to fight a woman?"

"Not just a woman," *she* said. "A wolf-woman."

"I won't."

"You'll do as you're commanded to."

"Let me see her."

"She's in training."

"So you've said. Why can't I see her?"

"Because you're going back to the dungeon. I have plans for you."

I suppressed a snarl. *She* was not stupid. *She* must know what I was capable of now, how my powers had grown. *She* wouldn't put me anywhere she thought I could escape from.

My only recourse was to not go back to that dungeon.

"Why? I can be of much more use to you here."

"You've not yet completed your training, Dante."

"Torture is not training"—I swallowed a lump—"my queen."

She smiled at me, shaking her head. "You really have no idea, do you?"

"No idea about what?"

"About how important you are. How you can change things for our people."

"By being tortured?" I bared my fangs. "If I'm some catalyst for great change, you should treat me as such, not torture me, not force me to fight for my very survival."

"But Dante—" *She* touched my cheek.

I resisted the urge to cringe.

"You can only fulfill your destiny if you're prepared. Everything you endured has made you stronger, and it will make you stronger still." She bared her fangs. "Are you hungry?"

Nausea welled in me, traveling like a centipede from my stomach up to my throat. "Not especially."

"*I* am." She moved toward my neck. "I've missed you."

No. Just no.

I stood still, my body rigid.

"Your pulse is rising," she said. "I can see the beat in your carotid artery, just waiting for me."

"Take me to Lucy," I snarled. "You will not taste a drop of my blood before I see her."

"Oh, Dante," she laughed. "Just who do you think is in control here?"

"Wasn't *my* blood enough for you?" I seethed. "How long had you been feeding from Erin before I escaped here?"

She laughed again. "Did you truly think you were my only sustenance? I don't have to tell *you* how sweet Erin's blood is."

"You took from her femoral artery. From her thigh."

"As I took from yours. Honey is always sweetest closest to the pot."

"Why? Why her?"

"Why *not* her? Her scent is irresistible." She sniffed.

"Come to think of it, I didn't scent her when she showed up in the entryway. Why is that?"

"Maybe your nose is failing."

She inhaled. "My nose is just fine, thank you. I can still smell the little wolf's musk. She is sweet as well, not that I knew that before she was brought here. I didn't take her blood above ground. Only Erin's." She inhaled once more. "I can't scent you, as you know, but your blood, Dante... Nothing has ever satisfied me quite so well. Made me yearn for more the way yours did."

"You'll get nothing. Not until I see Lucy."

"I'll take what I want from you and anyone else," she growled. "Who the hell do you think you are?"

I snarled, and my teeth snapped down farther. "Who am I? I am what *you* made me."

The dark energy bounced through me, as if it were a ball frantically looking for a landing place. I fought against it, snarling and snapping.

"Give in to it, darling," she said. "Only then will you be what you're meant to be."

Give in to it. Give in.

Yes. Give in. I'd let the darkness give me strength. And then I'd use that strength against *her*.

The black energy swirled through me, warming my blood as it raced through my vessels.

"Take. Me. To. Lucy."

Her eyes went wide for the tiniest of seconds. For the briefest of time, she'd been...frightened.

Good.

No way was I going back to that dungeon. If I could frighten her enough to show me where the women were, I could free them.

Then I'd deal with *her.*

"Again!"
I twisted my hips and kicked the boxing dummy under his armpit.
"Again!"
"Again!"
"Again!"
New kicks. New jabs. Then calisthenics until my body was ready to give out.
"Again!"
"Again!"
"Again!"
My whole body ached, but it was better than being chained down and readied for torture.
This new training at least gave me a tiny piece of freedom, a chance to exercise my body.
"Again!"
"Again!"
"Again!"
Then someone entered, clad head to toe in cushioned armor.
"Fight!"
I did not move.
"Fight!"
No. Would not move.
"Fight!"
My opponent moved.
And then I fought.
Roundhouse to the cheek, uppercut to the chin. Knife-hand

to the neck, front snap kick to the groin. Axe kick to the top of the head.

He went down.

Another opponent entered.

The same.

The same.

The same.

When I was sure I would drop to the ground if forced to work any harder, the trainer finally said, "You're ready."

Fight or die in the arena.

New memories always jarred me, and this one sent the dark energy from me like steam rising from boiling water.

I'd known someone must have trained me. I didn't learn how to fight by osmosis. And now I knew why my muscles didn't atrophy during my captivity. She had always told me it was her blood that kept my muscles healthy.

More likely, it was the forced training and workouts.

My body was robust, and the power growing within me was getting stronger. My ability to control it was strengthening as well.

How much did she know?

I'd keep it to myself as long as I could.

One thing was sure. I would *not* go back to that dungeon. She'd have to kill me first.

"Are you taking me to see Lucy or not?"

"No, Dante. The wolf is a disgusting creature. She has no self-control."

"A disgusting creature? She's a nurse. She cares for patients."

"Yes, and she's Erin's best friend. That's what this is really all about, isn't it? I can understand your concern for your sister, but Lucy doesn't deserve your concern. She's been nothing but trouble since she got here."

"Then why didn't you let her go? You let two of the others go. Why not Lucy?"

"Her wolf brain can't be glamoured into misremembering, and memory-altering drugs have had no effect. Taking her was a mistake that unfortunately can't be rectified by returning her."

"Let me see her," I said again.

"She's in training."

"Why bother training her? If she's of no use to you, why not just throw her in the arena and let one of your fighting vampires kill her?"

She huffed. "That's a tempting idea, and I did think of it. But I know Lucy. She would shift and then kill. Wolves are vicious and carnivorous creatures."

"Why not just kill her, then?"

"Dante"—she met my gaze, her blue eyes icier than usual—"I'm *not* a killer. I'm creating life here, not taking it."

NINE

Erin

"Ready?" River met my gaze and then Jay's.

"Ready," Jay said.

"Ready," I repeated.

River pointed his gun. "Let's roll." He opened the wooden door.

The fluorescent lights shone harshly, making me adjust my eyes once again.

I blinked, almost expecting to see Dante and Dr. Bonneville across the oblong room, which, I realized, was really more like a wide hallway.

River and Jay both held their pistols, and though they flanked me and I wore a bulletproof vest, I felt oddly exposed. "Dante and Dr. Bonneville went through that door." I pointed.

"Yup. And that's where we're going," River said.

I swallowed back my fear—or at least tried to—as we inched closer to the door that loomed in front of us.

"We should have asked Julian what to expect through this

first door," I said.

"We should have asked him a lot of things," River said. "He didn't stick around, though."

"He needs to be with Dante," I said. "The three of us have each other. Dante is alone in there."

"He's not with Dante, either," River said. "He's with that nutty voodoo lady. I hope he knows what he's doing."

"If Bea can get him through the shields, he can find the other women. His brother. Whatever else is hidden here," I said.

"We already know Em is here," River said. "The others have to be."

We reached the door on the other side of the room, and River opened it, again leading with his gun.

Another room ahead, lit with fluorescent lamps. I looked around. A door fabricated from stainless steel lay ahead.

We walked forward.

"It's locked," River said. "*Now* they decide to lock us out. Great."

My heart sped up, in a good way this time. "Dante is in there somewhere. I can feel it."

"What do you feel?" Jay asked.

"I don't know. I can't describe it. I just know it. We have a bond, Jay."

"Your bond isn't doing us any good," River said. "I can't pick this lock."

"Can you shoot it off?" I asked.

"I could if it were a padlock, but it's not. It's a double deadbolt."

"Shit," Jay said. "Now what?"

River sighed. "We look for another way in, unless either of

you can pick this lock."

"Crap," I said. "Now we really need Dante. Somehow he learned to pick locks."

"While he was here, no doubt," River agreed. "Why would he need to pick locks?"

"I don't know," Jay said. "But it sure came in handy. Do you ever get the feeling that we're rats in a maze? And someone keeps moving the cheese on us?"

"All the time, partner," River agreed.

A maze was one thing. A puzzle was another, and this was a puzzle. The biggest puzzle piece in my mind was how I would feed Dante—and Dante needed to feed soon. I could feel it. I could feel *him*.

I closed my eyes, urging my mind to recall the dream I'd had about the baby crying. About the blood bank full of B positive blood. Maybe I could find a clue in the dream.

No use. Right now, my fear and my need to feed Dante overwhelmed all else.

One thing I was certain of, though. We were meant to be here right now. *I* was meant to be here, to feed Dante.

I had to find a way in.

River and Jay were examining the lock on the steel door, so I looked around, scanning the room for anything that might lead us to something. I had no idea what I was looking for, but I was bent on finding it. I had to get to Dante.

The walls were gray-painted concrete, the floor covered in thin gray carpet, some kind of industrial grade textile. I started at the door and began walking around the edge of the room. I got down on my hands and knees to check the thin carpet, but it was tacked down pretty solidly. Still I wandered around the perimeter of the room, scanning every crevice.

Come on, Dante. Give me some kind of clue.

If only Bea were here. I'd welcome one of her statements cloaked in a Shakespeare or Thoreau quotation. At least it would give me something to think about, help me extrapolate what to look for.

Nothing. Nothing around the perimeter of the room gave me any hope.

When I returned to the door, Jay and River were both shaking their heads.

"No way to open this thing without a key or some very sophisticated lock-picking equipment," Jay said.

"Maybe we're going about this the wrong way," River said.

"I'm no detective, but I just walked around the perimeter, scanning every inch of this room. I didn't find any other way out."

"I suppose there's the door we came in," Jay said.

"That won't get us any— Oh!" I clasped my hand to my lips. "What if—" I walked quickly to the center of the room. "What if there's something *between* the doors?"

"Why would there be?" Jay asked.

"Between the doors of perception."

"We already used that," River said. "The old guy got us here."

"Maybe there's more to what he said." I bit my lip, urging my brain to recall. "What was the quote Bea used? It's from Aldous Huxley. I got it! 'There are things known and there are things unknown, and in between are the doors of perception.'"

"Yeah," Jay said. "I don't think that's going to help us at the moment, Sis."

"Not unless one of you has some mushrooms or LSD," River agreed.

"We know what's on the other side of that door." I pointed to the wooden door where we'd entered. "But we don't know what's on the other side of that one." I pointed to the steel door that was locked.

"Sis, you're a bright woman and a wonderful nurse, but right now, you're stating the obvious."

"Bear with me. Bea used that 'doors of perception' quote right before she told us about the 'most important work of all.'"

"Which is..." Jay said.

"She didn't say in so many words, but she was clearly talking about the *Vampyre Texts*."

"Why would the *Vampyre Texts* be the most important work of all?" Jay asked. "If there are truly so few vampires left, how could that book be the most important book ever written?"

"Maybe it isn't the most important book ever written," I said. "Maybe it's the most important book to *us*. Right now. For our perception. Perception is our reality. 'It's not what you look at that matters. It's what you see.'" I removed my backpack, unzipped it, and slid my hands around the leather-bound book my mother had given me.

"Say what?" my brother said.

"Thoreau." Never had I been so thankful for Bea and my post-high-school Thoreau seminar. "The doors of perception aren't supposed to be literal."

"The two doors we found above ground were pretty darned literal," River said.

"Yeah, true," I said, "but I think Aldous Huxley and Bea have more to teach us." I caressed the smooth leather of the book.

"It's worth a shot, Sis," Jay said. "See if you can open it."

I held the book for a few precious seconds. *Is it time? Will*

you finally show us your secrets?
The book fell open.

TEN

DANTE

Not a killer.

True. She'd returned two of the women she'd taken, and Em was alive and appeared to be well cared for—as well cared for as one could be while being held against her will, that was. Better cared for than I was when I was trapped here. Thank God.

But Bonneville *was* a killer. She was going to have Lucy thrown in the arena to fight for her life, and her odds were on the vampires.

"Maybe you don't pull the trigger, my queen, but make no mistake. You *are* a killer."

The words fell like poison from my tongue. I risked punishment for them, but I uttered them anyway. She'd turned *me* into a killer.

I hadn't yet remembered the murderous strike from each time I had fought in the arena, but I remembered everything up to that point. My brain was probably shielding me from it to protect me.

No longer.

I needed total recall now. I needed to know who I truly was.

You know *who you are.*

The dark energy. Always with me. Always part of me.

"I'm a physician, Dante. I'm a healer. I have been all my life."

"No. Whether you do the actual killing doesn't matter. You force others to do your dirty work. You have Decker, Giles, and the rest. You have Logan Crown. You have..."

Me.

The word sat on the edge of my tongue, but I couldn't say it. Couldn't force it to drop from my lips.

"Decker and his gang are thugs, but they're not killers. And Logan Crown is a physician as I am."

But what about me?

Say it, Dante. Say it. You deserve to know the truth.

No. Can't face it. Can't face the truth.

"We don't kill here, Dante. We have a much higher purpose. One that you'll understand in time. One in which you have a large role to play."

As a killer.

But I didn't feel like a killer. Even with the darkness inside me, I didn't feel I was capable of killing. To save my own life? Yes. To save Erin or anyone else I loved? Of course.

But in the arena, where I was only going to go back to my torturous existence?

Could I have killed?

Fight or die in the arena.

The darkness surrounded me. I must have killed. If I hadn't, I wouldn't be alive.

Fight or die in the arena.

Those words. They'd been the truth of my existence since she'd begun dropping me into that black cave of gladiator darkness.

Had she said them?

Had someone else?

They were so formed in my mind, such a part of me...

Where had they come from?

"It is time, Dante."

"Time for what?"

"You know what. It's time for you to return to your dungeon."

"No."

"I fulfilled my end of the bargain. I allowed you to see your sister."

I dropped my fangs in a painful snarl. "You will release my sister. You will release my uncle. You will release Lucy and the others, or I—"

Something bit at my neck.

A tug.

That undeniable tug.

ELEVEN

Erin

I gasped.

"Damn," River said. "What does it say?"

I scanned the two pages that were open to me. Most of it was in some sort of hieroglyphic gibberish, but one paragraph stood out.

In English.

I read aloud.

"Though no actual blood bonds have been recorded since prehistoric times, there are a few documented circumstances that could be attributed to the phenomenon. In 1446, a French woman known as Cecile Volande wrote of her power over English Lord Edmund Theophile, known to the council to be a vampire. 'I am his sustenance, his livelihood. Without me, he cannot exist, for I nourish him from my body, and he in turn provides for me. Our bodies and souls are entwined for eternity. I can bring him to me anytime simply by opening the door.' Volande and Theophile died within two days of each other in 1478."

"Opening the door?" Jay said. "What's that supposed to mean?"

River shook his head. "Not a clue, man. The door is fucking locked."

"The rest of it is gibberish," I said. "The shield must think we only need this paragraph. What door? And how do I open it?"

"What's the word for door in French?" Jay asked.

"I don't know. I didn't take French," I said.

"I did," River said, "but I don't remember much. Door, though. I think it's *la porte.*"

"Good. This is a translation, right? Is there any other meaning of *porte* in French?"

"The original *Texts* are in *Old* French," I reminded him.

He and River ignored me.

"Good, partner. I see what you're getting at." River scratched his head. "Yeah. Gate or gateway. Hatch."

An idea struck me like a lightning bolt. "What about portal?" I asked.

"Yeah. Probably. It makes sense. It sounds like *porte.*"

"Do either of you have a knife?" I asked.

"Say what?" Jay said.

"You heard me. A knife."

"What do you need a knife for?"

"I'm going to cut myself."

"Oh, the hell you are," Jay said.

"No, you don't understand. A portal is a door in a vessel. In this case, a blood vessel. I need to open the door to bring Dante here."

"I'm not going to let—"

"Hold on, Jay," River interrupted. "She might have something."

"I'm a nurse. I carry a first aid kit wherever I go. I have one in my backpack. I just need to cut myself and bleed. If what the book says is true—and it has to be, doesn't it? It opened to that page, and only that paragraph is legible. My grandmother said it would open when we need it, and right now, we need to bring Dante to us so he can open that damned door."

River riffled through his backpack and pulled out a Swiss Army knife. "Will this work?"

"If it has a blade, it will work." I removed an antiseptic wipe from my kit and rubbed it over my wrist.

"You're not really going to do this," Jay said. "Are you?"

"I don't have a choice. If this fifteenth-century woman had a blood bond with this guy, and if the blood bond worked the way it works with Dante and me, there's no door. There's a blood vessel. Makes perfect sense to me."

"She's right, Jay. We have to try. How else are we going to get through the door and find the women?"

Jay let out a huff. "Okay. Get it over with."

"I may have to bleed for a while. I don't know how far away Dante is."

"I'm not a complete pussy, Sis. I'm a cop. I've seen blood. I just don't really want to see *your* blood."

"There's one other thing we haven't considered," River said. "Dante didn't seem to know any of us when he went through that door with Bonneville. Your blood might bring him here, but what if, when he gets here, he's not himself?"

I hadn't thought of that. I bit my lip, fingering River's knife.

Dante was here. I knew that logically—I'd seen him—but I also felt it. Felt *him*. He was here, and he needed me. He needed to feed. He needed my blood.

Trance or no trance, I felt certain I could bring him here.

But what if that made things worse instead of better?

No.

Right now, we needed to get through that door, and this was our only option. Dante might not know us, but he would not hurt us. I believed that with all my heart.

I winced as I punctured my skin with the knife, careful to avoid an artery. Blood trickled onto my skin.

"I guess that's that," Jay said. "He's coming, and if he's not himself, we need to be prepared to deal with that." He cocked his gun.

"It won't come to that," River said. He didn't sound convinced.

"I hope it won't, but I'll protect my sister if I have to."

River nodded. "I understand."

The warmth of my blood oozing over my skin made me shiver in anticipation. My heart hammered, and adrenaline kicked in so I felt no pain.

Dante would come.

I knew he would.

Seconds passed.

Then minutes.

River and Jay paced on the gray carpeting.

"Come on, cuz," River said, looking at his watch. "We can't let her bleed forever."

Jay stopped pacing and stood next to me, his gaze glued to my bleeding skin. "I don't like this."

"I know," I said softly. "He will come. Trust me."

If I could be sure of anything in my life, I could be sure of Dante.

But he didn't know you…

I silenced the devil on my shoulder.

He would come.
He would come.

TWELVE

DANTE

The tug I'd tried to resist at first was now like a dream I could barely recall.

Words flowed into my mind, words in the voice of my grandfather, when he first told me about the blood bond.

The pull you feel isn't coming from you. It's coming from her.

My heart pounded as if a gargoyle were beating on a bass drum. The high hiss of my blood pumping out through my arteries became a red noise overpowering her voice.

You will obey me.

You will obey...

No. Love and light pulled me away from the darkness, away from *her*.

Erin. Erin was pulling me to her. I growled, a low rumble beginning in my abdomen.

My hunger for fresh blood curled into me like an eagle's talon. I inhaled. Yes, the dark chocolate, earthy truffles, lusty Bordeaux.

Erin's blood.

I turned and raced down the hallway.

I raced toward Erin.

I raced toward life.

Only the stainless-steel door separated me from Erin. From Erin's blood. I inhaled once more, letting her scent infuse every cell in my body.

Erin. Musky, sweet, dark, sultry Erin.

The deadbolt was latched, and I had nothing to pick the lock with. But Erin's blood called to me. I sent a coil of aching need toward the deadbolt, and it turned, unlatching. I burst through the door, a growl on my lips.

"Dante!"

Blood.

Yes, Erin was there. River. Jay. All three of them. How hadn't I recognized them before? The three blurred figures? Three people so important to me?

But I couldn't ruminate further. I was here for blood. Erin's blood. I stalked toward her, my fangs descending to their sharpest points.

Jay stepped in front of Erin, but River pulled him away.

"It's okay," River whispered to Jay.

But I heard him as if he were shouting.

Louder even than River was the flow of Erin's blood to her heart, and the higher hiss as it spread out again through her arteries. Then her capillaries burst with tiny pops, giving way to her alluring blush.

She was frightened.

She was also turned on.

She timidly held her bleeding wrist to me.

I yanked her toward me until our bodies were touching. So

warm. So right. I inhaled again, letting her scent melt into me, become part of me.

I brought her wrist to my lips and licked it, closing the wound. Then I pulled her hair to one side and sank my teeth into her milky neck.

"Shit! No!" Jay's voice.

Didn't care.

"Let him. It's our way." River's voice.

Didn't care.

No. My only care in this world was Erin, sweet lovely Erin. She had come to me. To feed me. To nourish me. To sustain me.

To save me.

Jay and River shuffled away from us, toward something. I didn't care what. I was too busy with Erin, letting her red gold flow onto my tongue, down my throat, into my body and soul, cleansing me of all the taint of this place.

All the taint of *her*.

No more blemish. No more contamination.

No more her.

Until—

"Dante!"

I snarled into Erin's neck, still sucking out the nectar that gave me grace when I didn't deserve it.

"Take me to my father, you bitch."

River's voice.

I withdrew my teeth from Erin's flesh, licking her wounds. I turned.

Jay was behind her, holding her arms. For some reason, she hadn't glamoured him.

River's pistol was touching her forehead. "Now. Or I *will* kill you."

"You're not a killer," she said. "You catch killers."

"I'm willing to make an exception for you." River cocked his gun.

"Dante," she said, her voice never wavering. "Remember the one rule of chess."

Chess? When had we played chess? The answer was we hadn't. I'd played with my father and Bill a few times when I was younger, but—

"Protect your queen." The words emerged from my mouth before I could think them.

"Yes, Dante," she said. "*Always* protect your queen."

"You're no quee—"

I let go of Erin, raced toward the others, and tossed River aside. He landed on his ass—

"Dante!" Erin gasped.

—but was up in a flash. "Nice, cuz, but this isn't you. Don't let it be you."

"Protect your queen," *she* said again.

Dark energy swirled within me, and the dueling swords clashed against each other once again.

"Control, son. Remember that part of you that *she* can't touch."

My father had returned.

But his voice didn't move me.

What did was the woman who touched my hand, her warmth a soothing salve to my tortured soul.

In a flash, I whisked energy toward *her*, pulling her away from Jay and knocking her against the concrete wall.

Her eyes shot into circles and she opened her mouth, but no words emerged. She was bound to the wall through the sheer force of my will.

"Quickly." My father. "Through the door. Take them with you. Lock it."

I grabbed Erin's arm and raced through the door, Jay and River following us. When we were on the other side, I locked it.

"She probably has a key," River said.

My father materialized. "She doesn't. Not on her. I made sure of that, with Bea's help."

"Still, she'll be able to get back in."

"She will," my father agreed. "We don't know how much time we have, so use it wisely."

"Dante?" Erin's face was pale, frightened.

"I'm so sorry, love." I cupped her cheek.

"It was like you didn't know me. Before."

Guilt knifed through my heart. How had I allowed myself to fall under that bitch's trance? I brushed my lips over hers. "I'm so sorry," I said again.

"No time for this," River said. "Take us to the women."

"I've only seen Em," I said. "I don't know where the others are."

"I know where Lucy is," my father said. "I'm not sure we can get there from here, but we have to find a way. She's in danger."

Erin jolted against me. "What? Why? What are they doing to her? She just had surgery!"

"They're training her to fight," I said.

"To fight?" River said. "What do you mean? She's weak right now."

"Apparently not that weak," I said. "I guess she's been a problem. She's resistant to all the sedatives they've given her, and she shifts at will and attacks."

"Of course she attacks," Erin said. "She's being held against her will! We have to find her."

"I can try to take you to her," my father said. "The others aren't in any danger at the moment." Then, he added sadly, "I have not yet found my brother."

River shoved his hands through his hair. "Damn."

"He's alive, River. I'd know if he weren't. But that's all I know."

"God, how am I supposed to choose between rescuing the woman I love and finding my father?" River rubbed his chin.

"We rescue Lucy," my father said. "Braedon has survived this long, and though his time is nearing an end, he will continue to survive until we find him. I have to believe that."

"What about Emilia?" Jay cleared his throat. "And the baby?"

"She's okay for now, and so is the baby," my father said. "Dante saw her."

"Yeah, she's okay. If you call being held against her will okay." I rolled my eyes.

"We have to hold on to the fact that she's not in danger right now. I will try to figure out how to get you to Lucy. I won't be long." My dad disappeared.

"All right," Jay said. "Then Lucy is the first priority."

"Agreed," River said. "Let's go."

I grasped Erin's hand, her warmth traveling through me. Her blood wasn't enough to sate me. I needed her body, her strength. Control. I needed control. Everything in me screamed at me to grab her and fuck her, but I couldn't take her right now with her brother and my cousin right here, especially not when Lucy was our priority. "I love you, baby. So much."

"I love y—" She clasped her hand to her mouth. "Oh, shit!"

THIRTEEN

Erin

"What is it?" Dante asked.

I fell against him. God, I was a complete moron. I'd just ruined everything.

"Baby?"

I inhaled, getting ready to disappoint three of the people I cared about most in this world. "The book. My mom's copy. I left it...out there."

It had tumbled from my lap when I'd cut my wrist, and after that, I'd been thinking only about Dante coming to find us.

I hadn't put the book back in my backpack.

"It's out there," I said. "With her."

Dante stroked my back. "It's okay, baby."

River didn't look convinced, but Jay had a grin on his face. "It's okay, Sis," he said. "Everything will be all right."

"How can everything be all right? I just lost a family heirloom! A family heirloom that we need right now."

"It's o—"

"It opened, Dante. That's how I knew how to get you to come to us. It opened to one page, and I could read a paragraph about the blood bond. God, how could I be so stupid!"

"Sis," my brother began again.

I wanted to punch myself in the face. "The shield broke, at least for the one paragraph we needed. And now—"

I gasped.

Jay held the book in front of my face. "Did you really think I'd let you leave that book out there? It's my family heirloom too, you know."

I hurled myself into my brother's arms. "Jay! I could kiss you." I planted a wet one on his cheek.

He wiped it away. "Don't get disgusting on me. We all have each other's backs, remember?"

"But how—"

"When Dante came through the door. I noticed the book on the floor, so I grabbed it and put it in my pack. I wasn't sure what we'd be dealing with."

Dante growled.

"Easy, man," Jay said. "The last time we saw you, you were catatonic."

"He's right, Dante," I said.

"Plus, we need the book," Jay said.

"Good work, partner," River said.

I grabbed the book from Jay and opened it. It still only opened to the same page. I handed it to Dante. "Read this."

He scanned it quickly. "That's how you got me here? Not by opening a door but by opening a vein?"

"That's what we figured it meant. In French, the word for door is— It doesn't matter. It worked. You needed to feed, and I needed to feed you. Plus, we needed to get through the door. I found a way to get you to me."

Dante shook his head. "This book is obviously full of useful information. Why in hell does Bill want to keep it from us?"

"We've read all of one paragraph, cuz," River said. "And only the paragraph Erin needed to get us through that door."

"It seems our mom was right when she said it would open when we needed it," Jay said. "The problem is it only gave us exactly what we needed at the time. We may never get to read the whole thing."

"Apparently not unless we need to," River agreed.

"There's something else, though," Dante said, scratching his ear.

"What?" I asked.

"The *Vampyre Texts* is supposed to be centuries old, but this was obviously written after the fifteenth century."

"That's still centuries old, dude," Jay said.

"Yeah, but it's like the Bible. It's supposed to predate almost everything ever written."

"Maybe it's been added to over the years," Jay said.

"No," River said. "He's right. Something's weird here. Bill always said—"

"Bill's not known for his truthfulness," Jay interjected.

River sighed, nodding.

"All I know is that this book gave me the information we needed when we needed it," I said. "It's the real thing, in my opinion."

"Whether it is or not really doesn't matter," Jay said. "It helped us once, and it might help us again."

"True," River said. "Plus, it's in English, and it's a quarter of the size of the other copy we have. No way could we have dragged that down here."

"Only one paragraph is in English," I said. "At least so far. That shield is obviously only going to give us exactly what we need. There might be something on this page that could harm us, as Bill seems to think."

Dante took the book from my hands and attempted to turn another page. To no avail. "It's spilled its only secret for now," he said. "Standing around here isn't helping anyone. We need to find Lucy."

River nodded. "Agreed. Let's go."

I eyed the place. Sterile-looking, as a hospital should be, but no staff milling about. "It's so quiet here. It looks so much like University, but no one is here. Where would Lucy be?"

We walked down an empty corridor, and—

A sign on a door—a door to a refrigeration unit.

Blood Bank.

Without warning, I turned and opened the door.

"Erin—" Dante said.

I walked in, rubbing my arms against the chill. The freezer storage lay ahead, where units were stored longer term.

Yes, a blood bank.

The blood bank from my dream. I eyed the shelves.

Filled only with B positive.

FOURTEEN

DANTE

"Erin, come on." I tugged on her arm.

"All B positive," she said. "Just look."

"Luckily I just fed and I can't smell this blood anyway," I said. "But think of River. He's going to need to feed soon."

"I'm ahead of you." River entered. "There's plenty here, and now I know where I can feed." He inhaled. "Human blood. I've never tasted it, believe it or not."

"Now's your chance," I said. "We'll look away."

"I brought a couple days' supply with me in my pack. It's in a small cooler." He inhaled again. "But God...this is tempting." He shook his head. "I can't. I fucking can't. What if..."

"What?" I said.

"What if...I *like* it?"

"It's stored blood," I said. "It's not the same."

It wasn't. I'd raided a blood bank that first night—that fateful night when Erin had come into my life. I'd feasted on the bags of stored blood at the hospital. It had sated my hunger, but it was nothing like—

I used to dream of severed human heads...

The reality. Not the dream. I'd forgotten it was a reality until recently. I'd thought Erin was my first taste of fresh human blood.

The nectar that had dripped from the human heads was still warm. Still fragrant.

Chills erupted on my skin. It wasn't my fault. I hadn't killed those human beings. *She* had. But I had drunk from them. I had lapped up their essence as it fell onto my face.

Erin stood next to me, her hair in a tight ponytail, her face pale and beautiful.

Taking Erin's blood had been unlike anything I'd experienced before, even from the suspended heads that I'd thought for so long had been a dream.

"You okay, bro?" River asked.

No. Not really. But I nodded anyway.

"Good. Because I have to get out of here before I fucking masticate this entire bank." River turned and left.

"He has a lot of willpower," I said quietly.

"Is it that...tempting?"

"Not for me. Not with you standing right here. Plus, I just fed."

"I'm sorry I came in here," she said.

"It's okay."

"I just had to know."

"Now we know. Your dream was a premonition, just like my dad explained. B positive blood is essential to whatever is going on here. Problem is, we don't know what to do with that information."

"Not yet, anyway," she said. "Come on. Let's find Lucy."

We left the blood bank and headed farther down the

corridor. I pointed to a turnoff. "Em is down that way. I assume the others are as well."

"I want to see her," Jay said. "I want to make sure my baby is okay, too."

"They're okay," I said. "Believe me, if I thought they weren't, we'd be heading there. But we need to get to Lucy. She's in danger."

Jay nodded. "All right. I'll take your word for it. For now."

I tensed, going rigid. Erin's presence next to me was a soothing warmth.

"There must be an exit somewhere," I said. "When I was here—"

An image erupted in my mind. The manhole I'd found. Was it truly the right one? When I'd escaped, the paths had been lit. This time, when I'd come down here, they hadn't been. Was I even in the right place?

Had to be. *She* was here.

But the place I'd been kept was dark and dank. Not a sterile hospital.

Yet these halls were familiar somehow. Had I been in this hospital...before?

I opened my eyes and squinted against the stark white light.

My face stung, not like when I was electrocuted. It stung with the bristly bite of antiseptic. I inhaled. Humans. Humans were near.

I tried to turn my head to look around, but I couldn't. Either I was being held in place, or my neck was so stiff I couldn't move. I could see only the ceiling—stark white textured plaster.

Stark white.

I hadn't seen stark white since—

Since I'd been taken.

How long had I been held here, captive against my will?

My body was numb. Had I been drugged? Surely, I should be able to feel something.

What had happened? How did I get here? Had I...

I settled my mind, opening it, urging it to recall even the smallest detail. Where had I come from? How had I gotten here? Why was I here? What was this place?

But...

Nothing.

Yes. I'd been here. Somehow, this hospital was connected to the other place. The horrid, hellish place where I'd been tortured, electrocuted, violated, forced to fight for my existence.

Think, Dante. Think.

If I'd been here, I'd gone from here back to the dungeon. If only I could force my mind to remember. If only I could find the pathway from the hospital to the...

No.

I couldn't go back there.

But I didn't have a choice. If Lucy was in training, she was there. Somewhere.

I cleared my throat. "I've been here before. I can't recall the details, but there must be a way through here to get to Lucy. We just have to find it."

"It's mostly hallways, so far," Jay said.

River pulled a bota bag out of his backpack and took a long

sip. Then he licked the blood from his lips. Jay looked away.

"You'll get used to it," Erin said.

"Sorry. A guy's gotta eat." River put the leather bag back in his pack and inhaled. "I don't think she's far. Or at least she hasn't been gone that long. I can still pick up her residual scent." He closed his eyes. "We've got to find her."

"Dad?" I asked tentatively.

No response. He'd found something else to occupy his time, clearly. Perhaps he was looking for Lucy. He could go places we couldn't. At least for now.

Then, "I'm here, son." He appeared. "I wish I had better news. I can get to Lucy, but you can't."

"A shield?" Erin asked.

"Yes. A strong one."

"Someone had to create the shield," Erin said. "Who else has that kind of power?"

"Any practitioner of magick who is also a medium," he said. "Bea's enhanced power comes from the energy of the ghosts who inhabit her. She did not create the shields down here, however. I've already ruled that out."

"How?"

"I asked her."

"Oh. Simple enough, I guess." Erin rolled her eyes.

"She can reverse the shields, but it will require dark magick, and she prefers not to dabble. She was able to get me in with my ashes. My energy can pass."

"Is there a doorway somewhere here in the hospital?" Erin asked.

"Yes," my father said, "but as I said, you will not be able to pass."

"We'll see about that." River bared his fangs, some of the

blood he'd ingested still visible on them. "I'm going to get to Lucy one way or another."

"Your strength and teeth won't get you past, River," my father said. "But there is another way."

"How?" Erin asked.

"We need to lure *her* to us."

FIFTEEN

Erin

"You mean like I lured Dante?" I quickly explained what we'd found in the book.

"Not exactly. No one here has a blood bond with Lucy, and even if one of you did, Lucy isn't a vampire. She won't be lured by blood."

"Then how?" River asked.

"You're the key, River. You and Erin."

"How are we—"

"If she shares your feelings, your scent will be the strongest to her. Erin's should also be strong. Since we have both of you, we're in good shape. There's only one issue."

"What's that?" I asked.

"She needs to be in wolf form to pick up your scent."

"Shouldn't be a problem," Dante said. "Bonneville"—he seemed to struggle with the name—"said Lucy's been forcing the change to get out of captivity."

"She is not in wolf form right now," Julian said. "She's

being forced to train to fight, and she's not changing. I'm not sure why she isn't."

"They've threatened her," Dante said gravely. "That's the only explanation."

"How do you know?" I asked.

"You. And River. Bonneville"—he cleared his throat to get the word out—"knows you're here now, and she's using you as leverage to get Lucy to do what she wants."

"Can't you tell her, Dad?" Dante said. "Appear to her and tell her she needs to come to us."

"Seems logical, doesn't it?" Julian agreed. "Problem is, I already tried that. Werecreatures are notoriously resistant to the ghostly plane. I'd heard rumors, and apparently, they're true. She couldn't see or hear me. I can get to her, but I can't do anything beyond that."

"Take us as far as we can go then, Julian," I said. "The closer we are to her, the better chance she'll be able to pick up our scent."

"She'll still be too far away if she's in human form," he replied. "Somehow, we have to get her to shift."

"What causes a shift?" Jay turned to River.

"What are you looking at me for?"

"Because you're dating her."

"And I had no idea she was a shifter until we found her in the cemetery. Although"—he lifted his brow—"she did shift when we had the car accident. She shifted and broke through the windshield."

"What caused the shift?" Jay asked.

"Fear. She said she shifted out of fear."

"We need to scare her?" I said. "If she's not scared already, just being here—"

"That's obviously not enough right now," Julian said. "I believe Dante is most likely correct. Bonneville is using your presence, River and Erin, as leverage to keep Lucy from shifting."

"So she's more frightened for *us* than she is of anything here," I said. "That sounds like Lucy. She always puts others before herself. It's what makes her such a great nurse."

"Then how do we get her to shift?" Jay asked. "If she can't see or hear a ghost, and we can't get to her, what chance do we have?"

"We have to show her we're not in danger," I said.

"How?" Jay asked.

"I don't know. You're the detective."

Jay rolled his eyes. "Good one. Honestly, I'm not convinced we *aren't* in danger here. The good doctor won't take forever to get past that door. Even without a key, she'll find another way in. She built this place, right?"

Dante nodded. "That's what she says."

"Then she knows it inside and out. I hate to be the bearer of bad news, kids, but we *are* in danger."

"Stating the obvious, Jay." I rubbed my arms. I'd been on high alert since we got here, and though I'd managed to tamp down the aching fear to try to reason and figure out our situation, still the emotion was there, coiled within me, ready to spring.

"Then we have to find another way to force her to shift." Dante turned to his father. "She can't see or hear you."

"Stating the obvious again," Julian said.

"Bear with me. I've seen you harness your energy to move something twice now."

Julian nodded. "But it's not anything I can control. No

other ghost that I know of exhibits this type of power."

"I have this type of power too. Maybe it's some kind of latent power in the Gabriel line."

"Perhaps," Julian said. "But if it were, wouldn't our ancestors have discovered it by now?"

"Not necessarily," Dante said. "Maybe it has to be… switched on. Maybe it happened while you were kept here. While I was kept here."

"And maybe it has something to do with the change in your Rh factor," I said.

"Bonneville"—Dante winced—"is conducting research here. I'm not sure what kind of research, but it has something to do with B positive blood. And the council—" He fingered his several days' growth of beard. "The council has something to do with it. Otherwise Levi Gaston wouldn't have prohibited Bill from telling us how to find the women that night at Napoleon House. And when Bill cautioned us about exploring a translation of the *Texts*, he said something like it had to do with what we're capable of. What if all vampires are capable of the things you and I are exhibiting, Dad?"

"We also know Gaston wanted vampire progeny, and that he was a geneticist and an alchemist," Julian said. "He was also a supremacist. He considered vampires superior to humans and weres."

I gasped. "She's keeping human women here. Human women with B positive blood. Plus a shifter with B positive blood. She's trying to breed vampires."

"Not only breed vampires, Erin," Dante said. "She's making vampires stronger."

"Somehow, B positive blood is the key," I said. "But how?"

"You're the medical professional," Jay said. "You tell us."

"How would I know?"

"I have no clue. Just getting you back for the 'you're the detective' remark."

"Ha ha. Bonneville did have me research physical characteristics and blood types, but there wasn't any correlation. At least not that I found."

"Maybe she was looking for something else," River said.

"Or maybe," Jay said, "she wasn't looking for anything at all."

"Do you mean she sent me on a wild goose chase?" I said.

"Exactly. She obviously knew you were with Dante, if she went so far to exchange your birth control pills with placebos."

"Still, why would she have me research something that doesn't exist?"

"She was dropping hints," Jay said. "It's a very common narcissistic tendency. She believes so fiercely that she's unstoppable that she intentionally drops clues, proving to herself that she can't be caught. She led you into suspecting her, and you did."

"Right on the money, partner," River agreed. "We see that all the time on the force."

I nodded. This was all making so much sense. Dr. Bonneville was a classic narcissist. She treated others like complete shit and lacked empathy for those around her. Except for her patients. She did seem to care about them. The woman was a puzzle of contradiction.

"So what do we—"

A crash thundered through the air, and then descending clatters, as if a rock had been thrown through a window.

I gasped.

SIXTEEN

DANTE

The clash and shattering rang in my ears. My fangs descended with a snap, and a growl left my throat.

"What was that?" Erin gasped.

The spiky scent of adrenaline permeated the air. "Riv?" I asked.

My cousin inhaled. "Nothing. Nothing but adrenaline."

"Vampires," I growled. "The thugs. I'll take care of them. You get Erin to safety."

"Are you kidding? I'm here for you. Let me help you. Jay can keep Erin safe."

"No, he can't. He can be glamoured. You can't."

"You two are wearing your potion, right?" River said.

"Yeah," I said.

Jay nodded.

"Just in case, you two should separate. Dante, take Erin. I'll take Jay."

"Are you fucking kidding me?" I snarled. "I'm taking those bastards out."

Footsteps clomped, becoming progressively louder.

"Are you crazy? They can't smell us, and they can't smell Erin and Jay. They have no idea where we are. Our best bet is to get out of sight."

"Take the hallway to your right," my father said to me. "There's a supply closet where you can hide. River, you and Jay go the other way, past the blood bank."

"Yeah, don't go near the blood bank," I said. "They'll sniff that out."

"They probably already know where it is," Erin said. "My guess is that they fill it for her."

"There's a small pharmacy where medication is kept," my father continued. "The vampires are her suppliers, and that's probably where they're going. To the right is a janitorial station. Go there, and River, see if you can hear what's going on in the pharmacy."

"We're on it," River said. "Come on, partner."

"Dad, why don't you go listen in?"

"I'm needed elsewhere. Hurry!" He vanished.

"Damn!" I grabbed Erin's arm. "Come on." I whisked her down the hallway to the right. Two doors stood ahead of us. Which one was my father talking about?

I grabbed the knob on the first one we got to and opened it. Inside were lots of cardboard boxes with labels that read *syringes, bandages, Ringer's solution*—whatever that was.

I closed the door so we were in darkness. I could still see, but Erin widened her eyes.

"Give it a minute. Your sight will adjust," I whispered.

"My heart is beating so fast." Her voice was a whisper.

"I know." Oh, how I knew. Each thump rang in my ears like the sweet strum of a harp. The sweetest sound ever.

I wasn't hungry, not for blood, at least.

Erin's black hoodie obscured her gorgeous breasts and belly, but her luscious legs were shapely in the black leggings and short boots. A backpack was strapped to her, and I relieved her of it.

She let it go. "It's heavier than it looks. We had to bring a few days' supply of food and water because we didn't know what we'd find when we got here. River brought a bota bag filled with blood."

"There's no shortage of water here. Or of blood."

"I know. Now. What about food?"

"She has to feed the people here. There's got to be food somewhere."

"What did they feed you when you were"—she hesitated, gulping—"here?"

I closed my eyes. The food had been good, actually, from what I could remember. I'd tried starving myself, but they'd forced me to eat. "A lot of red meat. Green leafy vegetables."

"Good sources of iron," she said.

I nodded. We both knew what that meant. Iron kept my blood in tip-top shape—for *her* to drink against my will.

Why *had* she taken my blood? Forced me to take hers? Vampires weren't supposed to drink from each other. That's what we'd always been taught, but why?

"Do you have the book?" I asked.

"Crap. No, I don't. Jay still has it. He put it back in his pack after he waved it in my face."

"Too bad. I have so many questions."

"Yeah, me too, but the book won't open unless we need it to." She sighed. "It's proven that."

"Yeah. I know." I cupped her cheek, her skin like silk

beneath my fingertips. "But at least it brought me to you."

"I don't think I've ever been so scared in my life. I'm shivering."

I drew her into my arms. "You don't need to be scared when I'm here."

"But you—"

"Shh." I placed my fingers over her lips. "It won't happen again. I won't let it."

"But—"

"I promise, Erin. I'm here now. I've seen her, interacted with her. She has no more power over me. Have faith."

Faith. That word I'd heard so often since I'd returned and had been so loath to use. Now I was asking the woman I loved more than my own life to have faith that I wouldn't succumb to the darkness again. That I wouldn't succumb to *her* again.

"She's a monster, Dante." Erin shook her head. "I don't understand how a physician could be so cruel. She's supposed to be a healer."

"If what my father says is true, she may feel there is a method to her cruelty. She may believe she's serving a higher purpose."

"Breeding vampires," she said.

"Exactly. Though I have no idea how her holding me captive and torturing me, forcing me to drink her blood, serves that purpose."

"Maybe it doesn't," Erin said. "Maybe there is no higher purpose. Maybe she's just cruel. Sometimes a cigar is just a cigar."

"Freud?"

"Yeah. It's attributed to him, anyway. Psychology was required in nursing school, obviously."

"I'm surprised Bea didn't quote Freud." I smiled.

Erin didn't return my smile. "'Dreams are often most profound when they seem the most crazy.'"

"Say what?"

"Oh, sorry. It's another quote from Freud. It popped into my head and seems apt to the dreams I've been having and the dream my mother had. Crazy, yes, but so profound. It's like your dad said. Dreams can be regressions or premonitions. I've experienced the latter." She fidgeted restlessly. "I wish we could at least sit down in here. It's so cramped. And we shouldn't even be whispering, should we?"

"Probably not."

"I'm just so frightened, Dante. It helps to hear your voice, even if it is just a whisper."

I swept a stray hair out of her eyes. "I know. But you don't need to be scared. I'll do anything to protect you."

She cupped both my cheeks. "Please, Dante, make the fear go away. Kiss me. Help me remember who you truly are."

I brought my mouth to hers softly at first, but within seconds we were kissing ferociously, our tongues sucking and swirling.

For a split second, I perked my ears and listened.

No more footsteps. The thugs were either standing silently nearby, or they'd gone the other way. I should be worried about River and Jay.

Should stop kissing Erin and make sure they were okay.

But I didn't stop kissing Erin.

I needed this, and from her response, she clearly needed it as well. We were ultimately here for each other, and neither of us could ever forget that.

I'd scared her—made her think, if only for a moment, that

I'd forgotten her.

I knew better.

Erin was always in my mind.

Erin was what brought me back.

I deepened the kiss, forcing myself not to groan into her mouth. Our silence was crucial, and I vowed to stay quiet even as my cock hardened into marble inside my jeans. I ground it into her belly, searching for release.

Erin, too, stayed quiet. No moaning into my mouth as she usually did. Though I missed the sound and the vibration, kissing silently was oddly arousing. With no sound and our eyesight hampered by the darkness of the closet, my other senses were heightened. Her mouth tasted fresh and minty, an intoxicating flavor I hadn't fully appreciated before. Her lips were soft against mine, their texture as velvety as the skin of a peach. And her nipples—the hard little knobs poked into my chest right through her bra and both of our clothes. Perhaps the latter was my imagination, as the tight little berries appeared in my mind as if she were naked against me.

Didn't matter. Emotion coiled through me, and my senses worked overtime. I inhaled her musk, that erogenous mélange of her natural dark and heady scent plus her pheromones and the juices her body created just for me. I drew in the scent, let it take over my body and my mind.

My cock hardened further.

I had to have her. Had to take her in this closet where we barely had room to move. I broke the kiss gently to avoid a loud smacking sound.

I put my fingers to my lips, indicating for her to stay quiet, and then I turned her around, letting her lean against a stack of boxes. I longed to undress her slowly, slide my lips over her rosy body warm with her blood flow, suck her turgid nipples, and finger her puckered asshole.

Not this time, and probably not until we freed the prisoners and escaped this wretched place. Right now, I'd fuck her. Fuck her hard. Fuck her quietly.

Show her she was still mine and I was still hers, no matter what our circumstances and no matter where we were or why.

I eased her leggings and panties over her hips and thighs. I inhaled again. Her ripeness filled the small enclosure and made my already concrete dick expand thicker.

I slid my hand between her thighs and fingered her slick folds. She shivered but remained silent. Good girl.

So wet, so ready. I slowly shoved two fingers into her heat. She pushed backward against my hand, undulating her hips.

I imagined the sounds she was holding back—the sweet sighs, the low moans, the whisper of my name from her lips.

Yes, those things were inside her, and she was using her strength of will to keep them from coming out.

I, too, wanted to groan at the feel of her milky pussy tight around my fingers, at my cock straining to be free from its confinement.

I could wait no longer. I removed my fingers, hearing in my mind the whimper that would have come from Erin's lips. I freed my aching cock and plunged it inside her sweet tightness.

With the last shred of my control, I suppressed my groan. I pumped in and out of her slowly, silently, inhaling and letting her musky scent envelop every part of me. Each ridge of her pussy gloved my cock. The urge to go faster, to thrust violently, swelled within me, but I couldn't, because it would make a smacking sound. Slowly was the way for now, slowly and sweetly and silently.

She matched my movements, our rhythm like a chorus of silent angels whose music was composed of scents and emotion instead of sound.

And then...

And then...

She clasped around me tighter, pulsing in orgasm.

That was all I needed. I thrust into her, exploding, opening my mouth in a silent roar as I released inside her. Inside Erin.

We stood for a timeless moment, each breathing deeply, trying not to pant loudly. After a few minutes, I withdrew and reached for the red bandana in my pocket to clean us—

It was gone.

SEVENTEEN

Erin

As I came down from the mountain high of my climax, I resisted the urge to say Dante's name. It lay on my lips like a smidge of cake frosting, sweet yet dangerous.

"I'm sorry I don't have anything to...you know," Dante whispered. "I had a handkerchief, but it seems to be gone."

"The red bandana?"

He nodded.

"It's in my pack. We found it on our way here. It helped lead us to you." As quietly as I could, I unzipped my pack and rooted around for the bandana. I quickly wiped myself clean and then handed it to him.

"I don't know why I grabbed this," he whispered. "Just seemed like I might need it."

"Fate," I said quietly, smiling.

We both adjusted our clothing until we were again fully dressed. There was so much more I wanted to say to Dante in this moment. I wanted to tell him how much this quiet interlude had meant to me, how much I loved and trusted him never to forget me again. How all of this had been worth it to me because it had led me to him.

But that grand poetic gesture would wait until we could speak freely without whispering.

"Do you think it's safe to get out of here?"

Dante pulled his cell phone out of his pocket. "Nothing from River."

"Is there even service down here?"

"Believe it or not, there is. I have no idea how. You guys brought your phones, right?"

"Of course. They're all on silent." I poked into my pack again and pulled out my own phone. "Nothing. I don't have service."

"Hmm. That's strange."

"That might mean River and Jay don't have service either. If they don't, they can't get in touch with us."

"But why would I—" He shook his head. "*She* did this. She must have."

"How can she make sure one cell phone has service and others don't?" I whispered, more harshly than I'd intended.

"I don't know how she does half the shit she does." He shook his head. "I can't talk about this right now. It will make me angry, and then I won't be able to control my voice. Or the rest of me, for that matter."

I nodded, entwining my fingers through his. "It's okay. Relax."

He stood stiffly and didn't respond, and I realized how ridiculous my command had been. He wasn't capable of relaxing any more than I was, even after an amazing orgasm.

We wouldn't truly relax until we had found the women

and Dante's uncle and gotten them out of here.

"I'm going to check the door," Dante said.

I gasped quietly. Or at least I tried to.

"There's no other way," he said. "We can't stay in here forever." He turned the knob slowly.

A stream of harsh fluorescent light hurt my eyes. I squinted.

"I don't see anyone," Dante whispered.

"Should we go?"

He nodded, extending his arm. I gripped his hand and followed him out into the hallway.

"We have to find River and Jay," Dante said.

"Your dad told them to go down that other hallway. Do you think they're still there?"

"Probably. There's no way to know, if their phones aren't working." He checked his phone again. "Nothing."

Then he cocked his head to the right. "Did you hear that?" he whispered.

I shook my head.

"Shit!" He pushed me back into the closet. "Stay here until I come for you." He closed the door quietly.

My heart thundered and my bowels churned. Not a good time. I had no idea where the bathrooms were around this place, and there certainly wasn't one in this tiny closet.

Dante, please! Don't leave me here!

I shouted the words in my mind.

Seconds passed. Then minutes. I strained, my ear against the door, trying to hear something, anything.

Nothing.

Sheer silence met my ear. I didn't even hear Dante walking away. Away from me.

No, Erin. Don't. Do not cry.

I gulped back the threatening tears. Dante would never put me in danger, so if he told me to stay put, I would stay put. I had food and water in my pack. I would be okay.

But I didn't want to be okay. I wanted Dante. I wanted to find Lucy. I wanted to find Patty Doyle and her baby who had been crying in my dream.

I'd heard a baby crying when we were underground, searching for this place. I'd also heard a woman scream. But this underground hospital was most certainly soundproof, so where had those cries come from?

I shook my head. Dr. Bonneville. It was all a trap, wasn't it? Oxygen was being piped in. Was sound? Had she piped the sound of a baby crying through that dark tunnel? She was staying one step ahead of us.

The minute hand moved slowly around the face of my watch, my eyes having once again adjusted to the darkness in the small closet. Minutes turned into an hour.

Something knocked against the door. I shrank farther into the shadows, though there wasn't anywhere I could really hide. For a moment, I was frozen in terror. Then two soft raps followed the first.

An enemy wouldn't knock.

"Erin, are you in there?"

Jay. My brother. Thank God! I opened the door and threw myself into his arms.

"Easy. I've got you." He kissed the top of my head.

"Where's Dante?" The voice came from River, who was standing behind Jay.

"He left an hour ago. He acted like he'd heard something, but I didn't hear anything. He told me to stay here until he came back for me. But he didn't come back." I gulped back a sob.

"Man." River shook his head. "I hope he didn't go after those thugs."

"They ended up at the pharmacy, like Julian said," Jay said. "But we couldn't hear anything."

"*You* couldn't hear them?" I said to River.

"Just small talk. I heard three distinct voices, but they didn't say anything important."

"Three of them. Did one of them have a beard?"

"We didn't see them. We didn't dare move out of the supply closet."

"We waited awhile," Jay said, "and when we didn't hear from you guys, we decided to leave. Has Dante's dad been back here?"

I shook my head. "And I don't want him here. I want him with Dante. God, where is he?"

My thoughts raced to the worst-case scenario. Dr. Bonneville had come back into the hospital, had found him, and had taken him captive again. Somewhere he was tied up and being tortured at this very moment.

"No," I said.

"No, what?" River asked.

"I'm just scared. I'm scared Bonneville got to Dante. He said he'd come back for me. He would have, unless something kept him from it."

River sighed, his lips a flat line.

He knew I was right.

"Look," Jay said, "I know you both love Dante, but whether he's here or not, we have a mission to accomplish. First, find Lucy. Or figure out how to scare her into shifting so she can find us. Then find the other women."

River nodded. "He's right. Dante will take care of himself."

"But—"

"You know I'm right, Sis."

Yes, I knew he was right. The women had to be our priority. But I wasn't sure River was right. *Could* Dante take care of himself? He'd been held captive somewhere near here for ten years. This place did something to him. I didn't want him to be alone, not when I could be with him, could help him when the darkness threatened him.

River sniffed. "I'm getting something."

"I thought you said vampires didn't have any scent," Jay said.

"They don't. But human blood does. That's what I'm smelling. Blood from a blonde, actually. Probably a female."

Jay's brows nearly shot off his forehead. "Lucy?"

River opened his eyes. "No, not Lucy. Doesn't matter. I was smelling it the whole time you and I were hiding because we were so close to the blood bank, and I thought it was just the memory of that scent, but now I don't think so. It's strong here. Someone has been here, someone with human blood."

"Maybe one of the other women?" I asked. "Except none of them had blond hair. Of course she could be holding other women we don't know about."

River shook his head. "I don't think so. It's not pungent enough. More likely it was the thugs carrying units of blood from the bank."

"Blood that came from a blond woman?" Jay said.

"Yeah. Maybe. Doesn't matter. It's definitely blood, and it definitely went down this hallway." He pointed. "That way."

"Then we should go the other way," I said. "Right?"

"No, Sis," Jay said. "If they're carrying blood, they're

probably going toward the women."

"Exactly." River nodded. "Let's roll."

EIGHTEEN

DANTE

I followed Decker and two others stealthily, until they came to a stainless-steel door on the other side of the hospital.

I recognized that door, though the memory had only recently surfaced.

I'd been through it before, more than once.

This was the doorway to true hell.

"She wants the blood for the wolf," Decker said. "I guess she got fucked up pretty bad and needs a transfusion."

The wolf. Lucy. Damn. If she needed a transfusion, she was in no condition to change. We couldn't force a change on her.

"You're not as quiet as you think, shithead." Decker turned around, meeting my gaze. He snarled.

My fangs dropped.

Decker gasped.

"Take me to the wolf," I growled. "And then, take me to the others."

"She talks about 'the chosen one' all the time." He eyed my

teeth. "Giles was right. Now I can see why. It's you."

The chosen one? Chosen to be put back in a dungeon, apparently. I growled. "I took you out once. I can do it again. I want to see the women you're holding here."

"Look, man, we have nothing to do with all that," one of the others said. "We bring her blood and meds. That's it. We don't know where they are."

"Wrong. Your boss here just said she wants the blood for the wolf."

"The wolf is a little bitch. I should have sliced her innards out that night in the cemetery," the third vamp said. "I say let her bleed to death."

A menacing growl rose in my throat. This was the vampire who had stabbed Lucy. "Take me to her now," I said in a voice not quite my own.

Decker shoved a small soft-sided cooler into my hands. "You want to see her? Fine. Take the blood in there yourself. We don't fucking care whether the little bitch dies. Open the door, Flynn."

Flynn, the vampire who'd wanted to cut out Lucy's innards, inserted a key into the deadbolt and opened the door. "There you go. Have fun."

Erin. She was still safely in the closet. She'd told me she had food and water. I hadn't meant to be gone long, but now I had gained entrance to another part of *her* lair. I had to take the chance while I had it. Plus, if Lucy was truly in trouble, both Erin and River would want me to take care of her.

I'm sorry, baby, I said silently. *I love you and I will return for you.*

Then I dropped the cooler and pounced on Decker with a right hook to his nose.

"Fuck!" he cried out.

The one called Flynn jumped onto my back, but I shrugged him off as if he were a toddler. I turned around quickly and slammed him against the wall. "You fucking stabbed her, you piece of shit."

"Little bitch had it—"

I choked him until he passed out, and I let his big body fall to the floor.

I turned to the other vampire.

"Hey, man. We're good here."

"Sorry. I can't leave you standing. You all need to be out cold." I executed a roundhouse to his kidney.

He doubled over, and I finished him with an axe kick to the small of his back. His head hit the tile floor, leaving him unconscious.

I returned to Decker, whose nose was spewing blood. I slammed him up against the wall, my fingers squeezing his neck. "How many more of you are there?"

"Fuck you!" he said with a rasp. He attempted to spit in my face, but he lacked the velocity and his saliva dribbled down his chin.

I squeezed harder. "There's Giles, right? That makes four. Any more?"

"Fuck—"

I squeezed harder. "Do you think I care if you live or die? You either tell me how many there are, or I find out another way. I can kill you right now. Right here."

"You...can't—"

One more pinch to his neck, and he caved.

"Six altogether. The other two...are...above ground. Getting drugs."

"And Giles?"

"She..." He wheezed. "She put him...in...the arena."

NINETEEN

Erin

"Shit!" I clasped my hand to my mouth.

Three men lay unconscious in front of a steel door.

A steel door that was cracked open.

River inhaled. "They're vamps."

"I... I recognize them," I stammered. "From my dream. He's the leader." I pointed to the bearded one, who was bleeding profusely from his nose. I knelt down and checked his wrist for a pulse. "He's alive. Just out." I quickly checked the other two. "Alive as well."

"Dante," River said. "Who else could take on three vampires?"

"I've seen him take on two," I said. "And he seems to get stronger by the day. But why wouldn't he come back for me?"

"He will," River said. "But if he found a way to get through this door, he probably took it. Just like we're going to do." He sniffed. "Lucy is in there somewhere."

"You've picked up her scent? Great! We can get right to her."

River inhaled again, closing his eyes. "I've missed her scent."

"You can get googly-eyed later," Jay said. "Let's go. Or as you like to say, 'let's roll.'"

I nodded. "Dante's in there somewhere. But what about these guys?" I pointed to the vamps.

"We leave them," Jay said. "They're criminals."

"Yeah. I know, but—"

"Don't get all nursy on me," Jay said.

"But I'm supposed to help people."

"Your boyfriend most likely did this. They're not on our side, Sis."

"Fine. Let's go." I reached toward the door.

"Nope, me first," River said, gently pushing me out of the way. His hand was on his holster. "You in the middle. Jay in back."

I nodded and followed River through the doorway.

The hallways looked the same, white and sterile. Perhaps this was another part of the hospital. I listened intently. Were Patty and the baby here?

We walked silently down the corridor, but we didn't meet anyone. No staff milling around. Nothing.

River led us, sniffing. "She's here. This way."

We headed down another hallway toward a doorway.

"In there," River said. He walked to a door and pushed it open.

"Hey! This is a sterile environment. Get out of here!"

I recognized that voice. I pushed my way past River and faced the man in the white coat and hospital mask. "Logan?"

And in a hospital bed, unconscious and battered was—

"Oh my God! Lucy!"

"She needs a transfusion. Someone is supposed to bring me blood."

"Who?"

"Her runners."

The vampires. The vampires who were unconscious on the other side of the steel door. Did they have packs? I couldn't remember.

"Take mine. I have her same type. B positive."

"I do too," Jay said.

"That's not protocol. Blood has to be tested and—"

"For God's sake, Logan. Is *any* of this protocol? I don't have hepatitis or HIV. I promise."

"I don't either," Jay echoed.

"I don't have the equip—" He turned abruptly. "Doctor."

Dr. Bonneville stood in the doorway of the room.

Chills of fear swept through me, and both Jay and River stepped in front of me.

"Where's my father, you bitch?" River demanded.

Bonneville entered, ignoring River and seemingly unconcerned about our presence. "How is our patient, Dr. Crown?"

"She needs the transfusion. Soon."

"The blood hasn't been delivered?"

"Does it look like it's been delivered?"

I couldn't help a slight smile. I was glad he got rude with her. "Dr. Bonneville—" I began.

She whisked past me, ignoring me. "Get these people out of here. This patient needs quiet."

"Where's Dante?" I demanded.

"Where's my father?" River demanded again.

"Get them out of here," Bonneville said again to Logan.

Logan turned toward us. "You heard her."

River stalked forward. "Oh, think again." He approached Lucy's bedside. "What have they done to you, sweetheart?"

I gulped. Lucy's face was bruised, her eyes closed and puffy. Lacerations etched the swollen contours of her cheekbones and jawline. A wound on her neck was bandaged, and the rest of her body was covered by the white sheet of her bed.

"Who the fuck did this to her?" River's fangs were long and sharp.

Dr. Bonneville ignored him. "Get them out of here."

Logan's face paled. "He's a..."

This time, Dr. Bonneville bared her fangs.

And I gulped.

I'd seen her like this before, only I hadn't remembered. But seeing her...her cuspids so thin and long and sharp, so different from Dante's. The images came hurtling into my head.

"You. I knew it was you."

"Yes, Erin. Your blood is delicious. I couldn't help myself. Blah, blah, blah. You won't remember any of this anyway, so it doesn't matter."

"*I'll* remember it, bitch," River said, holding Lucy's pale hand.

"Actually, you won't," Bonneville said. "Do you think I'd even allow you in this place if I thought you'd have any recollection at all?"

"Dante remembered," River said. "So did his father."

Bonneville smiled, her fangs a strange contrast to the saccharine oozing from her lips. "Dante remembered only what I allowed him to remember. He needed to remember enough to return to me, and now he has."

"Dante is—"

"Shut up, Erin!" she growled. "And before I need to say it again, the rest of you shut up as well. This patient needs blood." She looked at Jay. "You. Come here."

"I don't think so," Jay said.

"I need your blood for this patient. Sit down in that chair. Dr. Crown, take a unit of blood from that human." She sniffed. "He's B positive."

"No!"

Jay gestured for me to be quiet. "I'll be fine. Lucy needs the blood. You know that yourself."

"Doctor," Logan said, "this isn't protocol—"

"We don't have time for protocol. She needs blood now."

"I'll go back to the blood bank and get some blood," River said. "It will take less time than taking blood from Jay and then transfusing it."

"Go ahead," Bonneville said. "We'll be done here before you're back. I have sophisticated equipment here, things most doctors don't have access to."

"That's bullshit—" River's eyes glazed over.

I shot my brow upward. "Did you just glamour him? A vampire?"

"Your boyfriend has educated you well, Erin. You believe vampires can't glamour other vampires. Most can't. I'm not most, however."

"But Dante—" I stopped. Dante was remembering. Every day he remembered more and more. Did she know that? She must. She knew he'd come back, apparently.

Jay had taken a seat, and Logan was checking his blood pressure.

"No time for that," Bonneville snapped.

"But if his—"

"I said no time!"

Logan's eyes went glassy, and he swabbed off the crease in Jay's elbow. Jay closed his eyes and went rigid when Logan inserted the needle into his vein.

Jay went white. Was he afraid of the needle? No, it was already inside his skin. Was he glamoured?

He shook his head slightly at me.

No. Not glamoured. I wasn't glamoured either, which was odd.

But River...

River was the only one who could protect us, and he was incapacitated.

"Doctor," I said, "why are you playing with Lucy's life like this? River could have gotten B positive blood from the bank a lot faster than this."

"Erin, did I ask for your opinion?"

Then it hit me, what she was truly up to. "Oh my God! You want Lucy to die!"

"I'm a physician, for God's sake. I don't want anyone to die."

"You're lying. I always defended you in the ER. But the others. They were right. You do want her to die! Why?"

"Shut up!" Her voice came out in a ferocious growl.

"Where's Dante?"

"Erin, you're a smart girl. What part of 'shut up' don't you understand?"

"You know everything, don't you? You tried to get me pregnant with Dante's baby. You're trying to— Oh my God. That's why you took Emilia. That's why you took— You're trying to produce vampire children by mating vampires and humans. Admit it, Doctor. Admit it!"

"I'm sure your boyfriend has told you that a vampire child from mating a vampire and a human is impossible."

"That's what you're doing here. What Levi Gaston tried to do but failed. But why would you take Lucy? I don't underst—"

"Levi Gaston was an old fool."

"He was a genetics researcher."

"And an alchemist. Alchemy is not science. It's voodoo."

I opened my mouth to shout out my defense of voodoo, because of Bea, but quickly shut it. Not a good time, when Bea had allowed Julian access to all the shielded portions of this hellish place. Bonneville didn't need to know that.

"Something about females with B positive blood. You've been stealing blood from our hospital and having your thugs steal more of it. And the drugs, and the—" I regarded Logan. "The lithium. You're using it to control Logan somehow, because he's descended from a vampire."

"Erin, you're in way over your head here, and I could take you out with a swipe of my hand."

"Then why haven't you?"

"I have my reasons, and you have no idea what you're talking about."

"I may not, but I know you're doing something you shouldn't be doing. You're imprisoning people. You're killing peo—"

"I am *not* a killer!" Her voice morphed into a monstrously low volume. "I'm saving this little bitch's life, and she's been nothing but a thorn in my side since she was brought here."

"Then why did you bring her here? If you're trying to produce vampires, why on earth did you take Lucy?"

"She was figuring out too much."

My mouth dropped open. Was Bonneville telling the

truth? And if so, why would she admit it to me?

"You're trying to kill her. We could have gotten the blood sooner, and now—"

"I am *not* a killer!"

"Don't believe her, Erin."

Dante's voice.

My heart leaped as I turned. He stood in the doorway, large and magnificent.

"She's very *much* a killer."

DANTE

Rage whirled through me, and my teeth, already descended, lengthened and sharpened with a painful snap.

"Move away from her," I said to her, motioning to Lucy.

Logan Crown was catatonic next to Jay, who was sitting in a chair getting blood taken. I handed the cooler to Logan. "I have the blood she needs. Get it into her. Now."

His glamour released. I wasn't sure how I did it, but clearly I had. Then I turned to *her*. "What did you do to River?"

"Something *you'll* never replicate."

Anger pulsed through me with a roar. "Release him. Now."

"Or what?"

I lunged toward her, but River snapped out of his glamour and caught me. "Don't, Dante. Lucy might need her."

I inhaled, exhaled, inhaled, cooling myself off. Lucy. I didn't trust Bonneville anywhere near Lucy, but she was the priority at the moment. I turned to Logan Crown. "Get her transfused. Now."

He nodded. Erin rushed to help him. Within a few minutes,

Lucy was hooked up and the lifesaving blood was trickling into her vein.

I inhaled again.

Only Erin's scent in this room, despite the fact that Lucy, Jay, and the transfused blood were all here.

Still, I smelled only Erin. The blood bond.

I snarled at Bonneville. "If Lucy dies, her blood is on your hands."

"I am *not* a killer," she said again through clenched teeth.

"Keep saying that, and maybe you'll believe it yourself. I never will."

I knew, now, that she *was* a killer. I'd seen evidence with my own eyes. Evidence I could never forget. Evidence I had to eventually share with River, Erin, and Jay.

How could I? What I'd seen would break them. All of them. And though I hadn't killed, I'd reaped the benefit.

"How long will the transfusion take?" River asked Erin.

"It can take anywhere from one to four hours," she said. "I'm not leaving her."

"I'm afraid you are," Bonneville said.

I threw a lasso of anger toward her, and her eyes widened. She didn't move. She *couldn't* move.

"They're not going anywhere," I said, clenching my teeth.

Bonneville's mouth dropped open, but nothing came out.

River looked to Jay still sitting in the chair. "You okay, partner?"

"Yeah. I've given blood before."

"Get something out of your pack to eat, and drink some water," Erin said. "You need it."

Jay nodded and opened his pack.

She stood quietly, immobile. I was between her and the door.

"You put Lucy in that fighting pit with a vampire," I said.

"She was trained."

"Trained? In a day?"

"She was adequately prepared."

"You wanted to kill her."

"I am not—"

"Spare me. You used Erin and River as leverage to keep her from shifting, and you dropped her in the arena with one of your thugs. Just because you don't pull the trigger doesn't make you any less a killer."

"Think before you accuse, Dante. You've done some heinous things yourself. Or do you not remember?"

How many fights had there been? I'd lost count. I'd never kept count. As soon as I left the arena, all I wanted to do was forget what I'd been forced to do.

No.

What I'd done.

Yes, I'd been forced to do it.

But in the end, I had done it. I could have stopped. I could have let her kill me. That would have ended the madness.

My will to survive was strong, stronger than my desire to end what she was forcing me to do.

Dad! *I cried out in my head.* Where are you? Why didn't you come for me? Why didn't you find me? She's forced me to do heinous things. Things I can't even remember. Things I don't want to remember.

My father never came. My grandfather never came. My uncle never came. My cousin never came.

I was alone.

Forgotten.

Abandoned.

Lost.

Forsaken.

No one would come for me. If I wanted to get out of this horrible place, I'd have to do it myself.

I tugged at the leather bindings.

And I remembered...

Electricity poured through my body. "*I didn't kill anyone.*"

"Didn't you?"

"Dante," Erin said, "Logan and I need to monitor Lucy closely. Any conflict isn't good for her. We don't need *her* anymore."

"I'm not leaving her side," River said.

"I'm staying too," Jay agreed.

"This is my hosp—"

I grabbed Bonneville's arm and yanked her out of the room, closing the door behind us.

She growled, baring her teeth. "Have you forgotten who's in control here?"

I snarled. Her teeth were no match for mine, and the slight widening of her eyes showed she was aware of that fact.

Control. She still thought she had control. As long as I could rein in the darkness she'd put in my head, I could maintain control.

"Did you miss the part where I rendered you immobile? Twice now?"

She said nothing. What could she say? She'd made me what I was.

"You say I did some heinous things," I said. "I don't deny it. I fought. I took men I didn't know to the ground to save my own ass. But I did *not* kill."

"You will never know for sure." Her lips curled into a serpentine smile. "I've made certain of that."

"I already know. You put me in that pit with vampires. Vampires, your own species that you're trying to recreate. You wouldn't allow a vampire life to be taken. Those men were sperm donors, weren't they? There's a reason I never remember the strike to kill." I clenched my teeth. "Because. It. Didn't. Happen."

Her lips slid into another snakelike smile. "You will never know for sure, though. Will you?"

"I already do. I have faith." That word again. Everyone told me to have faith, and finally, I did. I had faith in myself. I had never killed. If I had, I would know.

"You're forgetting who has the power here, Dante. Everything that is happening is because I have willed it."

"You willed Erin, River, and Jay to come here?"

"Of course."

No. That was a lie. "I don't believe you. You're bluffing. Your power over me is waning, and it scares you."

"I have power you can't even begin to imagine."

"It pales in comparison to what I have," I said.

"Everything you have is a gift from me."

Was it? The darkness. These new powers that were manifesting. Maybe they *had* come from *her*. But my real power, my true power, came from love. From faith. Those were the virtues that allowed me to harness the energy inside me for good. Those were the virtues that had allowed me to immobilize *her* twice now. Those were the virtues that were the true me.

And they had come from Erin.

My Erin.

Our blood bond.

Only Erin had shown me what was possible for me in this world, and no matter how strong my dark energy became, I would always be able to turn it. To use it for good.

Power coiled within me, and—

River and Jay burst out of the room. River's eyes were rimmed with red.

"What is it?"

"They—" He gulped. "They made us leave. They— They—"

Jay laid his hand on River's shoulder. "They're losing Lucy."

TWENTY-ONE

Erin

"BP is dropping quickly," I said to Logan after River and Jay had been forced out the door. "Damn! Help her, Logan."

"I'm doing my best. I've got the blood going into her as quickly as possible."

"Her heart rhythm is erratic. Oh my God!"

"Erin, I need you. Hold yourself together."

I nodded. The doctor needed me. Lucy needed me. I would not let them down.

"Get the paddles ready, Erin. I'm going to try to shock her back into normal sinus rhythm."

I nodded again. The paddles were not without risk. Lucy was in a weakened state, but we had no choice.

I would not lose my best friend.

"Ready, Doctor." I handed the paddles to Logan.

"Come on, Lucy." Logan placed the paddles onto Lucy's chest.

Nothing.

"Logan?"

"They're not working. What's wrong with the power?"

I eyed the machine. "It all checks out. Try again."

Again, nothing.

"Damn it!" Logan tried again.

"The power isn't getting through to the paddles," I said. "Must be a faulty wire or something."

"Damn!"

Dr. Bonneville burst into the room. "What's going on here?"

"We need to shock her back into a normal sinus rhythm, but the defibrillator is malfunctioning."

"Let me see that."

"Logan, no!" I screamed. "She'll kill her!"

"I am *not* a killer!" Bonneville took the paddles from Logan.

Tears formed in the corners of my eyes. I'd seen Dr. Bonneville save patients in the ER. I'd trusted her then. But now? Now that I knew everything she was capable of?

River rushed back into the room, plunging into Bonneville, knocking her off balance, and tackling her to the ground.

"Logan, do what you can! Please!" I yelled.

Then I fell to the floor and punched Dr. Bonneville in the nose. She was a vampire, so she was stronger than I was, but I didn't care at the moment. Strength came from within, coiled up through me, and burst out of my fists. I punched her again. Again. Again. Blood spurted from her nose and mouth, and her fangs were long and sharp.

Her lips were curled upward slightly. She was letting me do this to her.

I didn't care.

She had taken Dante. She had taken Lucy. She would take nothing else from me.

"Erin."

Logan's voice.

"Erin. She's okay."

I jolted, as if a current of electricity had struck me. I stood as quickly as I could.

Lucy's EKG had returned to normal.

Dante stood next to her, his hand on her bare chest.

Shock. Couldn't move.

Even Dr. Bonneville, who stood as though I hadn't just been beating the shit out of her, lifted her brow as blood oozed from her nostrils.

Logan checked Lucy's vitals. "She's okay. I don't believe it. She's going to be okay."

"Dante?" I said. "What happened?"

"It was him," Logan said. "He touched her chest, and..."

"Dude," River said. "Get your hand off my woman's breasts."

Dante moved his hand away. "I don't know what happened. I followed Bonneville in, and when nothing was happening, I just..."

"You saved her, Dante," I said, taking his hand.

"I don't know what I did."

I squeezed his hand. "Thank you."

"But I don't know what I did."

"You did what you always do." I turned. I didn't want to say anything more in front of Bonneville, but she was gone. "Where did she go?"

"I'm glad she's gone for the moment," River said.

"Don't be fooled," Dante said. "She knows exactly what she's doing."

"You can control her, Dante," I said. "She's running scared."

"Sorry, but you all need to get out of here," Logan interrupted. "I need to keep a close eye on the patient. Erin, if you could stay, please."

I hadn't come here to be a nurse, but this was Lucy, and she needed me. Plus, maybe I could get some information out of Logan now that Lucy was out of harm's way. "Of course." I squeezed Dante's hand once more. "Are you okay?"

He nodded, though the expression on his face was noncommittal at best.

"We've got him," River said.

Dante kissed my cheek quickly and then followed River and Jay out of the room, closing the door quietly.

I checked Lucy's IV site and recorded her vitals on a chart. Then I turned to Logan.

"All right. Start talking."

TWENTY-TWO

DANTE

*S*he was nowhere in the hallway by the time River, Jay, and I left the room. No trace of *her*, and I wasn't about to go chasing her down. I was staying right here, where Erin was in the next room.

"You okay?" Jay asked me.

I nodded, though I wasn't sure the response was accurate. I'd been angry. So angry. Energy had bubbled within me, beginning in the very core of my gut and emanating throughout my body. I'd been ready to knock *her* senseless, take from *her* all she'd taken from me, when Erin's voice had crept into my psyche.

She had been distraught, crying for help.

She had gone into the room, acting all doctor-like. As if she truly cared. And Erin had pounced.

The energy had sizzled inside me, and before I knew what I was consciously doing, I was at Lucy's bedside with the palm of my hand against her cold chest.

Logan Crown had jolted in surprise, and then he rushed

around, checking machines. "Normal sinus rhythm. Damn. How? How?"

I didn't know how. I held my right hand in front of me and stared at it. It was a large hand, long fingers, a few black hairs across the knuckles. A hand that had dealt crippling blows in the fighting pit. A hand that had caressed the soft skin of Erin's cheek. A hand that had slapped her bottom, bursting capillaries and bringing forth a gorgeous rosy pinkness.

A hand.

Simply a hand.

"What about you?" Jay asked.

I jerked.

"I'm good," River said. "I mean, now that she's going to be okay and all. I can't lose her."

"It's really love then, huh?"

My cousin nodded. "I think so. Maybe not forever love, but it's something. I know it hasn't been very long."

Jay clapped him on the back. "Time doesn't always make a lot of sense where love is concerned. At least that's what I've heard."

"I'd like to fucking mutilate whoever did this to her."

"The arena," I said quietly.

"Huh?" River asked.

"They put her in a fighting arena with a vampire. Made her fight for survival. At least that's what they probably told her. She thought she'd die."

"Damn." River shoved his fingers through his unruly hair. "They did that to you too?"

"Yeah. A lot."

"And you always won?"

I nodded. "But I never killed my opponent. I know that

now. *She* just made me think I did."

"Damn," River said again.

I shook my head. "I don't know what's happening to me. When I fight the dark energy, I'm not as strong. When I embrace it, I sometimes succumb. But this last time... I didn't succumb. I embraced it, and I stayed in my mind. And I... Damn. I healed Lucy."

"Yes, you did, son."

My father appeared next to River.

"Uncle Jules! Where have you been?"

"I followed a lead, but unfortunately it led me nowhere."

"What lead?" Jay asked.

"It's not important. Not now, at least. I have news." His voice was low and sad.

"What is it, Dad?"

He sighed, a wistful sound coming from a ghost. "I've found my brother."

River's eyes shot open. "Is he okay?"

"He's alive."

But not okay. The words my father didn't say. Perhaps couldn't say.

"Take me to him," River said. "I need to see him."

"It's not that simple. He's in an area that is shielded."

"We'll get to him," River said. "We have to."

I nodded. "I can get to him, Dad. I don't know how, but I can do it. I have to."

My father nodded. "This won't be easy."

Getting to him? Or seeing him? My father undoubtedly meant both.

"I found someone else as well," my father said.

"Who?" I asked.

"It's not pretty," he said.

Emilia was safe. Erin was safe. Lucy was safe. Uncle Brae was...well, he was alive, if not exactly safe. Who else was there?

"Dad, I've been to hell, remember?"

My father nodded. "I found your homeless friend. Abe Lincoln."

THE QUEEN

Why do I call myself the queen, you might ask?

You've learned many of my secrets, Dante, but you haven't learned that one.

I admit, your power has surpassed even what I dreamed of, and your mind is strong. Very, very strong.

But I assure you, I will triumph in the end. I will have everything I've worked for.

And you will help me.

For I have one weapon you don't know about yet.

BLOOD BOND SAGA

PART 14

Erin

"You saved her, Dante," I said, taking his hand.

"I don't know what I did."

I squeezed his hand. "Thank you."

"But I don't know what I did."

"You did what you always do." I turned. I didn't want to say anything more in front of Bonneville, but she was gone. "Where did she go?"

"I'm glad she's gone for the moment," River said.

"Don't be fooled," Dante said. "She knows exactly what she's doing."

"You can control her, Dante," I said. "She's running scared."

"Sorry, but you all need to get out of here," Logan interrupted. "I need to keep a close eye on the patient. Erin, if you could stay, please."

I hadn't come here to be a nurse, but this was Lucy, and she needed me. Plus, maybe I could get some information out of Logan now that Lucy was out of harm's way. "Of course." I squeezed Dante's hand once more. "Are you okay?"

He nodded, though the expression on his face was noncommittal at best.

"We've got him," River said.

Dante kissed my cheek quickly and then followed River and Jay out of the room, closing the door quietly.

I checked Lucy's IV site and recorded her vitals on a chart. Then I turned to Logan.

"All right. Start talking."

ONE

DANTE

I shook my head. "I don't know what's happening to me. When I fight the dark energy, I'm not as strong. When I embrace it, I sometimes succumb. But this last time... I didn't succumb. I embraced it, and I stayed in my mind. And I... Damn. I healed Lucy."

"Yes, you did, son."

My father appeared next to River.

"Uncle Jules! Where have you been?"

"I followed a lead, but unfortunately it led me nowhere."

"What lead?" Jay asked.

"It's not important. Not now, at least. I have news." His voice was low and sad.

"What is it, Dad?"

He sighed, a wistful sound coming from a ghost. "I've found my brother."

River's eyes shot open. "Is he okay?"

"He's alive."

But not okay. The words my father didn't say. Perhaps couldn't say.

"Take me to him," River said. "I need to see him."

"It's not that simple. He's in an area that is shielded."

"We'll get to him," River said. "We have to."

I nodded. "I can get to him, Dad. I don't know how, but I can do it. I have to."

My father nodded. "This won't be easy."

Getting to him? Or seeing him? My father undoubtedly meant both.

"I found someone else as well," my father said.

"Who?" I asked.

"It's not pretty," he said.

Emilia was safe. Erin was safe. Lucy was safe. Uncle Brae was...well, he was alive, if not exactly safe. Who else was there?

"Dad, I've been to hell, remember?"

My father nodded. "I found your homeless friend. Abe Lincoln."

I kind of liked old Red Rover. Erin was fond of him, and he'd helped me out the night I escaped. But right now, Braedon had to be our priority.

"We get Uncle Brae first," I said.

"Actually," my father said, "Abe Lincoln is easier to get to. The place is shielded, but it's closer and he's not tied up."

"But Uncle Brae—"

"Is not in any immediate danger that I can ascertain." His voice was low and grave. "Abe Lincoln, however, is."

"Uncle Jules," River began, "you can't really be saying some homeless guy is a priority over my father."

"Don't bother baring your fangs, River," he said. "I understand your anger."

"Do you? I don't care what kind of shield she has over my dad. I'm getting to him."

I nodded, energy still crackling through me. "I'm with Riv on this one."

"Not that I'm entitled to an opinion," Jay said, "but I agree. After the women, River's dad is the priority."

"Of course you're entitled to an opinion," my father said. "You're the father of my grandchild, so you're a part of this family. But Braedon isn't going anywhere, and we can't help him until we can get through the shield."

"How...is he?" River asked, his voice cracking a little.

"I wish I could tell you he's fine, but you wouldn't believe me if I did." My father sighed. "He's in shackles, and he's scarred. But inside, he's still Braedon. I'd know if he weren't."

"Yeah," River scoffed. "The twin thing."

"Your father would be the first to tell you it's real," my father said.

"What are they doing to him?"

"Torture," I said softly. "And they're making him fight, aren't they?"

"Honestly, I don't know," my father said. "They never made me fight while I was here."

"That you remember," I said, more to myself than to the rest of them. "I'm only remembering it gradually."

"True," my father said. "I do have lapses in my memory from when I was here."

"They mutilated you," I said, clenching my teeth. The image of my father's bare genitals was something I could never unsee.

"Actually, that's a memory that just recently resurfaced," he said. "No one here mutilated me. It must have been done after I died. I have no memory of it, but I'm certain I left here intact."

"How do you know?" River asked.

"I'm not going to go into detail," he said. "Suffice it to say I know, and that even at my age, certain things...arise when you'd rather they didn't."

"Then..." Rage consumed me. Decker and his gang had mutilated my father's dead body. But why?

Why else? So that I would see it.

So that I would be consumed by rage.

Rage at *her*.

My mind raced as thoughts bounced around like a pinball. "If she's trying to breed vampires, she needed you intact, so you could—"

"Oh my God," River said. "Is she using my father as breeding stock? Making him fuck these women? He would never..."

"No, your father is not a rapist, River." My father laid a ghostly hand on River's arm. "Neither am I. Neither is Dante."

"I never had sex with anyone while I was here," I agreed. Though there had been times when I'd wished for it, when *she* had ground on me, a young male with virtually no experience, and I'd wanted it. Wanted *her* even through my hate. Damn her.

"Neither did I," my father said. "But if she's trying to breed vampires, she's certainly not going to mutilate one of her prime males."

"Those bastards." I seethed.

"I'm not my body, Dante. I felt nothing."

"Still. You were a person, Dad. They shouldn't have done that to you."

"It wasn't me," he said again.

"Do you think that matters? Those thugs—"

"Either they did it because they were thugs, and that's

what thugs do, or they did it at her command," he said. "Either way, it was done to punish you, Dante. To bring your anger to the surface. Don't let them get what they were after."

No, they weren't after my anger, though that was certainly a side effect. They wanted to bring the dark energy to the surface. The dark energy *she*, or someone else here, had somehow planted within me.

Or awakened in me.

What if the darkness had always been there? What if she'd only activated it?

Energy crackled in my veins. Erin was still in the room with her friend and Logan. I peeked through the small window in the door to the room. She was sitting down, talking to Logan.

Possessiveness rose in me, and my fangs dropped with a painful snap.

"Dante?"

My father's voice.

"Dante?"

Then River's.

"Cuz, come on. This is important."

I snapped back into myself. "What?"

"My brother is in no immediate danger, as I said," my father said. "Abe Lincoln is."

"Why?"

As soon as the word left my lips, I knew.

I used to dream of severed human heads.

The dream that wasn't a dream after all.

Abe Lincoln was here to feed the winner from the fighting pit.

TWO

Erin

"I remember everything when I'm here," Logan said.

"Do you remember talking to River and me?"

"River?"

"Dante's—my boyfriend's—cousin. He was just in here."

"Bits and pieces. I was in a car?"

I nodded. "River glamoured you to try to get you to tell us where you'd been when you disappeared, but you resisted the glamour in some way. You came out of it and then went back in."

"Yeah. Bits and pieces. Damn Dr. Bonneville."

"Did you ever work at the free clinic over on Gravier Street?"

"No. Wait. Yeah. Once. No, twice."

"One of the women who disappeared and then returned mentioned you. Her name is Bella Lundy. You took blood from her."

"I might have." He scratched his head. "It's all a blur from when I'm back there, above ground. It seems like this is my life now."

"But you don't remember all of this when you're up there?"

"No. It's the same here. Like right now, I can't recall everything from up there. What the hell has she done to me?"

"Are you a competent surgeon, Logan?"

"Yeah. I did a surgical residency before my ER residency."

"This is starting to make sense now. Bonneville isn't a surgeon. She needs you for the complicated stuff."

"She's a bitch."

"We already knew that," I agreed. "She took my blood without my consent. She admitted it."

"She forced you to donate blood? Are you B positive?"

"Yeah, but that's not what I mean. She fed from me, Logan."

"Fucking bitch."

I inhaled. "Stating the obvious again. Is there anything else you can tell me? Is there a baby here? A girl?"

He nodded. "I operated on her. Nothing serious. A double inguinal hernia."

Relief swept through me. "So she's okay?"

"I haven't seen her in the last day or two, but yeah, I think she's okay."

"Is her mother here? Is her name Patty?"

"Yeah."

"I treated her at the ER. She and I bonded. I need to know she's okay."

"The people here in the hospital aren't in danger, Erin. She's doing some kind of research."

"First, they *are* in danger. They've been taken from their lives against their will. That's not right, and it's dangerous in itself. As for her research, we already figured that out. She's trying to produce vampire children by mating humans and vampires. B positive blood seems to be the key."

"Not just B positive blood, but B positive women," he agreed.

"Human women, yeah. According to Dante, vampire women are rare, so it's easier for her to get vampire sperm than vampire eggs. Plus a vampire male can reproduce pretty much all the time while a vampire woman is only fertile once every couple of years."

"There's a vampire woman here."

"I know. She's Dante's sister."

She's already pregnant, I added silently. *By my brother.*

I had to be careful. I wasn't sure how much Logan knew. Clearly, Bonneville was using him as a surgeon and attending physician for her captives. At least I knew he was a good doctor.

"What is it about B positive blood?" I asked. "And human women? She let two of the women go. Why?"

"I don't know, Erin. I guess they weren't useful."

"And why Lucy? She's a—" I clamped my mouth shut. Did Logan know?

"She's a what?"

"A...wolf shifter. She's a wolf shifter."

"For God's sake." Logan removed his glasses and began frantically cleaning them with a cloth from his coat pocket. "Vampires? And now shifters? How much am I supposed to take?"

You have no idea. "I met your great-grandfather."

"That's interesting, Erin, since he's dead."

"It wouldn't be outside the realm of possibility," I said, "but you're wrong. He's alive. He's a hundred and one years old."

He shook his head. "Impossible."

"Is your dad's name Hector Crown?"

"Uh...yeah."

"And your grandfather's name was James?"

He nodded. "I never knew him. He and my dad didn't speak, and the old guy's dead now, which means his father can't possibly be alive."

"Parents sometimes outlive children, Logan."

"Rarely."

"It's less rare when the parent in question is a vampire."

"Oh, for God's—" He stood. "I need to check on Lucy."

I nodded and stood to assist. We checked her vitals. She was resting comfortably.

"She looks normal," he said.

"She looks like she's been pummeled," I said.

"No. I mean she looks like a normal woman. Not a werewolf."

"Apparently they prefer the term shifter."

"Apparently my life isn't anything like what it seems."

"Trust me. I hear you. But surely you figured out..."

"Yeah. At least I know when I'm down here. Then, like I said, it's all hazy and I think it's mostly a dream."

"You're under a glamour to forget. Simple."

"Erin, nothing about any of this is simple."

I couldn't help a chuckle. He had that right. "Do you know what happened to Lucy? Who did this to her?"

He shook his head. "I'm only here to treat patients. I think." He cocked his head. "Sometimes..."

"What?"

"Sometimes I think I might do more here. I have dreams about this monstrous thing."

"What kind of monstrous thing?"

"I don't know. But it's so clear, clearer than a normal dream, you know?"

"Can you describe it?"

"It's human. Maybe. But it's big and mean, and it hates me."

"Why would it hate you?"

He swallowed. "Because, in the dream, I torture it. Big time."

THREE

DANTE

"I know what they have planned for Abe Lincoln," I said.

"So do I," my father said. "It's another memory that surfaced recently in my consciousness."

I used to dream of severed human heads. How could I say this in front of River and Jay? Especially River, who'd never tasted a drop of human blood?

"Don't keep us in suspense," River said. "What is it?"

Endorphins flowed through my body, making me float on clouds even though I was tied down to a table. As I floated, I lapped up the red gold that dripped down on me. It gave me sustenance. It gave me strength.

It gave me the will to go forward.

That was her mistake.

She killed to feed me, but in so doing, she fed not only my body but also my soul.

My soul gained no sustenance from her blood. But these humans who had been sacrificed to feed me... Without knowing, they strengthened me. Preserved my will.

Their deaths were not in vain.

I would see to that.

I would escape.

And I would end this.

Once and for all.

I cleared my throat. "The thugs. They prey upon the homeless. Bea must know this. Why did she never tell us?"

"Don't assume she knows," my father said.

"How could she not? These are her people."

"Bea doesn't know every homeless person in New Orleans. Perhaps they're not all homeless. They could be patients from hospitals who were freshly dead. Anyone who couldn't or wouldn't be traced."

"Uncle Jules," River said, "what the hell are you talking about?"

"Yeah," Jay agreed. "I don't like where this is going."

"Dante?" my father said. "Should you tell them, or should I?"

My father was dead. A ghost. Still very much here, but not bound with the nausea that was pouring through me at the thought of what I—apparently both of us—had done.

No wonder she'd made sure we didn't remember at first. Clearly, I had needed sustenance her blood hadn't given me.

Or had it simply been a reward?

No, my father said he hadn't fought.

It was sustenance we required. Vampire blood didn't have all the nutrients we needed. We required human or animal blood.

"She has to feed the vampires she keeps here."

"You said you drank her blood," River said.

"I did. She forced me to. But I also..." I swallowed down the bile inching up my throat. "I was forced..." No, that wasn't true. I could have shut my mouth, refused the blood. "I drank from freshly dead humans."

Jay turned around and heaved, though nothing came up.

River, already pale, simply stared at me.

"I was tied down," I said. "Their blood dripped onto me. I should have—"

"Don't do this to yourself, Dante," my father said. "You had a physiological need. I did as well."

"You tasted fresh blood before Erin," River said.

I nodded. I had nothing more to say.

"You didn't kill anyone?" Jay asked.

"No!" My fangs dropped in anger. "I didn't. I know that now. I *absolutely* know that."

I felt no better, though. Even though I hadn't killed, I still drank from the disembodied heads hanging over me.

"Do not blame him," my father said. "You don't know what it was like to be here. Right now, the important thing is to find Abe Lincoln and the others who were brought here as sustenance and free them."

River cleared his throat. "Right. You're right, Uncle Jules."

Jay stood weakly, pale and sick-looking.

"You going to make it, partner?" River asked.

Jay nodded unconvincingly.

I tamped down the anger that threatened to rise. This was

Erin's brother. He might be one-quarter vampire, but he didn't understand the lure of blood. Fresh blood.

"What do we do, Uncle Jules?" River asked.

"Abe is in a shielded area that Bea was able to get me access to."

"Who else has been in and out, if anyone?" River asked.

"Just the thugs, as you call them. The Claiborne vampires. They can obviously pass through the shield."

"Wait a minute." I reached into my pocket and pulled out the lapel pin with the vampire fleur-de-lis etched on it. "Were they wearing this when they entered?"

"I think so," my father said. "They all have them."

"I wonder..."

"We only have one," Jay said.

I cleared my throat. "You and I will go, Dad. Riv, you and Jay stay here with Erin."

"Are you kidding?" River shook his head.

"Dante has been here," my father said. "His memories are returning. Soon he'll know his way around this place. You won't. Besides, we don't yet know if the pin will work."

But I knew. The small gold trinket burned like a hot coal against my flesh. It was telling me something. Something I already knew. "There's a reason Decker and the others were so freaked when they couldn't find this pin at Em's place. They didn't want any of us getting our hands on it."

Look to your left.

Someone had guided me first to the small vodka bottle and then to the lapel pin. Had it been *her*, as I originally thought?

Or had it been *me*?

The darkness inside me. The darkness that had helped me find my way back here once I'd let it in. Once I'd proved I didn't fear it or what it might do to me.

Why would *she* care if one of the thugs lost their little lapel trinket?

Because it had another use—one I would take advantage of now.

"I'm going in," I said. "It has to be me. My father and I are the only ones who've been here. Between the two of us, we can find our way."

"But—"

"He's right, River," my father interrupted. "Plus, he has those strange powers that you don't. This is how it has to be."

"What exactly do you propose we tell my sister when she comes out of Lucy's hospital room and finds you gone?" Jay arched his eyebrows.

"You tell her the truth," I said. "That my father and I have gone to rescue Abe Lincoln. She knows he's in danger. She was with me when Bea told us he was going to be drained."

Jay nodded, sighing. "All right. She won't be happy."

"She'll be happy about Abe," I said. "She has a soft spot for him. He was her patient at the hospital a couple times. Plus she won't want any more innocent blood shed. But don't..." I couldn't finish.

"Don't what?" Jay asked.

"Don't tell her I drank fresh human blood. Please. That is for me, and only me, to tell her."

"But—"

"Don't!" I said through clenched teeth. "Just don't." I turned to my father's ghost. "Let's go, Dad."

FOUR

Erin

Logan's face was paler than I'd ever seen it. He was naturally fair, like I was, but right now he was white. Like a ghost.

But not like a ghost after all. I knew a ghost. Julian looked like a person when he appeared. He was not white. He was Dante's father, a vampire, so he was fair, but not white like a ghost.

Perception is reality. That fact became more ingrained in my head the further I delved into this mystery.

Logan had tortured something monstrous. In a dream. Or maybe not in a dream. I swallowed the nausea that threatened to come barreling up my throat.

He was suffering right now. He'd been unable to save Lucy due to the defibrillator malfunction, and now he was convinced he'd tortured some monstrous creature.

Lucy was still resting comfortably, so I focused on Logan.

"It could just be a dream, Logan."

He shook his head. "No. It's like all the others. A dream, until I'm back, and then I remember."

"You're here now, though, and you said it still seems like a dream."

"It's like..." He paced around the small room, avoiding Lucy's equipment, his heels clicking on the cold tile floor. "It's like I'm not myself. Like something has been transposed onto me. Something...not nice. Something almost..."

Evil?

I didn't want to say it, but that was the feeling Logan evoked in me. He was not an evil man. But he was not as he seemed, either. He'd been able to resist River's glamour to a certain extent, and then there was the time when I'd wanted to leave the hospital cafeteria, but he'd talked me into staying.

Chills coursed through me. Something wasn't right. I needed to go.

I stood. "Thank you for the coffee, but I have an appointment I need to get to."

"You're not leaving yet."

My eyes shot open. "I assure you I am. We're off duty. I don't have to follow your orders, Dr. Crown."

"Sit down, Erin."

Without knowing why, I sat. I didn't want to, tried not to. But somehow my ass ended back down on the hard cafeteria chair.

"Thank you," he said. "I won't take much more of your time. You're just...so easy to talk to."

That conversation was still hazy in my mind. What had we talked about? And why couldn't I recall it?

Logan's great-grandfather was a vampire. That made him one-eighth vampire, which shouldn't give him any special powers. I was one-quarter vampire, and I didn't have any. Did I?

He seemed truly remorseful that he might have caused another creature harm, even if it was a monster.

Or had it become a monster because of his torture?

We had Lucy to attend to, but I'd come here to help solve this mystery. Logan was clearly part of the key. I just didn't know how.

"What do you know about the properties of B positive blood, Logan?" I asked.

"Surely they taught you about blood types in nursing school, Erin."

"Yeah. But you went to med school. Maybe you got more information."

"There isn't anything other than what you already know." He spouted off a lecture I remembered from Biology 101.

Nope, nothing new there.

"But you've obviously noticed that the only blood type Bonneville stocks here is B positive. And that all the women here, except Emilia—"

"Emilia?"

"Dante's sister. The vampire woman. She never told you her name?"

"I haven't dealt much with her. Bonneville keeps her separated from the others."

"Oh." I wasn't sure why that surprised me, but it did. "Anyway, B positive blood has something to do with what she's doing here. Do you have any ideas?"

"Vampires are almost always Rh negative," he said.

"I know. Dante told me. But he's positive. B positive."

"So? There are exceptions, as I understand it."

"I know. But it's genetically impossible for him to have a positive Rh factor. Both of his parents were negative."

Logan wrinkled his brow.

"Any ideas?" I urged.

He sighed. "I don't know. Why would he even know his blood type?"

"Oh." I nodded. "You don't know, do you?"

"Know what?"

Dante was held captive here. For ten years. I couldn't say the words. Dante probably wouldn't appreciate me telling his story to Logan, a person he didn't particularly like. After all, they first met when I was about to take Logan into my bed to get my mind off Dante. Better to change the subject.

"Do you still hear voices, Logan?"

He dropped his mouth open. Yup, that was enough to take his mind off Dante's blood type.

"What are you talking about?"

"You told me you heard voices. Why do you take lithium?"

He rose and checked Lucy's vitals.

"Are you going to answer me?"

"This isn't any of your business, Erin. My mental health is fine."

"I'm sure it is. You're being treated. Are you bipolar?"

His lips formed a thin line as he wrote some notes on Lucy's chart. Then he turned back to me. "Maybe I should ask a question now. How did your boyfriend jump-start Lucy's heart into a normal rhythm?"

"If I knew, I'd gladly tell you. See? I answered you. Now will you answer me?"

He sighed and sat back down. "Yes, I'm bipolar. Happy now? Keep it to yourself, please. How do you even know about the lithium?"

Good question, and one I didn't want to answer. I'd been looking in his medical file for his blood type and had stumbled upon the medication by accident.

No. That was a lie. Of course I'd see any meds he was on if I got into his file. No use trying to make myself feel better.

"All right. Here's the truth," I said. "When you went missing, I checked the hospital files to see if you had a record. You did. I found an ER visit."

"You could be fired for that, Erin."

"I'm well aware of that, but I had my reasons."

"What were they?"

"I wanted to find out your blood type."

"Why would you— Oh."

"Yeah. I wanted to know if you're B positive."

"And I am."

I nodded. "You are."

"You think she only brings people here who are B positive?"

"That was my hunch at the time."

"Seems you might be right. Built-in blood donors for all these people."

"True. Now...I answered your question honestly. Will you tell me about the voices you hear?"

"It's under control," he said succinctly.

"I'm sure it is. I'm just trying to figure out why you had such a strange response to River's glamour. Dante's father said he'd heard that schizophrenia could cause such a reaction to a glamour."

"Sometimes diagnoses aren't accurate. I'm not schizophrenic, Erin."

"I'm not accusing—"

"Do you think I could have gotten through medical school

and two residencies as a schizophrenic?"

"Many schizophrenic people live normal lives, Logan."

"Normal lives as doctors?"

"Probably. I don't know. Look, like I said, I'm not accusing you of anything. I'm just trying to figure everything out. Why you're here. Why you and not another doctor? Why you seemed to pull out of River's glamour."

"And why did River glamour me in the first place?"

"That I know. We wanted to find out where you were when you went missing and what you did while you were there. Whether it was connected to the missing women."

"Clearly it was." He sighed. "The voices are silent most of the time. The lithium controls my mood, and also seems to quiet the voices. I'm a doctor. I know what they are. I'm not delusion—"

"Erin?"

Lucy's voice.

I turned to regard my friend.

And I gasped.

FIVE

DANTE

I followed my father's ghost to another steel door. It was unlocked. I raised my eyebrows.

"Locking isn't necessary. No one can get through the shield."

I looked down at the gold pin I'd attached to my shirt. "I guess we'll see about that." I opened the door.

My father swept in front of me and through the door.

I stepped through tentatively, almost expecting a jolt of electricity or some other punishment for what I was doing.

My father laughed. "It's okay, Dante. You wouldn't have been able to open the door against the shield."

I nodded and entered. The hallway was dark and dank.

Yes. *This* I remembered.

"Only you can hear me," my father said, "so I can speak freely. I'd advise you to speak in whispers."

"Understood," I whispered.

"Just follow me," he said.

We walked through the narrow corridor to another

hallway where several wooden doors stood.

Bile clawed at my throat.

I'd seen doors like this.

I'd been kept behind a door like this.

"It's okay, son. I was here once too. Easy. You can do this."

I nodded. Had my father gone through what I had? He'd clearly been tortured, but had he been forced to drink her blood? Been forced to give his own to *her*? Not that he'd ever told me. No. My father had been here for a different reason. One I didn't yet know. He probably didn't know either.

Had my sole purpose been to feed her?

And why had she taken my blood? What had it done for her?

As I followed my father quietly, these thoughts pattered in my mind.

Why?

Why?

Why?

I shivered. I was close to finding answers. Close to finding the truth.

Though I wanted that, it scared the hell out of me.

I knew now that I hadn't killed my opponents in the arena. I hadn't killed the humans sacrificed for my nourishment.

But what if I'd done something else just as horrid? Or worse?

My father cut those thoughts short, thank God, when we came to one of the wooden doors.

"Are they here?" I whispered.

He nodded.

I raised my hand to open the door, but left it suspended in midair.

"What are we doing?" I asked my father. "How do we get them out of here? We can free them, but what if she has the thugs gather them all up and imprison them again? We don't have a plan."

"Ah, but we do," my father said.

"Mind letting me in on it?"

"You're going to shield them and lead them out."

"I'm going to— What the fuck?"

"You have my ashes, right?"

I nodded. I'd brought them with me. I didn't know why, other than I wanted my father with me. Wanted his protection. Wanted some tangible part of him to hold on to.

"Good. You'll brush each of their foreheads with the ash and then lead them out the way we got here. Bea assured me you would get through undetected."

"Bea?"

"Apparently vampire ashes are more powerful than she led us to believe."

"How many people are in there? What if the ashes I brought aren't enough?"

"The ashes, along with your energy, will be enough."

"Will they get through the shield?"

"The shield keeps people from getting in. It doesn't keep people from escaping. You and I are proof of that."

"But she let me—"

"That's what she says. Maybe she did, and maybe she didn't. But one thing I know for sure is that no one let *me* escape. I escaped on my own."

"How do you know?"

He stayed silent for a few seconds.

"Dad?"

"Because I've seen my brother. He has paid the price for my escape."

SIX

Erin

"Logan! What's happening to her?"

"She was fine a minute ago." Logan rushed to Lucy. Her EKG was running amok.

"Erin?" she said again, her voice more like a growl.

"She's changing," I said. "Lucy, will you be able to understand us if you change?"

She nodded.

White fur sprouted on her cheeks and neck.

"Lucy, are you changing on purpose?"

She shook her head.

"Shit. I don't know what to do. Logan?"

"You think I do? We didn't exactly study werewolf physiology in med school."

"Are you in any pain?" I asked Lucy.

She shook her head. Then she nodded. Then shook it again.

"Can you talk?"

Again, she shook her head.

"The change must happen from the inside out. Her vocal cords can't produce speech anymore. We'll take care of you, Luce. Okay?"

She nodded again and then cried out something between a whimper and a scream as her nose began to elongate.

Damn! She was finally conscious, and now we couldn't talk to her. Why was this happening?

Dante had healed her, fixed the erratic rhythm of her heart. Could that be part of this? I had no idea, but it was the only working hypothesis I could think of.

"This might be a result of Dante's healing," I said to Logan.

I tried to close my ears to the pop of Lucy's bones snapping and reforming as she howled. Definitely a howl this time. A sharp howl. She must be in pain. How could she not be?

Then again, was a caterpillar in pain as it morphed into a butterfly? No, but that happened over many days.

Lucy was changing before our eyes in a matter of minutes.

"What can we do for her?" I asked Logan.

"Nothing. Her heart rhythm is changing, but it could be a normal canine rhy—"

The EKG flatlined.

Panic welled within me, until Logan spoke.

"It's okay. The electrodes popped off her chest."

Her chest was now covered in white fur.

A wolf stood on the hospital bed where, just minutes earlier, my best friend had been resting peacefully.

"Lucy?"

She gave a nod.

"Are you in any pain?"

She turned her head to the left. She looked fine, so I

figured that was her way of shaking her head no. She'd been badly beaten. Either the pain meds were still working or wolves had fewer nerve endings than humans.

"Did you change on purpose?"

Another head turn to the left. No.

"Okay. We'll figure this out, Luce. The important thing is that you're okay."

The white fur on her face and body covered her bruising and lacerations, so indeed, she looked better than she had earlier.

"Remember, you're still recovering, so don't run off or anything," I warned.

She nodded with a whimper.

"She still needs rest," Logan said.

"I agree. Lucy, you need to lie down on the bed."

She remained standing.

"I thought she said she could understand us," Logan said.

"I think she can. She just has other stuff on her mind."

Lucy gave another canine nod, looking downward.

"Do you want to show us something?"

Another nod.

"What?" Logan asked.

I scoffed. "She can't talk, Logan. Geez."

"Right. Sorry."

Lucy jumped off the bed, walked to the door, and pawed at it.

"She wants to take us out of this room," I said.

"She needs to be resting," Logan said.

"I know, but what can we do? She says she isn't in pain."

"How do we even know what she says? I've seen dogs move their heads thousands of times."

"She's not a dog, Logan. She's a sentient being. We need to see what she wants to show us."

"She couldn't do this as a human?" Logan asked.

"She said she didn't shift on purpose. Weren't you listening? Jeez!" I went to Lucy and stroked her soft head and then stopped abruptly. Was that okay? She wasn't a dog. She was my best friend. Were you supposed to pet your best friend?

She ignored my petting and continued to paw at the door.

"All right, Luce." I opened the door. "Show us."

SEVEN

DANTE

The door was locked with a double deadbolt. Not a problem. I grabbed the small screwdrivers out of my pack and went to work. In less than two minutes, I had unlocked both of them.

"That's a great skill to have," my father said.

"For a criminal."

"You're no criminal. You're about to save the lives of the people behind this door. Get my ashes ready."

I sighed as I pulled out the plastic bag containing my father's remains.

"There will be enough," he said. "There will always be enough."

"How do I explain this to them? How do I make them understand?"

"They'll be thrilled to get out of here," he said. "Did you like being held against your will?"

He had a good point. Slowly, I pushed the door open.

Abe Lincoln sat in one corner of the dark room. Only three

others were in the room. Another man and two women, one who looked like she could still be in her teens. They all wore old and dingy clothes.

If I had to guess, I'd say they were all homeless, picked up on the streets by the Claiborne thugs.

"Abe, you okay?" I asked.

He squinted at the dim light streaming in from the hallway. "Who's there?"

"It's me. Dante. Erin's boyfriend."

"There were more here earlier," my father said gravely. "We were too late for them."

"Do you know where they took the others?" Abe asked.

"I'm sorry. I don't. We need to get you out of here." I opened the bag of ashes and dusted some between my fingers. Then I touched my fingers to Abe's forehead.

"What's that?"

"You don't want to know. Just know that it will protect you. Bea says so."

He nodded. "You'll get my cooperation. I can't be sure about the others. The young one only stopped screaming about a half hour ago. Her voice is too hoarse now."

I turned to them. "I'm here to help. You're getting out of here."

The man stood. "Let's go, then."

I walked to him and reached toward his forehead.

"What the hell are you doing?"

"Protecting you."

"You some kind of priest or something? I don't believe in all that laying hands bullshit."

Do you believe in getting out of here before you're vampire food? I held back the words. "Just do as I say, and you'll get out of here. Resist me, and you won't."

"Who the hell are you? Why should I go anywhere with you?"

So much for holding back words. "I'm getting you out of here. If you stay, you'll die. Is that good enough for you?"

"Why the he—"

"You're welcome," I said, my voice a low growl. "One more word and I'll leave you here."

The two women stood and didn't resist as I touched the ashes to their foreheads. Finally, the man allowed me to smear the ash on him as well.

"Lead them out, Dante," my father said.

"Who's that?" Abe Lincoln asked.

"Nothing, Abe," I said.

"I heard—"

"You heard me," my father said. "The others can't hear me. I'm Dante's father. Don't let on that I'm here."

"Are you—"

"What did I just say?" my father roared, his voice thundering through the cell.

Abe shut his mouth and said nothing, though his eyes shone with a mixture of fear and something else I couldn't identify.

He stayed quiet, though.

I opened the door. "Follow me and don't make a sound. Absolutely no talking. I can't protect you if you make any noise." I didn't know if that was true, but it sounded good. Besides, I didn't want any distractions.

"Take them back through all the doors and out the way we came in," my father said.

That's a lot to remember. I didn't say the words. That

would only invite questions. I could remember, though. Back to the door leading here, and then back through the second sterile place, through the hospital, through the outer room, and back out through the tunnel leading to the ladder and the manhole.

Sure. No problem.

"You've been here before. You'll remember," my father said, seeming to sense my apprehension. "Trust yourself. They won't be seen. They are shielded. Bea assured me that this will work."

Was I shielded as well? Just to make sure, I dabbed a bit of my father's ashes on my own forehead. As morbid as the act was, immediately I calmed, as if a ray of sunshine shone down on me.

And I knew.

We *were* shielded. We would get through this maze, and these people would escape their fate.

She was around, of course. As were the thugs, though perhaps they were still out cold from my beating. I'd won every fight she'd forced on me when I was here.

I was undefeated.

I would remain undefeated as I led these innocent people out of hell and back to their lives. I would prevail.

I would also prevail against her and anyone else in my way.

I would get these people to safety. I'd release all the women and get them to safety. Then I'd find my uncle, save him, protect him, and get him to safety.

That was why I was here. Why I'd come back into hell.

And why I would leave it behind forever once I'd accomplished those goals.

EIGHT

Erin

Lucy scampered down the hallway, slipping on the tile floor.

"Easy," I said. "You're recovering. Remember?"

She didn't slow down. Logan and I followed her down the hallway to a closed door. She pawed at it.

"In here," I said to Logan. "Lack of opposable thumbs getting you down, Luce?" I opened the door.

"Unlocked," Logan said. "Interesting."

"Why would it be locked? Everyone here works for Bonneville."

"This is... I've been here before. I think. But I can't remember why."

"Maybe you have been, and she glamoured you into forgetting."

He raised his eyebrow. "You said I was resistant to glamouring."

"What makes you think I know what I'm talking about?

That's just a theory based on how you reacted to River. You can be glamoured, Logan."

"So can you."

"I know. Which is why we can't get caught here."

"Then we'd better be quiet."

"Lucy will warn us. She'll hear anyone coming long before we do."

"How?"

"Dog ears, genius. Her sense of smell and hearing are heightened when she's in wolf form."

"And you know this because..."

"Jesus, Logan. Let's just see what's in here." I found a light switch on the inside wall and flipped it on.

Logan followed me into the room, Lucy at our heels.

"This is a file room," Logan said.

"What was your first clue, Logan? The file cabinets? Good thing the computers were here to confirm your genius theory, huh?" I sat down at one of the computers and tried to log on, but access was denied. Big surprise there.

"No need to get rude, Erin."

I scoffed at him. "What did you want to show us in here, Luce?" I asked.

This time Logan scoffed. "Good luck getting an answer out of her."

I ignored him. "Is there information in here we need?"

Lucy did her nodding thing.

Where is it? I bit my lip to keep from asking. Plus, it was a stupid question anyway. The information was either in the file cabinets or in the computer database. My guess was the computers. The file cabinets probably housed old files.

Old files.

An epiphany hit me. Old files. How long had this hospital been down here? Doctor Bonneville was only forty or so. Who built this place?

I walked over to the file cabinets and pulled open a drawer. The smell of musty paper wafted up.

Yep. Old files. The manila folders were yellow with age. Each file had a name on it, but I didn't recognize any of them.

Logan sat down at the other computer and started tapping on keys.

I turned. "Logan?"

"I'm in," he said.

I rushed to him. "How?"

"Hell if I know. I just knew the access code."

"If you do work down here, you must enter records," I said. "Then she glamours you into forgetting."

"Maybe." He tapped the keyboard. "Here we go. Patient files."

"See if there's one on Lucy."

"I'm looking. Here it is. Lucy Cyrus." He clicked. "It's empty."

"Shit. Let me see." I sat down in the other chair and wheeled over to him, pushing him over so we could both see the screen. "Go back."

The list of names reappeared.

Most I didn't recognize, but some I did.

Cyrus, Lucy

Downey, Sybil

She was the appendectomy who had disappeared.

Doyle, Patty

Doyle, Baby Girl

Yes! Now I knew for sure that Patty and baby Isabelle Erin were here.

I continued glancing down the list, which was in alphabetical order by last names.

More names I recognized.

Gabriel, Braedon

Gabriel, Dante

Gabriel, Emilia

Gabriel, Julian

I froze.
The next name.

Gabriel, River

He was here. He'd descended right into her trap. "Logan, we have to find Riv—"

But then I turned to ice.

Hamilton, Erin

NINE

DANTE

We'd stepped over the thugs who still lay unconscious outside one of the doors.

We'd walked quietly down the hallways of the hospital. A couple of staff members had passed us without reaction.

She had been nowhere in sight, but if we'd come across her, I knew instinctively that we would get by undetected.

I trusted myself.

I had faith.

The word I'd dreaded for so long—I finally understood its true meaning. Faith was freeing. It freed me to believe in myself and do the right thing.

We even passed Jay and River, who stood outside the blood bank. I motioned for them not to speak, but neither of them reacted at all. Not even a brow lift. They didn't see us, and that finally convinced me.

I truly believed and had faith that we were shielded.

We moved through the hospital, through the attached rooms, until we finally came to the tunnel that would lead us to the ladder and manhole.

"You'll need to join hands," I said quietly. "We need to go single file, and it's dark. Your eyes will adjust, but just in case, stay joined."

I led them through the dark, dank tunnel until the ladder appeared in the distance.

"Abe," I said, "go up the ladder. You'll need to move the manhole cover at the top out of the way. It's heavy, but you can do it."

I nodded to the other man. "You go last. I want the women between you. It's a long way up, but you can all do it."

"Aren't you coming with us?" the older woman asked timidly.

"I can't. I still have work to do here. Abe, I'm counting on you to take care of these people."

"They're just going to capture us again," the teenager moaned.

"They won't," I said. "You're shielded."

"But what if the shield doesn't work?"

"It's worked so far, hasn't it? No one noticed us as we walked out of there."

She nodded, gulping. "I'm scared."

"You'd be nuts if you weren't," I said. "But trust me. You are shielded from ever being brought back down here again."

Was I telling the truth? What if they washed the ashes from their foreheads? I didn't dare ask my father. I wasn't even sure if he was with us any longer.

I warmed as a feeling of supreme peace settled over me. *They are protected.* In the depth of my bones, I knew. This shield would hold for as long as necessary.

"Thank you," Abe Lincoln said. "We all owe you."

"You owe me nothing. Just get out of here and live your lives. Get off the streets, Abe. You were made for better."

"The streets are all I know," he said.

"Then learn. And stop letting the Claiborne vamps feed from you."

"But they—"

"They aren't your friends, Abe. They brought you here. Do you know why?"

He shook his head.

"Do you think it's normal for 'friends' to take you somewhere and lock you in a room?"

"When you put it that way..."

"Right. Your life was in danger down there."

"But I—"

"Damn it, Abe!" I pulled him away from the others so we were out of earshot and whispered urgently in his ear. "They were going to kill you, cut off your head, and hang it over trapped vampires so they'd be forced to drink human blood."

He stiffened against me, his eyes wide with fear.

"Get it? Finally?"

He nodded.

"Now go."

He returned to the others and began to ascend.

I stayed until all four had reached the top and the manhole cover had been placed back over the entrance.

"Good work, son."

My father wasn't visible.

"You were here the whole time?"

"I was."

"River and Jay didn't seem to notice us. Isn't that strange?"

"Not at all. You were shielded. You were their protection."

"No. It was your ashes."

"My ashes helped, but you were the main shield. You, Dante. Your belief. Your power."

"But I felt that it was— How could I have been wrong? I told them they'd still be shielded above! How could you let me lie to them?"

"Because it wasn't a lie, son. It wasn't a lie."

"But—"

"Have faith in your strength. They carry *your* protection now."

TEN

Erin

"Y ou want me to open it?" Logan asked.

A cloak of ice continued to envelop me.

My name.

I hadn't been here, so why did I have a file?

I didn't want to know.

Yet I needed to know.

I nodded slowly. "Open it."

The first page was simply my name, age, and physical characteristics. Nothing out of the ordinary. But why was I in this database at all? My skin crawled with invisible caterpillars. I felt violated. Really violated.

"Keep going," I said.

"You want to look at it yourself? I can step back."

"Yeah, if you don't mind."

"Not at all. Though you did peek at my records."

He had a point. Plus, his medical opinion might come in handy. "Actually, please stay. Just scoot over and let me have the mouse."

He obliged, and I sat in front of the desk while he stayed beside me in another chair.

The next page was my medical history. I'd been pretty healthy, so this was just current physical exams and meds, my annual gynecological visits, and my birth control pills.

Next, though, was a family history.

Jay was listed, as were my mother and father.

Then,

Maternal Grandmother: Sharlene Ray Bennett Jackson (Bennett line vampire)

Bonneville *knew*. She knew about my ancestry.

"So you're...?" Logan said.

"A quarter vampire. I've got you beat. You're only an eighth."

"I wonder why I don't have a record?" he said.

"My guess is she's only interested in male vampires, not descendants. But females... Are all of us descended from vampires?" I clicked back to the page of medical records.

Sure enough.

Lundy, Bella

North, Cynthia

Among other names I didn't recognize.

"She's taking women who are descended from vampires. She can't produce a vamp baby from a female vampire and male human because vampire females are so rare and can only reproduce once every couple of years."

"So she's...?"

Logan truly didn't know.

"She's trying to produce a vampire by mating a human and a vampire," I said. "We already figured that much out. It has something to do with B positive blood. Now it looks like there's a second criterion. The woman must be a vampire descendant."

"This is crazy," he said.

"True enough." Then something dawned on me. "Where are River and Jay? They were outside Lucy's hospital room, but when we left, they weren't in the hallway."

"I don't know."

Panic rose in me, but then I looked over to Lucy, who was standing sentry at the door. Surely she would know if River was in danger. Or would she? She was a wolf, not an empath. Could a wolf smell fear and danger? Or could she only smell creatures?

"Luce, is River okay?"

She didn't respond.

"Okay, nod yes if you smell him."

She bowed her head slightly. Good.

"Nod if you smell him strong, shake your head for light."

She cocked her head to the side.

"All right. He's here, but he's not close to us. Is he okay?"

No response.

She didn't know, but she didn't seem overly concerned, so I went back to the computer screen.

The next page was entirely devoted to my physical characteristics and blood type.

Skin: fair

Hair: dark brown

Eyes: green

Height: 5 feet 7 inches

Weight: 135

Blood type: B

Rh: positive

VO: positive

Genetic screening: negative

What kind of genetic screening? That could mean anything, though I hoped "negative" was a good sign.

"Logan, what does 'VO' mean?" I pointed.

He studied the screen. "I have no idea."

"Are you sure? Something to do with blood? Think back to med school. Hematology. Did you do a hematology rotation?"

"Yeah, I did, actually. I've never seen anything called 'VO' related to blood. We studied diseases of the blood. Stuff like that."

"It's got to be some sort of genetic marker," I said, "but I've never heard of it before."

"There's no search engine in this database or on this computer that I can see." Logan took out his phone. "I'll do a quick search."

I bit my lip as he tapped on his phone.

"Nothing's coming up on the search engine relating the initials VO to anything blood related."

I opened a new window and pulled up Bella Lundy's file.

Blood type: B

Rh: positive

VO: positive

Genetic screening: positive for BRCA1

BRCA1 was the breast cancer gene. Not great news for Bella Lundy, though it wasn't a guarantee of contracting the disease. Bella had been returned—possibly because the genetic marker for breast cancer made her an unsuitable subject?

What about Cynthia North? I opened another window.

Blood type: B

Rh: positive

VO: positive

Genetic screening: positive for ApoE4

"Logan, do you know what this genetic marker is?" I pointed to the screen.

"ApoE4. Yeah. That's Alzheimer's."

Another unsuitable candidate. Poor Cynthia.

I scrolled back to Sybil Downey and Patty Doyle.

Both had negative genetic abnormality screenings and were VO positive. Apparently why they were still here.

A quick look through the rest of the records showed that all the other women were VO positive with negative screenings for genetic abnormality...and all had a vampire somewhere in their ancestry.

Bonneville was collecting the best of the best B positive vampire descendants as far as genetics went.

She was hoarding potential breeders.

ELEVEN

DANTE

I headed back through the maze and into the hospital and found Jay and River where I'd left them, at the blood bank.

"Hey, where have you been?" River asked.

"Didn't you see me walk through here before with four people?"

"Uh...no."

"We walked right past you two."

"You see anything, partner?" he said to Jay.

"Negative."

"I had four humans— Wait! You should have been able to smell them."

"That was part of the shield, son." My father appeared. "They are shielded from vampires."

"For how long?" I asked.

"Only you can break the shield, Dante."

"But I didn't do anything!"

Except that I had. I'd known at the time, known the truth in my bones when I told them they were safe. I was no longer slave to the darkness in me. Somehow, I'd learned to control it, to use it for good.

"You're learning to control the new powers that have manifested," my father said.

"But...how?"

"Instinct. Need. It's how we all learn. It's how a baby knows to suckle for nourishment."

"But no one else has these abilities," I said.

"Which is exactly why you're using instinct to control them. A baby comes into the world without sentience. No one teaches him how to draw nourishment. He uses instinct. Since you're the only one we know of who has these new powers, no one can teach you how to use them. Instinct has kicked in, Dante. Today, you began to control what has previously been only instinct."

"They are truly safe?"

"Don't you already know?"

"How would I know, Dad? You tell me to have faith. You tell me I'm their shield." My hands tingled with energy. At least I assumed it was energy. I was beginning to recognize the signs of this newfound power.

"You are, Dante. Bea assured me it was true."

"It's crazy, cuz," River said. "These things that are happening to you. But it's great, too. You saved Lucy."

Yes, I had. My hands had been the conduit for the energy that saved Lucy. But my hands weren't the only conduit. I'd used my eyes as a conduit before. And in the courtroom, a mere thought had served to reverse Bill's glamour.

I wasn't sure I was ready for this.

Didn't matter. I had work to do here, and the control I was now exhibiting would be a huge help.

"Where's Erin?"

"She and Logan Crown are taking care of Lucy."

"Why did you leave her?" I forced my teeth not to descend. The tingling itch was unbearable.

"River heard some vampires talking. We followed them here."

"What happened?"

"Nothing. They just deposited some blood in the bank and then left. We were on our way back to Lucy's room when you got here."

I inhaled. Erin's scent was always with me, but something had changed. She was worried. Or scared. Sharp adrenaline had spiked her normal dark and seductive scent.

"If something happened to her—" I growled.

The urge for Erin rose within me, and this time my fangs elongated. I was hungry, and not just for her blood. Her spicy fragrance drew me in, and I stalked toward the intoxicating aroma. Was it her scent? I'd smelled her a thousand times, with and without adrenaline.

Was it the result of the energy still tingling through me?

Whatever it was, it didn't matter.

"Where are you going?" Jay asked.

I didn't answer.

I needed Erin. I needed sustenance in more ways than one.

This time, we'd find a bed. We'd take a vacant room and lock the fucking door, and then I'd take her roughly. Then softly. Then roughly again.

"Hey!" Jay again.

"Let him go," River said. "I know that look."

"Shit," Jay replied. "I'm afraid I do too."

Then their voices were unintelligible as I increased my pace.

She was here. Somewhere. Perhaps she was watching me. My every move.

Didn't care.

My nose led me to a closed door in the same hallway where Lucy was. As I reached for the knob, a wolf howled.

My heart stampeding, I turned the doorknob.

The white wolf. Lucy. And Logan Crown sitting next to Erin, both of them staring at a computer screen.

She turned. "Dante!"

"Come with me," I said. "Now."

TWELVE

Erin

"Wait," I said. "We've found something strange in the database here. I—"

"I said, 'come with me.'" He grabbed my arm and yanked me toward him.

I let out an *oof* when I hit his hard chest.

Oh, God, his eyes. They were dark and sexy, the rims of amber burning like circles of fire.

My insides sizzled, little flaming arrows coursing through me and landing between my legs. Was it feeding time? Maybe. I didn't care. He wanted me. Needed me. And I'd be there for him.

He pulled me outside the door, ignoring Lucy, still in wolf form, and Logan. Once we were free of the room, he headed straight for another door and went in without knocking, pulling me in as well.

A sterile hospital room with two beds. Unoccupied.

Dante glared at the door, and it slammed shut by itself, the lock clicking.

My mouth dropped open. But why was I surprised? I'd seen Dante levitate us, indeed our whole bed. But this had been intentional.

Dante had controlled his power this time.

He was growing, learning.

I opened my mouth to tell him how happy I was for him—

"Oh!"

His lips came down on mine in a violent kiss. I opened for him without thinking twice. I'd always be there for him, and right now, even though we were in a strange place with a person who wanted to do people harm—do *us* harm—our needs could not be denied.

I brushed his pack off his shoulders, thinking for a millisecond that I'd left my own back in the records room with Logan and Lucy.

I couldn't worry about that now.

Dante would take care of me. Would see that I had food and drink.

And I would make sure he had the nourishment he required.

I broke the kiss with a loud smack and tilted my head, baring my neck for him.

I moaned when he sank his teeth into my flesh. First the sharp pain, and then the intense pleasure. Those sweet tugs of his mouth on my neck made me shiver, and I trembled, my legs nearly crumpling beneath me.

"Take what you need from me, Dante. I'll always be here for you. Always."

A low growl vibrated against my flesh as he continued to feed.

"Always, Dante. I love you."

He sucked once more and then removed his teeth, licking over the puncture wounds. Then back to my mouth. The coppery tang of my own blood only increased my desire. Memories swirled in my mind—all our kisses, all the intense flavors when our mouths were joined. And the most intense of all—after I'd tasted his blood.

My nipples hardened, and my breasts swelled against the bulletproof vest I wore. My body turned to flames. Too many fucking clothes. I'd been wearing these black clothes for how long now?

I pulled away. "Need to strip. Now."

He roared. Yes, it was a roar, and his eyes burned into me like hot coals. "Strip, Erin. Quickly."

I obeyed. I wanted to, but I also had an ulterior motive.

If I didn't, he'd shred my clothes, and I needed them here. I didn't have any spares other than panties.

Stripping took longer than normal with everything I wore, but as soon as humanly possible, I stood naked before him, my tits bulging and my nipples puckered. Already juices had moistened my inner thighs.

My clit was hard and aching. I squeezed my thighs together, hoping for some relief, but to no avail. I was on fucking fire.

Dante closed his eyes and inhaled. "God, Erin. You smell like a feast."

"Then devour me, Dante."

He scooped me up and placed me on one of the hospital beds. "Spread those legs for me, baby. Show me that feast."

I was only too eager to comply.

He adjusted his groin but made no move to remove his clothes. Didn't matter. I liked being before him, a feast for all his senses. I imagined myself not on a hospital bed but on a giant silver platter, soft clouds of cotton candy as my pillow.

My pussy throbbed, aching for attention, aching to be filled.

"So fucking beautiful," he growled, his teeth still tinged with my blood.

Oh, God, he was magnificent. So beautiful. So primal and majestic and full of lust. Full of love.

"I want to fill every part of you, Erin. Fill you with all that I am."

"Dante," I whispered, closing my eyes. "Fill me."

Two fingers plunged deep into my channel.

And the orgasm hit me as if I'd been transported straight into the eye of a hurricane. One kiss, one bite, two fingers.

All it took to send me to nirvana.

"That's it, baby. Damn, you're so wet. Come for me. Your climaxes turn me on so much." He thrust, stretching me, finding that spongy spot that made me crazy.

"Yes, please, yes."

"Don't move. You are at my mercy."

Fine with me. I wasn't bound. Only Dante's innate power kept me still. He continued fingering me as my climax ebbed. I lifted my hips, spread my legs farther apart, everything I could to get him to go deeper, deeper, deeper.

Then a *zing* of his zipper...

And his cock was invading me, filling up every bit of emptiness I'd ever felt. So big, so amazing, so Dante.

I opened my eyes.

His teeth were clenched, his eyes still blazing, and sweat had emerged in clear drops on his forehead.

Take off the rest of your clothes. I want your skin touching mine.

But the words never left my lips. I couldn't destroy this moment. Couldn't bear the thought of his cock no longer in my pussy.

As if he'd read my mind, though, he withdrew. I whimpered at the profound loss. But he undressed in a flash, and soon he was back, flipping me over onto my stomach.

"On your hands and knees, baby. Present yourself to me."

I was happy to obey.

"So swollen and pink." He stroked the folds of my pussy. "So fucking beautiful."

And so fucking empty. I gritted my teeth.

He swiped his fingers into my channel briefly and then used the juices to lubricate my asshole. With his other hand on my butt cheek, he forced his cock back into my tight cunt with a growl.

A soft sigh escaped my throat.

He thrust once, twice, once more, and then began massaging my asshole with his finger. And suddenly I wasn't full enough. I wanted him everywhere. My mouth, my pussy, my ass.

I lifted my hips farther, trying to give him access.

And he breached my tight rim. I inhaled the sharp pain, waiting for him to say something.

He didn't. Just moved the finger in and out of my tight hole, and just as I got used to the invasion, he added another.

"Good, baby?"

"God, yes. Please. Fuck me, Dante. Fuck me hard."

No answer, just a powerful thrust into me that touched my heart. He fucked me harder and harder, probing my asshole in tandem, until another orgasm rose within me.

"I'm going to come, Dante. Oh, God!"

It hit me like an explosion, sending shards of me catapulting into oblivion.

"That's it, baby. That's it." He thrust harder, pummeling me, tunneling into me and reaching my core.

A groan on the tip of a snarl. And—

He thrust deeply, releasing. As he contracted into me, every pulse of his cock thrummed against the walls of my pussy. Every beat of his heart mirrored my own.

He leaned down, brushed his hair against my shoulder blades, and sank his teeth into the other side of my neck.

Such completeness. Such intensity.

I quivered, my orgasm still barreling through me, his feeding making it even more intense and strong.

The soft tugs, the satisfied groans rumbling from his throat, his slick body pressed against mine—it was pure rapture.

After he'd withdrawn his teeth, fingers, and cock from my body, I lay limp, my face burrowed into the stark white pillow.

"Do you have any idea how beautiful you look right now?" he asked gruffly.

I turned onto my back and stared at him. He stood naked, his cock still hard and springing from his black nest of curls. His body was muscular, and the shine of perspiration made him dazzle, as if the harsh fluorescent lighting were actually the natural rays of the sun. His hair was a mass of unruly waves, strands sticking to his cheeks and forehead. His lips were full from kissing and smudged with my blood.

He'd never looked more gorgeous.

I smiled. "Did you get your fill?"

"I'll never get my fill of you, Erin." His eyes were heavy-lidded. "Never."

I opened my arms. "You'll never have to."

He came to me, sitting down on the bed, and he caressed my cheek. "I love you so damned much."

"I know. I love you too, Dante. So much."

"I'll do anything to protect you."

"I know that too."

He inhaled, letting the air out slowly. "That's why I need you to leave here. Now."

THIRTEEN

DANTE

"You've got to be kidding." Erin moved from the bed indignantly and began gathering her clothes.

"Do I sound like I'm kidding?"

"Don't overestimate your power over me, Dante. I'm happy to obey your command in the bedroom, but outside? Not so much."

"This is for your own protection, Erin."

"What about you? You need me to survive!" She whipped her hands to her hips, an adorable stance considering she was stark naked, her body flush with blood at her skin's surface, her scent irresistible.

I couldn't help the slight curve of my lips.

And the hardening of my cock.

Then a curve of her lips as she noticed her effect on me.

She advanced toward me slowly. "I'm not going anywhere, Dante, and you can't make me."

I pulled her naked body against mine and kissed her fiercely. The thrumming of her blood to her heart drowned out all other noise, and I took her with my lips and tongue.

Her aroma wafted around me, the dark and exotic scent of her blood and the musky apple tartness of her arousal. Plus something new. Something vibrant and intense. Yes, the testosterone rising from her anger with me, but it was laced with something more this time.

Something dark and irresistible.

Intoxicating.

I had no idea what it was, but I was powerless to resist it. I was hard, and she was in my arms, still wet from me coming inside her. I slid my fingers through her slick folds and then broke the kiss, turned her around so she was against the bed, and shoved my cock into her from behind.

"You *will* obey me, Erin," I commanded through clenched teeth in between thrusts.

"I'm *not* leaving," she replied.

"You *are*."

"I'm *not*."

My whole body throbbed. Her disobedience, her indignation—it all made her more attractive to me. More irresistible. More determined.

I thrust harder, deeper, gripping her hips and panting.

Obey me. Obey me. Obey me.

Not leaving. Not leaving. Not leaving.

She didn't utter the words, but I heard them as if she had.

When she shattered beneath me, clenched around my cock, I thrust deep into her body, taking her, making her mine, willing her to obey.

When my orgasm finally subsided, I withdrew and joined her on the bed, pulling her into my arms.

"Still not leaving," she said against my neck.

"You are."

"No, Dante, I'm not. Don't you understand? I need to be here. Not just for you but for me. This is something I have to do."

I nudged her away slightly so I could meet her gaze. Her peridot eyes sparkled with fire. She was serious. Dead serious.

"Try to understand," she continued. "I understand where you're coming from, but I need you to understand where I'm coming from. I love you. This place is hell for you. I need to be here. For you."

A warm blanket of love and devotion cloaked me. I always knew she loved me, but right now, for the first time, I understood that her need to protect me was as great as mine to protect her.

She might obey me during lovemaking, but outside, we were true equals with equal responsibility to love and protect each other.

This was the blood bond.

Bonded by blood, body, and soul, bound to love and protect each other until death separated us.

Even death wouldn't separate us. Our energies would be bound for eternity.

This I knew, as if I'd always known. As if it had always been a part of me.

"Let me stay," she whispered.

I kissed her forehead. "As if I'd be able to make you leave."

She chuckled. "I suppose you could ball up your energy and force me out of here."

"No, I can't."

"You can. You forced me out of our bedroom when I wanted you to get me pregnant."

"That was necessary at the time. You can't be pregnant

right now. Not until we figure out what's going on here. Besides, you're not fertile. I'd know if you were."

"Oh!" She jumped from the bed and began pulling on her clothes. "Logan and I found medical records."

"You hacked into the system?"

"Are you kidding? Like I'd know how to do that. No. It was all Logan. He sat down and logged on. Said he didn't know how, but he knew the passwords."

"So he's used the system before."

"Yeah, that's my guess. Only he doesn't remember doing it."

"Or that's what he says."

"I think he's telling the truth, Dante. His memories are fragmented. He explained it as when he's here, it's like his time above is a dream, and vice versa. It could have something to do with his schizophrenia. His mind works differently, which probably affects the way he reacts to a glamour."

"Maybe, but I'm not sure I buy it. River thought he was either manipulating us or someone else was manipulating us through him. What did you find out, though?"

"Bonneville is taking B positive women who have vampire ancestry and holding them here. If they have a genetic marker she doesn't want, she lets them go. For example, Bella Lundy tested positive for the breast cancer gene."

"Why?"

"Breeding. That's my guess. Why else would she be concerned with genetics?"

"So it's something to do with B positive women with vampire ancestry. That would be a lot of women, I'd think."

"Yeah, but there's something else. All the women down here, including me, are VO positive."

"What's that?"

She sighed. "Tell me and we'll both know. Logan didn't know either, and he did a hematology rotation."

"Are any of these women pregnant?"

"I don't know. I haven't seen any of them other than Lucy, and she's not. I'm still not sure why Bonneville took her. She said Lucy was onto her, but that doesn't compute. Bonneville could have just glamoured her. Lucy has B positive blood, but it's unlikely that she has vampire ancestry. Did vampires ever mate with shifters?"

"I don't know about vampires mating with shifters, but Bonneville told me she couldn't release Lucy because she wasn't able to glamour her."

"She's in wolf form right now. At least she was. Something caused her to change. She didn't seem to have any control over it. I wonder..."

"What?"

"What you did to her, your healing energy. Maybe it forced the change."

"Then wouldn't she have changed right away?"

"I don't know. This is all just theory at this point." She snapped a strange-looking vest on. "Bulletproof vest. Jay and River insisted."

"Good call."

"I suppose. They're kind of binding. You should get dressed."

I nodded and got myself together. "I guess we should find River and Jay and fill them in."

"And Logan," she said.

My hackles rose. "Hell, no."

"He's part of this now, Dante. He helped Lucy, and he

helped me. He doesn't deserve to be down here any more than the rest of us."

As much as I hated to admit it, Erin was right.

But one thing bugged me. Bugged me big.

She had been absent for too long.

FOURTEEN

Erin

"Come on." I tugged on Dante's arm once he was fully clothed, trying not to let myself get hypnotized by his dark and dreamy eyes.

He nodded, and I followed him out the door. River and Jay were sitting on some chairs at the end of the hallway. Lucy, in wolf form, was with them.

"Any sign of Bonneville?" Dante asked as we approached.

"No," River said. "Seems kind of odd, doesn't it?"

"You have no idea." Dante rubbed his temple.

My brother stared at Dante with pursed lips. Pretty clear he knew exactly what had transpired between Dante and me. I glared at him.

He broke away from my gaze and held up the book from my mother. "Another page opened, but only two words are clear, and we have no idea what they mean." He handed me the book.

Vampyr Omega

VO.

"Oh my God."

Everything else on the page was illegible. I handed the book to Dante.

"Vampyr omega?" he said. "What's that?"

"VO, Dante. Remember I told you about the records?" I quickly explained everything to River and Jay.

"You think it's some kind of genetic marker in a B positive vampire descendant?" River said.

"That's my guess."

"Vampyr obviously means vampire," Jay said. "But what about omega? It's the last letter of the Greek alphabet. Does this mean the end of vampires? That doesn't make any sense. She wouldn't be condemning her own species to extinction."

"No." Julian appeared.

I jolted.

"Sorry. I didn't mean to startle you. But there's another meaning for omega."

"Don't keep us in suspense," River said.

"Destruction," Julian said. "The end of everything."

"The end of humanity," I said softly. "She wants to breed us out, and she thinks this vampyr omega thing is the key."

FIFTEEN

DANTE

"You don't know that, baby," I said.

But *I* knew.

Erin was right. This was *her* doing. I'd find her, and I'd get the truth out of her. "Stay here," I said through clenched teeth.

"Where are you going?" Erin asked.

"I'm going to find that bitch and have it out with her once and for all."

"No!" Erin grabbed my arm. "We can't risk the safety of the others."

"If what you theorize is true, *she* won't risk their safety. They're human incubators. She needs them."

"You're going to weigh the safety of innocent people, including your sister, against my theory?" Erin shook her head. "I can't let you."

"Then what, Erin? We let her get away with this? If you're right, she has no intention of letting any of these women go."

"Why Emilia?" Jay asked. "She's already pregnant with my child."

"I don't know."

"And why you, Dante?" Erin asked. "Why hold you here for ten years? What does that have to do with breeding vampires?"

"Oh, God." Nausea erupted in my stomach and clawed its way up my throat.

"No, son," my father said.

"What if, Dad? And you? And Uncle Brae?"

"Would anyone care to explain what the hell you're talking about?" River said. "We're not mind readers here."

"Dante is afraid Dr. Bonneville harvested our sperm," my father said.

"Oh, God." From Erin this time.

"Where would sperm be kept?" I asked Erin.

"A cryobank. Fancy word for a freezer." She swallowed. "The blood bank has a freezer in the back. Units of blood are stored there for longevity."

"Dad, Andrew Gaston told us that his father considered you and Brae to be perfect vampire specimens. He was obsessed with you. You'd be the perfect sperm donors. This is so fucked up!"

"You think that's why they were taken?" River said.

"Bill once told me he didn't think I was the primary target," I said. "What if he was right? What if she knew taking me would draw Dad and Brae out? And she was right."

"Then why keep you, Dante?" my father asked.

"I don't know. She got her jollies from feeding me and forcing me to drink from her, I guess. From dropping me into a fighting pit and making me— But no. She told me I *did* have a purpose, and that if I failed, there was another." I looked to River.

"Keep me out of this," he said.

"Braedon and I might have been the targets, but once we got here, she didn't let you go. And she thinks River could replace you if need be." My father shook his head. "It must all add up somehow."

Images and thoughts buzzed through my mind at a rapid pace. The feedings. The fights. The rewards.

Once bonded, never broken.

Fight or die in the arena.

Darkness rising.

And we shall rise again.

The last five words popped into my head after those I'd heard so often while here. Yes. New words, except they weren't new. She had uttered them many times while I'd been in captivity. Each time after I'd proved victorious in a fight. Each time after she'd fed from me...

"And we shall rise again," I said slowly in a voice not quite my own.

The dark energy rose inside me, churning my insides into goo and forcing its way to the surface.

But I knew it now, could control it now. I could use it for my own purposes. "I need you all to trust me," I said. "To have faith."

"In what?" River asked.

"The dark energy that tries to take me over—I'm going to let it come through. I need you to have faith that I can control it."

"But Dante," Erin said, "you didn't *know* us."

"That won't happen again, baby. I promise."

"But—"

"Please. Have faith."

I knew what I was asking. People had been asking me to

have faith for so long, and I'd resisted. I understood now. I was asking for complete trust and confidence when I hadn't shown I'd earned it. At least not where the darkness was concerned. Days ago, if someone had told me I wouldn't recognize Erin—or River or Jay, for that matter—I'd have scoffed in his face and told him he was nuts.

But it had happened. They were justifiably afraid. And so was I.

Erin grabbed my hand. "If I can have faith in anything, Dante, I can have faith in you."

"Me too, cuz," River agreed. "You haven't let us down yet, and if that dark crap possesses you, Erin can bring you back. We know how now, thanks to this." He pointed to the book that Jay still held.

I grabbed it from Jay, trying to pry open its pages. "Show me!" I yelled. "Show me your secrets! What did she do to me? What effect did her blood have on me?"

To my surprise, the book opened.

SIXTEEN

Erin

I stared at the page that had opened before Dante as he read aloud.

"The blood of a female vampire is a powerful philter. When ingested by a male, it increases muscle mass, strength, and accuracy. All senses become more enhanced, and additional powers emerge. However, it should be used only in the direst circumstances, as the negative side effects outweigh the positive. The male fed on female vampire blood will eventually undergo a metamorphosis—a profound change in form, psyche, and temperament that will eventually end in an inevitable painful death.

"The blood of the female vampire, however, pales in comparison to the much more potent blood of the male, especially that from a young vampire on the waning moon of maturity."

The rest of the paragraph was illegible.

I attempted to swallow the mass clogging my throat.

An inevitable painful death.

Dante had ingested female vampire blood for ten years. His muscles were certainly strong, and his senses acute. Additional powers? Check. Strong glamouring and telekinesis, for starters. As for a profound change in form, psyche, and temperament? The dark energy that lived in him was most likely the beginning.

And inevitable painful death?

No. Just no. Dante would *not* die.

He said nothing for what seemed like an eternity.

Then—

"Bonneville did say she'd found a way to combat the negative side effects."

"You haven't died a painful death, thank God," Julian said. "That seems proof enough that she has negated the side effects."

"But the darkness," Dante said. "It could be..."

"Don't let this change what you know, Dante," Julian said. "You just got done telling us that you could control it. That we should have faith. We *do*. *You* are stronger than anything she did to you. Never forget that."

He nodded, his Adam's apple bobbing when he swallowed. "It doesn't mention anything about my change in blood chemistry."

"Blood types weren't discovered until 1900, and the Rh factor in 1940," I said. "This was probably written way before then. It's still possible that ingestion of her blood caused the spontaneous change. And the change doesn't harm you. That's a plus."

"I suppose that's something," he said.

"Dante, we trust you," I said. "We have faith, like your dad said. You are stronger than all of this."

"Am I?" he said, shaking his head. "Am I truly stronger than everything here? Because apparently male blood is much more potent. She drank from *me*, remember? A young vampire on the waning moon of maturity."

SEVENTEEN

DANTE

"*Your blood is a gift,*" *she said.* "*If only you would give it freely.*"

I said nothing. She could take my blood. I couldn't stop her. I'd chafed my wrists bloody struggling against her leather bindings.

"*You have no idea how precious you are,*" *she said.*

"*Then let me go,*" *I said through clenched teeth.*

"*Would I let the Hope Diamond go if I possessed it? The crown jewels of England? The* Mona Lisa?"

"*I'm not yours.*"

"*You are. You are mine. You represent what all vampires are capable of. What we can become. You will see, Dante. You will see.*"

Something in this book had spooked Bill.

The portion of the Texts *I'm talking about has nothing to do with our history. It has to do with what we're capable of.*

"She's not only trying to breed vampires," I said, "she's trying to make us stronger. If drinking female blood strengthens our muscles, and she's found a way to negate the other side effects..." I shook my head. "Maybe she's trying to create a vampire army. It's like Erin said. The end of humanity. *Vampyr omega.*"

"Not so fast, son," my father said. "Don't get ahead of yourself. That might be what she wishes could happen, but it's impossible. Even with a few potential breeders, we're still vastly outnumbered by humans. The only realistic thing she can accomplish here is to increase the vampire population by a small percentage."

"I need to find her. She *will* answer to me, Dad. She will."

"She'll answer to all of us eventually. We'll see to that. But we need more information. The book hasn't told us what feeding on male vampire blood can do. We need that information so we can figure out her strengths and her weaknesses."

"I've controlled her. I kept her behind that door."

"You did," my father said. "That's a good thing, and it probably scared her."

"Why won't the book tell us what male vampire blood does?" I shoved my hands in my pockets.

"Apparently the book doesn't think we need that information yet," Erin said.

I grasped the book, my knuckles white, ready to hurl it down the hallway, when—

Lucy howled. We all turned toward her as the snapping of what could only be bones breaking filled the air. Her howls morphed into cries and then into screams. She changed. Fucking changed right before our eyes.

And God, it looked and sounded like bone-crushing pain.

Finally, a soft whimper, as she lay, stark naked, on the cold tile floor.

"Lucy!" River ran toward her, stripping off his jacket and placing it around her shoulders. "Sweetie, are you okay?"

She nodded timidly.

"Luce," Erin said, "your face. Your body. It's all healed."

Lucy looked down. "I...don't understand."

"I don't either." Erin turned to me. "Maybe what you did healed Lucy in every possible way."

I shook my head. "I have no idea."

"What did you do?" Lucy asked.

I couldn't speak.

"Your heartbeat was erratic," Erin explained. "Logan wanted to try to shock you back into a normal rhythm, but the paddles wouldn't work. Dante came in, put his hand over your heart, and it went back to normal."

"What?" She closed her eyes, obviously disoriented.

"It's okay, honey. We've got you. Can you stand?" River helped her to her feet.

"Logan's here?" she asked. Then, "Right. I remember now. The change clogs my brain a little at first."

Erin nodded. "He helped save you when you were injured. Although your injuries seem to be healed now. You were beat up pretty badly."

"I tried to fight..."

"We know, honey." River rubbed her shoulders. "You should never have been in that situation."

"I've been fighting every step of the way since I got here. Their drugs didn't work on me, and I'd escape by shifting. I tried to get out. I ran more than once, but the doors were always locked." She looked down. "Oh!"

"What is it?" Erin asked.

"My stab wound. It's healed also."

Erin approached her. "Let me take a look."

I looked away. I'd already seen Lucy's breasts when I healed her, but I didn't want to be rude. Besides, River was giving Jay and me a look to kill.

"I think you performed a miracle here, Dante."

"Thank you, cuz," River said.

A miracle? I'd healed a person.

"I know what you're thinking, son," my father said.

Did he? Did he know I was considering the words of my mother in his dream?

A nearly divine purpose?

I'd resisted the godlike definition of divine, but if I was truly performing miracles...

No. I was not becoming a god. Certainly not with the darkness inside me.

"Supremely good," was all my father said.

I nodded. Supremely good. Whatever powers her blood had given me, I'd use them for supreme good. I could control the darkness. Hadn't I just begged them all to have faith in my ability to do just that?

"Yes, thank you," Lucy said. "I don't remember much until I changed in the hospital bed. I'm not sure why I changed, except that I have fewer nerve endings as a wolf, so maybe it spared me some of the pain of healing so quickly."

"Maybe," Erin said. "You still had bruises and lacerations when you changed."

They all looked to me, as if I were supposed to make some grand declaration or announcement.

"You're welcome?" was all I could come up with.

"We need to find you some clothes," River said to Lucy.

"There should be scrubs around here somewhere," Erin said. "If it's a real hospital, which it seems to be. Logan will know. Lucy, go back to the records room. He's probably still there."

"Okay."

"You're not going anywhere without me," River said.

"We should all go," I said. "I want a look at those records. Then I want to check on Em. We still haven't located the others."

A baby's cry pierced the air.

Erin turned. "Patty and the baby." She ran off.

EIGHTEEN

Erin

Dante grabbed me. "You're not running off alone."

"But the baby! Didn't you hear her?"

"Of course I heard her. My hearing is better than yours."

"I need to find her."

He sighed, cupping my cheek. "This is important to you." A statement.

"Yes."

"We'll go together. I'll see the records another time." He turned to the others. "You go ahead. Find clothes for Lucy. I'm with Erin."

River nodded. "Got it."

Dante took my arm, and we raced toward the sound of the wailing infant. We passed several rooms with locked doors. No windows in the doors.

Were the women we searched for behind them? I had no way of knowing. Right now, I followed the wails.

Dante stopped at one of the doors. "She's in here."

I put my ear against the door and could hear the infant's cry on the other side. "Yes! Can you open it?"

"I can." He quickly picked the lock and opened the door.

The girl in the bed let out a shrill scream.

Patty Doyle. In her arms was a bundle. A crying bundle.

"Patty, it's me. Erin. From the hospital. We're not here to hurt you."

"You can't take my baby! You can't take her again!"

"We're not here to take her," I said. "We're here to help."

Patty's face was red and her eyes swollen from crying. "I just want to go home!"

"I know. I know. Dante, could you get me a cool washcloth?"

He nodded and went to the sink. When he returned, I wiped Patty's face.

"They take her sometimes," she said.

"We're going to get you out of here."

"Now?"

"As soon as we can figure out how."

"I can get her out," Dante said. "I can shield her."

I nodded. "I need to check her out first. Make sure she's physically able. Is that okay, Patty? May I examine you?"

"I don't know."

"You do remember me, right? I was there when Isabelle was born."

"Yeah. I remember. Thank you for remembering her name."

I smiled. "It's a beautiful name. May I take the baby? I need to have a quick look at both of you."

She held on tight at first, but eventually let me take the infant, who had stopped crying, from her arms. "She's beautiful, Patty."

Indeed she was. Pink skin, a nub of a nose, full red lips, and a tuft of black hair. Tiny ears and delicate features. She would be a beauty.

Holding her felt nice. Like a comforting slice of warm apple pie. I turned to place her in the bassinet, but Dante stopped me.

"I'll hold her."

I smiled again and handed him the bundle.

He was so big and strong but took great care handling Isabelle. I couldn't help but stare at him for a moment as he gazed at the baby. Dante would be an amazing father. An amazing father to our children.

"Is he...?" Patty asked, her voice shaking.

"He's fine. He's my boyfriend. He won't hurt her."

Patty nodded as I removed the sheet and began to examine her. I felt the lymph nodes in her neck and then listened to her heart with a stethoscope I found on the table next to her. I checked her vitals, and all were normal.

"All right, Patty. You're in good health as far as I can see."

"What about Isabelle? She had surgery."

"She had a hernia repaired. The doctor told me about it. I'll check her incisions before we go, okay?"

She nodded, chewing on her lip.

"Dante," I said. "She's okay to go. I'm going to see if I can find her some clo—"

I gasped. Dante was touching the baby's lips, forcing her into a pucker.

"What are you doing?"

"Just check—" He stiffened.

"What is it?" I moved toward him, peering at the baby's sweet face.

"Erin," he said softly so only I could hear. "This baby is vampire."

NINETEEN

DANTE

Little white nubs on her upper gum line. They would grow into vampire canine teeth. My father had taught me long ago how to recognize a vampire baby. Most humans wouldn't even notice.

Erin's eyes shot wide open. She motioned me to be quiet. "Don't alarm Patty," she whispered.

"She might already know. She must be a vampire." I looked over at her. "If River were here, he could tell us if she has a scent. But—"

Erin took the baby from me and set her gently in the bassinet. "Patty, Dante and I are going to step outside for just a minute, okay?"

"I thought you were getting me out of here!"

"We are. We'll just be a minute."

"Well...I guess."

She pulled me out the door and closed it. "I saw Patty's records, Dante. She's VO positive and descended from a vampire, which seems to indicate that she herself is *not* a vampire."

"We still don't know what VO positive means."

"It's some kind of genetic marker," Erin said. "That part seems pretty obvious. All the women Bonneville has brought down here are VO positive, and those that have some kind of genetic abnormality are returned. Somehow, Patty gave birth to a vampire baby. How is that possible?"

"Don't look at me. I have no idea how our genetics work. I have a genetically impossible blood type."

"Damn!" She pushed a stray strand of hair out of her face. "Her baby must have been fathered by a vampire. I think she said his name was Liam, and that he wouldn't marry her."

"But that wouldn't— Oh."

"Right. This VO marker in a B positive human woman with vampire ancestry must mean she will produce a vampire child when she mates with a vampire male."

"Bonneville is keeping breeders. You were right. And Patty was a test case."

She shook her head. "I don't think so. I think this happened naturally. She came to the ER in labor. Wait! I remember Dr. Bonneville checking the baby's sucking reflex by putting a gloved finger in her mouth. At least that's what she said. Could she have been checking for vampire teeth?"

"The nubs? Yeah. They're almost always present at birth."

"How would she have known to check? Is there any other way to tell?"

"I don't think so," I said. "Not that I ever learned, anyway. But remember, I was gone for ten years."

"Something about this baby made Bonneville check," she said. "Then Patty and the baby disappear— Oh my God!"

"What is it?"

"Dante, Bonneville has a file on me. *I'm* VO positive."

The beautiful image of Erin handing me a baby boy surged back into my mind. The dark hair, the sweet cherubic face...and the canine nubs.

He was vampire.

"No wonder Bonneville took my pills. No wonder she wanted me pregnant."

"Not just pregnant," I said. "Pregnant by *me*."

What did all of this mean? Especially considering the new powers I'd developed? If I made a baby with Erin, it would be vampire.

My son.

My vampire son.

Erin interrupted my thoughts. "You said vampire females are rare."

"Yeah, eighty percent of vampire babies are born male. Shit." I ruffled my fingers through my hair. "We've got to get the baby out of here."

Would I let the Hope Diamond go if I possessed it? The crown jewels of England? The Mona Lisa?

She had eventually let me go, and she never did anything without a valid reason in her own mind. Did she know I'd find Erin? That I'd form a blood bond?

No. My father was certain that she hadn't counted on the blood bond. Perhaps it was the bond that was helping me force the dark energy down. Perhaps it was the bond that was keeping me from metamorphosing and then dying.

I didn't know whether any of those things were true, but I did know something.

She would not let this vampire baby girl go without a huge fight. This child was way more precious than the *Mona Lisa*. Way more precious than I was.

"See if you can find clothes for Patty," I said. "I'll stand guard out here. We've got to get them above ground as soon as possible."

Erin nodded and went back into the room.

God. Patty probably had no idea her child was a vampire. Someone would have to tell her.

But not now. Right now, she had to get out of here before Bonneville found out what we were up to.

She would not let the baby go.

"You're right, Dante."

I gasped.

She stood before me. She must have come down the hallway quietly as a mouse.

Had I been speaking out loud?

Didn't matter. She was here, and I would protect that woman and her baby with everything I had.

"I'm taking the baby and her mother out of here," I said on a growl, my teeth lengthening and sharpening.

"I'm afraid you aren't. I've allowed you to think you might be in control here. It was a fun little game, actually. But it's over."

"You've allowed me?" I snarled, my skin burning. "The power balance has shifted here, my *queen*. I know what you're up to."

"It was never a secret," she said.

"Was Levi Gaston working with you?"

"That fool? I already told you he was an alchemist. I'm a scientist."

"Who then? Who is helping you? You couldn't have done all this alone. You said this place took decades to build. How old are you, anyway?"

"It's rude to ask that question of a woman," she said wryly.

"Are you related to the hematologist Zarah Le Sang?"

"In a manner of speaking."

"Did she help you build this place?"

"In a manner of speaking."

"Why are there no records of you anywhere? You've been working above ground at the hospital. According to Erin, you're a gifted physician. Why aren't you anywhere on the internet?"

"I choose to be discreet, for obvious reasons."

"I want answers, damn it. What does VO positive mean?"

No response.

"What does vampyr omega mean?"

Her eyes narrowed. "*Where* did you hear *that*?"

A-ha! That got to her.

"Vampyr omega," I said again, this time slowly with exaggerated enunciation. "The end. What are you planning, *my queen*?"

"Sarcasm does not become you, Dante."

"You're no queen. Yet you consider yourself royalty. Why?"

"I'll speak no more of this until you're back in your right mind. For now, you will not take that woman or that baby anywhere. They are vital to what I'm accomplishing here."

"It's a vampire baby. How? Who's the father?"

"Did you not just hear me? I said I'll speak no more—"

"Dante!" Erin opened the door. "I need help. Patty's hemorrhaging."

Bonneville whisked past me into the room. "What the hell is going on?"

"She... When she got up," Erin said.

"She shouldn't be getting up!" Bonneville hurried to Patty's bedside. "What's happening, Patty? Where does it hurt?"

"Everywhere," Patty sobbed.

"Vaginal bleeding," Erin said, going into nurse mode. "It began quite suddenly."

I looked away as Bonneville examined the woman. "It's most likely from the birth," she said.

"I'm a nurse," Erin said indignantly. "I know what postpartum bleeding looks like. This isn't it. She's going to need to go to the OR."

"I'll decide what she needs," Bonneville said.

"What about—"

"Quiet, Erin! You're not even supposed to be here yet. But you are here, and I need your assistance. It's probably placental remnants. Crown will operate."

Yet. She had said Erin wasn't supposed to be here *yet.*

She had plans to bring Erin here.

This was going to stop now.

I blew into the room like a raging wind, the small pouch of my father's ashes in hand. With a mental gesture while I still held the baby, I threw *her* across the room.

She landed with a thud, her mouth dropping open.

"Dante!" Erin said. "I need a doctor. Patty is bleeding!"

I quickly fingered a pinch of my father's ashes and then touched them to the baby's and then Patty's foreheads. That would shield them from her. Then I closed my eyes and pictured Logan Crown in my mind, forcing him to come to us. He appeared in the room a few seconds later.

"What the—" he began.

"No time to explain," I said. "You need to help this woman. Erin can assist you."

I grabbed the baby. What would I do with her? No time to worry about that. I'd figure something out.

"That baby is mine!" Bonneville shouted, still sprawled on the floor, immobile.

"We need to get her to the OR, Erin," Logan said. "Come on. Help me. There are other nurses and assistants here."

"Where?" Erin asked.

"In another wing."

"There's *another wing*?" she said.

"Yeah. We need to hurry."

They wheeled Patty's bed out of the room.

"Put the child down, Dante."

"Think again."

"Release me!" her voice rumbled in a low, demonic tone.

Damn! I should have shielded Erin while I had the chance. What had I been thinking?

"What has happened to you?" she demanded. "How are you able—"

My rage boiled, and I forced energy toward *her*. She stopped talking and just lay there. I had no idea how long whatever I'd done would last. I needed to get the baby out. But who would care for her? Her mother was being operated on.

I was able to control *her*. Now I had to figure out how to control my control of her.

Only then could I put a stop to all of this nonsense.

I knew how to shield and get people out of here, so I'd do it. I'd find someone who could take the baby to the surface. Emilia. My sister could care for the child, or maybe one of the other women.

I had yet to find the other women, but I was sure they were behind the locked doors. Right now, my priority had to be this child.

The baby began wailing. Now what?

TWENTY

Erin

Logan led me to yet another wing of the hospital, and this one was bustling. While the other wings had been sterile and isolated, clearly this was where most activity happened down here. Scrubs-clad people milled about, all with glazed looks in their eyes.

A glamour. They were here to do a job, and they'd been glamoured into doing it.

"Coming through!" Logan shouted. "I need OR one!"

"Yes, Doctor." An orderly led us into an operating room.

Logan and I scrubbed up quickly while two others prepped Patty for surgical intervention.

"Get a transfusion ready," Logan said.

"Uterine atony?" I asked.

He shook his head. "She's several weeks postpartum. The uterus should have already contracted back to normal size. It's most likely placental remnants causing the bleed. She needs an immediate D and C."

I was gloved and ready to go. "I'm not an OR nurse, Logan," I warned.

"You're what I've got. You'll do fine, Erin. Just listen carefully and do what I tell you."

I nodded, swallowing a lump in my throat.

"Let's give her some Pitocin, twenty milligrams," he said. "Get the IV started. I want her on fluids now."

"Erin," Patty said. "What's happening to me?"

"We're going to take good care of you, Patty," I said.

"My baby!"

"She's in good hands." I prayed I was right. Dante had incapacitated Dr. Bonneville—for how long, I didn't know—so he was likely caring for Isabelle. He knew nothing about babies, but he could find Lucy. She would take care of the child.

"Point five milligrams of Versed, Erin. She needs to calm down."

"I'm going to give you a sedative," I told Patty.

"No! I need to stay alert for my baby."

"Your baby is fine, but we need to take care of you right now, okay? Please let us do what we have to do, so you can go back to your baby."

My words seemed to calm her, and she nodded. I administered the medication, and soon she was relaxing into sleep.

Logan worked diligently, dilating her cervix and then beginning to scrape Patty's uterine lining.

I held back a gasp. Too much blood. The curettage wasn't helping.

"I don't understand," he said. "Get her transfusion ready. Add plasma to help with clotting."

An orderly handed me a unit of B positive blood, and I set

up the transfusion.

"I'm opening her up," Logan said. "Erin, prepare for laparotomy."

God, no. If Logan couldn't stop the bleeding, he'd have no choice but to—

Once Patty's abdomen was open, Logan massaged the uterus with his gloved hands.

Come on. Stop bleeding. Please.

"Damn!" Logan huffed. "Come on!"

After a few more seconds, he pulled his blood-covered hands out of Patty's body. "We have to stop the bleeding, or she won't make it. Erin, prepare for hysterectomy."

"No! You can't do that to her. She's only seventeen. She won't be able to have another child."

"She won't be able to have another child if she's dead, Erin. Let's allow her to be a mother to the one she has."

"No." I was adamant.

"Do you have a better idea?"

"Dante," I said.

"Quit thinking about your boyfriend. You're on duty."

"He can help."

"He's not here, and he's not a doctor."

"You saw what he did for Lucy."

"That could have been a fluke. Besides, how do we find him? He could be anywhere in this damned compound by now. We're losing precious seconds, Erin. Do your job!"

"I can get him here. I can get him here fast." I grabbed a scalpel off the table and cut the skin of my forearm.

"Christ, Erin! What the fuck! I've got a bleeding patient here!"

"Dante's on his way. He can help her. I know it."

I continued to monitor Patty's vitals. Dante would have found someone to care for the baby by now, right?

It didn't matter, because he was coming. I felt it.

"Bandage that up!" Logan yelled. Then, "You!" He pointed to a young man in green scrubs. "My nurse is indisposed. I need your assistance with a hysterectomy."

"I'm just an orderly, Doctor."

"Do I look like I care? Get over here!"

Dante burst through the door.

I gasped. "I knew you'd come!"

He inhaled. "You. Now."

Oh, shit. I hadn't thought about the potential side effects of my actions. "No, Dante. We need you. We can't stop Patty's bleeding. Help her. Help her like you helped Lucy."

He growled, baring his fangs. "Hungry."

Damn! What had I done?

"Come on, Patty. Come on!" Logan turned to the young man assisting him. "Sponge, please. Hurry!"

Dante glared at me, burning two holes in my skin with his fiery eyes. "Erin." His voice was low and primal.

"Please, Dante. For me. Help her."

"Erin."

"Please!" I squeezed my eyes shut to force back tears. "Please! This is important to me. Help her!"

He snarled and then walked toward the operating table.

"Get him out of here, Erin," Logan said. "He's not wearing a mask. He hasn't washed up."

Dante growled at Logan, but Logan didn't flinch.

"Do what you want to me," he said. "My concern is for my patient."

Dante ignored him and pushed him out of the way. He laid

his hand on Patty's abdomen.

Energy sizzled in the room.

"Damn," Logan said.

I ran to the table.

Patty's bleeding had stopped.

TWENTY-ONE

DANTE

My skin radiated heat, and every nerve within me was jumping with energy.

Erin had wanted Patty to stop bleeding, and I'd do anything for Erin. Now that Patty was out of danger, though, I could only think of what brought me here.

Erin. Her blood. She'd called me here with our bond, and now I'd take what she'd promised.

I removed my hand from the young woman and then turned to Erin.

"Now," I said through clenched teeth.

"Dante, no. I need to see to—"

"Erin," I snarled. "You called me here with your blood. Don't expect me not to answer that call. I won't say it again. *Now.*"

"But Patty—"

"Logan and the others will deal with her. She's out of danger. You're forcing my hand here. You woke the beast within me. Now you must sate him."

She nodded, gulping. I yanked her out of the operating room and into the first alcove I came across.

Then I brushed her hair away from her neck and sank my fangs into her milky flesh.

Sweet red gold. As it trickled over my tongue and down my throat, I calmed.

But only a little.

Blood was not enough to sate my lust anymore. I needed all of her. I inhaled. Her musk was thick in the air. The dark truffly scent of her, the fruity arousal. I released her and then gazed at her.

She was still dressed all in black, vest and all, and she was wearing rubber gloves. Her beautiful face was obscured by a white surgical mask.

I ripped the mask from her and crashed my lips down onto hers. Yes, a kiss. A ferocious, raw kiss. I dived into her mouth, tangling my tongue with hers, groaning, my cock a granite bulge in my pants.

I wanted to lift her in my arms and thrust into her against the wall, but all these damned clothes!

I broke the kiss and turned her around, shoved her leggings and panties over her hips and down her thighs, and then released my cock.

I didn't check to see if she was wet.

Didn't ask what she wanted.

Didn't think about anything other than sating my own animal lust.

I pushed into her, hard.

"Dante!" she cried out.

"That's right. Say my name. Say my fucking name, Erin."

"Dante!" she screamed again.

"Who is fucking you, Erin?"

"You. Dante."

"Who do you belong to?"

"You. Dante."

"Who did you call to you with your blood?"

"You. Dante."

"And who came to you?"

"You. Always you. Dante."

"That's right."

Thrust.

"I'll always come to you."

Thrust.

"So you'd better always be fucking ready for me."

Thrust.

Thrust.

Thrust.

And then—

Sweet release. Sweet release into Erin's perfect body. With each contraction of my cock, I came closer to nirvana, closer to pure peace, closer to heaven itself.

Heaven. Erin was heaven.

But this place was hell.

With that abrupt realization, I pulled out of her and helped her clean up. When she looked up at me, her cheeks were streaked with tears.

My stomach dropped. What had I done? I cupped her cheek. "Erin."

She closed her eyes. "I'm so sorry."

She was sorry? "What for, baby?"

"I called you here for..." She shook her head. "I didn't think. I wasn't thinking. I just knew I couldn't let Logan sterilize Patty.

She's only—"

"What? *Sterilize* her?"

Erin sniffled, nodding. "He couldn't stop the bleeding, so his only choice was to remove her uterus. A hysterectomy. It would have saved her life but left her unable to have any more children."

"That's why you called to me with your blood?"

She nodded again. "I'm sorry."

"Baby, don't be sorry for wanting to save a young woman's ability to have children. You're a nurse. A very good and caring one. That's what you do. But why me?"

"I was desperate. You healed Lucy. I knew you could heal Patty."

"I wasn't sure I could. I don't know what I did."

"Oh, Dante, that doesn't matter. *I* was sure. And you did."

"You believe in me that much?"

"Absolutely."

I thumbed Erin's soft cheek. God, she was so beautiful, so perfect. And her belief in me... I was unworthy of it, with the darkness that threatened to control me.

But the last few times it had creeped up, I'd allowed it to surface, and I'd controlled it.

Was that energy part of what gave me these odd powers? The ability to heal was certainly not a dark power. It was an amazing power of love and light.

And it hit me, like a brick falling on my head.

I had control over everything in me—the light, the darkness. The black, the white. The beginning, the end.

It was all part of me.

It was all me.

She might have fed me her blood and tortured me and

forced me to fight for survival for her own purposes, but in the end, *I* could control the powers she'd given me.

I could control *her*.

Already I'd incapacitated her twice simply with my anger. She knew I had the upper hand now. She *knew*.

"Are you okay?" Erin asked.

"Yeah. Why?"

"You haven't said anything in a few minutes." She adjusted her clothes.

I adjusted mine as well. "Just thinking. Let's go see how Patty is."

"I'd like that," she said.

We walked back to the operating room.

Logan was just walking out, looking haggard. "Patty's in recovery. She's going to be okay. I don't know how you do what you do, but thank you."

I said nothing until Erin nudged me.

"You're welcome."

"I'd like to bottle whatever you have inside you, man," he said. "You've saved two lives down here."

Again I said nothing. What could I say? I had no idea what the hell I was doing.

"I know we didn't meet under the best of conditions," he continued, "and not that you care, or that it even matters, but I'll have your back from now on, if I have anything to say about it. Down here or up there."

I nodded. I supposed I should reciprocate, but I still remembered catching him about to fuck Erin.

"Anyway"—he rubbed his hands together—"thank you again."

"Can we see Patty?" Erin asked.

"Yeah. She'll ask about the baby as soon as she's coherent. Where is she?"

TWENTY-TWO

Erin

Dante cleared his throat. "I had the chance to get the child out of here, and I took it."

I gasped. "What?"

"She's fine. She's shielded."

"What do you mean shielded?" Logan demanded.

"You seem to think I can perform miracles," Dante said. "I shielded her, her and Lucy. I sent Lucy above ground with the baby. She's in good hands."

I sighed in relief. Both Lucy and Isabelle had gotten out of here. Good news indeed. "Lucy will take good care of her, but what will we tell Patty?"

"We'll tell her that her baby is safe. She'll be happy about that."

Logan shook his head for a second and then stopped abruptly, a glassy look taking over his gaze. "I'll leave that to the two of you to work out. I need to take a break." He ambled off.

"Did he look okay to you?" I asked.

"Wasn't really looking that closely," Dante said. "I still can't stand the guy."

"After that speech he just made?"

"Call it a flaw in my character if you want. I'll always have a problem with guys who tried to fuck you."

"I'll remind you that it was entirely consensual."

He let out a sarcastic laugh. "You think that matters?"

"Apparently not. Did you think Logan looked a little weird just now?"

"I think Logan looks weird all the time."

"I'm serious, Dante. He seemed to gaze off into nowhere and leave suddenly."

"He's probably tired."

"Maybe. I feel like we should follow him, but I need to look in on Patty."

"When will she be able to get out of here?"

"She just had surgery. Her abdomen was opened up. A few days, probably."

He sighed. "All right. I want to get Em out of here right away. Then the others. They're in those rooms behind the locked doors. Now that I know the shield works, we need to accomplish what we came here to do."

I nodded. "I agree."

"After that, you and the others can leave. I'll take care of Bonneville."

I had no intention of going anywhere, but arguing with Dante on the point wouldn't be productive. "Is she still in Patty's room?"

"I have no idea," he said. "I don't know how long whatever I did to her will work."

"Are you sure Lucy and the baby got out? Did you

personally see them?"

"No. I sent River and Jay with explicit instructions to see them safely to the ladder to the manhole."

"Okay. They're coming back, right?"

He nodded. "They won't leave. Not as long as you and Em are down here."

"None of us can leave until all those women are safely out of here. If you've found a way to do it, let's get it done. Then we find your uncle."

Dante stayed eerily silent.

"Dante?"

His eyes widened. "Nothing. Yes. Let's get the women out of here. Unfortunately, Patty won't be able to go until she's—"

"You can heal her, Dante. You healed Lucy. Her injuries from the fight are all better. They healed while she was in wolf form."

"Erin, I have no idea how I did any of that."

"But you—"

I gasped as Julian appeared.

"Damn, Julian!"

"I'm sorry, but I need the two of you. Dr. Bonneville has taken River."

TWENTY-THREE

DANTE

"What?" Rage surged through me.

"I would have stopped it if I'd been there. I was with your sister." He shook his head. "Though I don't really know how I've channeled my energy before."

"I hear you," I said. "I have no idea how I do it either."

"Wait. Wait," Erin said. "If you weren't there, Julian, how do you know Bonneville has him?"

"Your brother, Erin. He said he was paralyzed, incapable of helping River. It was a glamour I'd never heard of before. He remained in his own mind but couldn't move."

"Oh!" Erin clasped her hand to her mouth. "That must have been terribly frightening for him."

"It was, but he's okay. He's resting in Emilia's room."

"I want to get Em out of here, Dad," I said.

"I agree. Jay can take her out of here. You will shield them both."

"I need Jay here," Erin said, but then she shook her head. "I'm sorry. You're right. He should go. He should be with the mother of his child."

"That's the only way he would agree to go," my father said. "He wants you to accompany them, Erin."

As much as it pained me, I nodded. "I agree, baby. You need to leave while you can."

Erin whipped her hands to her hips, taking that indignant stance that set my loins on fire. I breathed in. God, yes. Angry testosterone coupled with everything else Erin drove me to the brink of madness.

"I'm not going anywhere," she said defiantly, holding out her bandaged forearm. "You need me, Dante."

Her blood beckoned me. I'd just had a taste—of her blood and of her body—yet now I wanted more. I tamped down my desire as best I could. I had to think of River.

"Erin, please."

"I'm *not* going."

"All right, Erin," my father said. "Dante will protect you. And so will I."

"Good. Now let's get those women to safety."

"Now is the time," my father said. "The thugs have gone above ground. Dante can unlock the doors and shield the women, and you two lead them to safety. Then get some rest if you can. You will both need your strength for what is to come."

But I would get no rest. Not as long as River was missing.

Three hours later, Emilia, Jay, and twelve other women, including Sybil Downey, were safely above ground. I glamoured the women, except Emilia, to forget where they'd been. Right now, having cops sniff around would only hinder what we had to do.

We'd accomplished our primary objective—free the women.

The next objective was my uncle, and now we had another. River.

She'd warned me. Warned me if I didn't cooperate, she would turn to River. Had I taken her seriously? Apparently not enough.

Erin desperately needed to sleep. She fell against me, her legs no longer able to hold her. What could I do? She'd been awake for days, and so had I.

She trusted me to protect her. "Dad?" I whispered.

Nothing. Damn him.

I held on to Erin and went into the first unlocked room. I removed her pack and laid her gently on a bed and sat down next to her. I'd wake her in a few minutes. Hopefully a catnap would be all she needed. I couldn't afford to waste any more time. In the meantime, I tried to force more memories from my time in captivity. Nothing. The memories presented themselves when I didn't want them, but now, when I wanted them? They were nowhere to be found.

Even *she* had stopped speaking to me.

That was a good thing. It meant I had exerted control over her and over the darkness that was part of me. All good.

But no longer could I count on her to force me into action.

I was me.

Only Dante.

Then I smiled as I buried my nose in Erin's soft hair and inhaled the apple-mandarin scent.

Not just me after all. I had Erin. Always Erin. Erin, who chose me over her own safety. Erin, who I loved more than anything.

Time had no meaning in this place. Only darkness. I'd figured out early on that I was underground. Darkness became a friend to me. My only friend in this hellish place.

I always felt ill after she forced me to take her blood. My throat was raw, as if her blood had crawled down, sinking its talons into my esophagus. My stomach churned and coiled, growling at my body. My muscles tautened and tightened, and I flexed against my bindings. My bones creaked. And my vision became so acute that I almost forgot the darkness for a moment.

For a moment, I saw light.

But only for a moment.

Perhaps I forced the light away to make room for my old friend, the darkness. Or perhaps the light was only a brief side effect of ingesting her blood.

Each time, though, something in me changed. It happened gradually, but it happened. I felt it in the marrow of my bones. I felt it in the core of my brain.

And for one horrid second after each feeding, I found myself smiling.

I awoke with a start, jarred.

Shit! How could I have fallen asleep?

But it had given me a memory. I'd tried to force a memory but had no luck. When I finally drifted off to sleep, one came to me. I ran through it in my mind. What was its purpose? I'd always felt sickened after taking her blood, but I'd assumed it was psychological. Now, with this memory, and after reading the deciphered paragraph in the *Texts*, I knew it was indeed physical.

She always told me she'd found a way to combat the negative side effects of ingesting vampire blood. Had that been a lie? Most likely. I *did* change. The darkness had become part of me. She'd expected it to take me over.

It almost had, until I accepted it, embraced it, and now worked to control it.

I would be successful.

I would take her down.

For myself. For Erin. For all.

I turned to kiss Erin's head.

She wasn't there.

Erin

"Let me go!" I pulled against the straps holding me down.

"I can't, Erin," Dr. Bonneville said. "You've cost me all the women I've collected. They're all gone, save for Patty. I'm afraid you're all I have left."

Dante truly was powerful. Bonneville had been running this operation for months now, and Dante had freed the women in a couple of days. Inside I smiled. Not on the outside. I would not give her the satisfaction.

"You know Dante will come for me."

"Indeed. In fact, I'm counting on it."

Damn! *Don't come, Dante. Please, don't come.* Could he hear my silent plea? He had so much power. I had to believe he could hear me.

It didn't matter, though. He would come for me anyway. He'd walk right into her trap.

"Why are you doing this? You're a physician, for God's sake. You took an oath to do no harm!"

"I'm not doing any harm, Erin."

"You are! You're holding people here against their will. Performing experiments."

"All for the greater good, I assure you."

"How is any of this for the greater good? So you increase the vampire population. It will take centuries for any of that to have any effect at all. And even then, humans will still outnumber you."

"Look at this from my perspective, Erin. Would you let your own species die out?"

An anvil hit me in the gut. Nothing like getting right to the point. "I wouldn't kidnap innocent people for any reason."

"Sorry, Erin. You didn't answer the question. Would you let your people become extinct if you could prevent it?"

"Not if it meant—"

"Yes or no!"

"This isn't a courtroom drama. Nothing is absolute, Zabrina." The first time I'd used her given name. After what she'd done, I no longer felt comfortable calling her Doctor. "There's still the issue of right and wrong."

My use of her first name didn't seem to faze her. "There's also the issue of the end justifies the means."

"Not if it infringes on people's rights."

"Rights? Don't my people have the right to survive, Erin?"

"Don't *mine*?"

"I've taken no lives. None. I'm a physician for God's sake."

"Maybe not personally. But you've tortured innocent people. You held Dante here for ten years, forced him to—"

"Everything Dante has been through has made him who he is today. The man you love."

Wow. How did I argue with that? Easy. Put me in fucking

chains and I'd argue with anything. I opened my mouth to speak, but she cut me off.

"I could glamour you, you know. I don't have to listen to your petty whining."

"Go ahead. You glamoured me all those times you fed on me without my permission."

"A woman's got to eat. Why not choose the sweetest fruit?"

I seethed, rage eking out of every pore in my body. *Calm down, Erin. Get some information. Get anything.*

"What is VO positive?"

"None of your business."

"Why not? You can always glamour me into forgetting it."

"You won't understand."

"Why wouldn't I? I'm a nurse. A medical professional. And whatever this VO thing is, apparently I have it."

"Fine." She put down the file she was perusing and sat down in the chair next to the bed I was strapped to. "VO is—"

"Short for vampyr omega?"

"Where did you hear that?"

"A little bird told me."

"Fuck off, Erin." She stood. "I have work to do."

Shit! She'd been about to tell me. I could handle this. She was a narcissist through and through. All I had to do was bring that out. "It's nothing, isn't it? Something you made up so you could indulge in your psychopathic fantasies about kidnapping innocent women. Feeding off a potent male vampire. You're nothing!"

Yup. That did it.

She turned back to me with a snarl, baring her teeth. "You dare insult me? My work is legendary. It will change the world!"

"How? You're nothing but one vampire woman. How can

you change the world?"

"VO, Erin, is a marker that occurs on the twenty-third chromosome in a small minority of B positive women who have vampire ancestry."

"I've figured out the rest, Zabrina, despite the tiny little mind you think I have. You wanted me pregnant by Dante. You think we'll have a vampire baby."

"You *will* have a vampire baby if you get pregnant by a vampire male, but that's not why I wanted you pregnant by Dante."

"Why then?"

She snarled. "Dante is very special."

"One thing we can agree on," I said.

"The father of Patty's baby is a vampire," she said.

"I know. His name is Liam."

She chuckled. "That's her boyfriend's name. He's not the father, however."

Rage surged into me again. "You had her *raped*?"

"*I* had nothing to do with anything! I don't control what another vampire does any more than you do."

"You got that right. You thought you could control Dante, but he's stronger than you ever imagined, isn't he?"

She bared her fangs to me once more, but I was done fearing this woman.

"Dante will come to see the truth. So will the others. Even the women. Even Patty."

"Patty doesn't know, does she? She thinks her boyfriend is the father. Whoever raped her glamoured her into forgetting it. No wonder Liam refused to marry her. He must doubt that he's the father."

"Or he's just an asshole," Bonneville said.

I couldn't fault her observation. Still, there was a vampire rapist on the loose. "Is it one of your Claiborne drug-runner thugs?"

"I don't know who it was. Believe it or not, this happened totally by accident. I already told you I had nothing to do with it. It was as big a surprise to me as anyone else when she gave birth to a vampire baby, but it proved my theory. I tested her blood, and Patty has the VO marker. Therefore, her baby is vampire. A vampire *female*, no less. Very rare."

Did Bonneville not know yet that the baby was gone? I wasn't about to tell her. "You're keeping all the VO women who don't have any genetic abnormalities. I saw the records, Zabrina."

"My work is more important than the liberty of a few women."

"More important for whom?"

"For everyone."

"Really. For me?"

"*Especially* for you. Your children will be fathered by Dante, as fine a vampire specimen as was ever created. Your children are the future of my species. You'll be the mother of greatness."

"Not if you force me to get pregnant and give birth down here. No child of mine will be born imprisoned."

"You won't have that choice, I'm afraid."

And then I knew.

This wasn't about saving her species. If that were her only goal, she could accomplish it above ground. She could use her glamour and inseminate VO positive women with vampire semen. She had a whole hospital at her disposal.

Saving her species was only the beginning.

With us down here, she could monitor everything. Bring things to whatever conclusion she wanted. She could force breeding. Harvest our eggs and implant embryos fertilized by vampire seed into surrogates.

"You're lying to me," I said.

"About what?"

"Vampyr omega. There's a reason you used that name for the marker. You're a supremacist, aren't you? Just like Levi Gaston."

"He was a stupid old fool."

"Maybe, but you share his philosophy. You think vampires are the superior species."

"We *are* superior."

"If you are, wouldn't evolution have proved that? Wouldn't your numbers increase instead of decrease?"

Zabrina approached me, growling, and slapped me hard in the face. I cringed as my cheek numbed for an instant and then burning pain spread over my skin.

"Enough!" she yelled. "That's enough! You have no idea what we're capable of. No idea what *I* am capable of. No idea who I truly *am*!"

My body buzzed with her glamour—yes, I remembered it now—and then my mind went blank.

TWENTY-FIVE

DANTE

Rage tumbled through me. At *her*, for taking Erin, but mostly at myself.

I'd gotten cocky. I might have power, but I was still a mortal being—one who required sleep. I'd let myself be weak for a moment, and *she* had swooped in and taken the one person who meant more to me than my own life.

She'd taken the person who *was* my life. My everything. My blood. My body. My soul.

"Dante." My father appeared.

"Where is she, Dad? Where?"

"She's in a hospital room, strapped to a bed."

"No!" I roared. "Why didn't you stop her!"

"I was searching for River. I'm sorry, son."

"Where is he?"

"I haven't found him yet. A new shield has been erected around certain parts of this compound. I'm going to have to go above ground and get Bea to allow me through."

I fingered the vampire fleur-de-lis pin on my shirt. "Will I be able to get through?"

"I don't know. Most likely, unless she doesn't allow her thugs to get through."

It was a miracle *she* hadn't noticed the pin yet. I quickly unpinned it from inside the collar of my shirt and pinned it to my boxer briefs, where it would be less likely to be discovered.

"Dad, please understand. My first priority has to be Erin."

"I do understand, son. I can take you to her. She's not shielded, but she is tied down."

"Not for long. Show— Wait!"

Erin's pack lay on the floor where I'd tossed it, her book peeking out from the unzipped top. Whoever came and took Erin while we were sleeping either hadn't noticed it or didn't think anything of it. Which meant it probably hadn't been Bonneville. Who else could have gotten in here without my knowing?

The answer?

No one.

No fucking one.

I would have heard anyone who tried to take my love away from me, and no one could stop me with a glamour.

"Dad? Something doesn't add up here. How could Erin—"

"There's only one answer. She left voluntarily."

"But why?"

"I don't know. Maybe it wasn't voluntary. Maybe she got up and went to the bathroom or something."

"But I would have heard her."

"Not if what she was doing was normal. You were asleep."

"I'm also down here. I'm on high alert."

"True. I admit it's a riddle."

"One I'm going to solve. I was sure, Dad, that I'd conquered the power that bitch had over me. What if I haven't? What if she can still find a way to control me?"

"I think that's why she took Erin, son. She knows she can control you if Erin is at stake."

"But it still doesn't answer how she got Erin in the first place. She wouldn't go voluntarily."

"Then somehow she left this room in a normal manner, and then she was taken."

"Or..." I rubbed at a tender spot on my neck. "Damn."

"What is it? Let me see." In an instant, my father was in front of me. "That explains it. You were injected with something."

"How long was I asleep?"

"I don't know. Several hours."

"Time doesn't have any meaning down here."

"Time doesn't actually have any meaning at all, Dante."

"You know what I mean, Dad. I get that you're noncorporeal and time is all relative and all that bullshit. But I'm a physical body that ages with the passage of time. Time has meaning for me, okay? But down here, there's no telling what time it is." I huffed. "What could she have given me that would put me out for a few hours? And why don't I remember her coming in to do it? I should have heard her."

"A lot of drugs give you retroactive amnesia for a few minutes. You probably wouldn't remember the few seconds it took her to come in and inject you."

"But she'd have to incapacitate me before she could even come close enough to inject me. My reflexes—"

"Maybe aren't as strong as hers. There's much we don't know about her. Erin hasn't been able to find her anywhere online. She's kept her tracks well covered over the years."

"That bitch! No, it wasn't enough for her to violate me for ten years. Now she drugs me? That was the last time, Dad. I swear to God!" I curled my hands into fists and let my teeth lengthen and sharpen to their most lethal points. *She* would not get away with this. I would shut this fucking place down. "Take me to Erin," I said in a voice I hardly recognized.

"Easy, son. If you want to be any help to Erin, you need control."

"Fuck control."

"Dante—"

"I said 'fuck control.'"

My father disappeared.

I didn't care. I was alone in this now. No Erin. No River. No Dad. No Uncle Brae. She'd taken everything from me.

Everything.

And now I'd make her fucking pay.

TWENTY-SIX

Erin

Darkness shrouded me. I couldn't see. Couldn't make my eyes adjust.

Tied down. Still tied down.

"Dante!" I screamed. "Dante! Help me!"

I pulled against the bindings. I lay on my back, my wrists and ankles bound. This was no hospital bed, as I'd been in earlier. This was...

This was...

Oh, God. This was where Dante had been kept. Perhaps even the same room.

"I can't see!" I cried. "Dante!"

The door opened, letting in just a sliver of light, but not enough for me to see anything except a dark figure.

"Stay away from me! Dante! Help!"

"He can't hear you." A male voice.

"Who are you? You leave me the fuck alone!"

"I do what I'm told."

I squinted but still couldn't see. How was it so dark that my eyes couldn't adjust?

He released my wrists and pulled me into a sitting position. "It's time for your meal."

"I'm not hungry."

"Doesn't matter. You'll eat." He wheeled a table over and placed it in front of me.

I inhaled. Beef, maybe? Or pork? Without the ability to see, I couldn't be sure. Funny how the senses were all connected. Didn't matter. I wasn't eating. With a grand gesture, I tossed the tray to the floor.

The man chuckled. "You think you're the first to do that? You get to go hungry now and enjoy the stench of rotting food until someone decides to clean it up. That someone won't be me, by the way."

"Fuck you."

He came close to me, our faces inches apart, and finally I saw something. The blue of his eyes was so light it seemed to glow. Then he opened his mouth.

No fangs.

This man was human. He wouldn't steal my blood, but he could still inflict a lot of harm.

"Why are you doing this? What did she do to you to make you do this?"

"I don't know what you're talking about, little one. I was told to feed you."

"Who told you?"

He furrowed his brow. "No one's asked me that before."

"Who?" I said again.

"I...don't know."

"How long have you been here?"

"I...don't know."

"I can get you out of here."

He guffawed. "Now that's funny. You're tied up at the moment, as far as I can tell."

"If you untie my legs, I can get you out of here. I swear it. All I need is a knife."

"Right. I give you a knife, and you carve out my heart."

"I won't say it's not tempting, but I won't. I swear it. I'm a nurse. I don't harm people. Get me the knife, I just need to..." God, how to say this?

I need to cut myself open so my vampire boyfriend will smell my blood and come to me.

Oh, what the fuck?

"I need to cut myself open so my vampire boyfriend will smell my blood and come to me."

"You're crazy. I'm done here." He pushed me down and bound my wrists once more.

"No! Help me! I can get you out—"

The door slammed, leaving me with only the darkness.

Until it opened once more.

Again, I could only make out a dark figure entering.

"Hello, Erin."

A voice I recognized. "Hello, Zabrina."

"I hear you didn't eat your meal."

"Not feeling hungry, thanks."

"You need nourishment, Erin, if you're to bear vampire children. Plus, you need to prepare for the harvest."

"Prepare for the...what?"

"The harvest. You'll only feel a slight prick."

Damn! I couldn't see! "Whatever you plan to do to me, think again! Dante! Dante!"

Fingers massaged my thigh. Was it bare? I had a shirt on, but my legs. God, they were bare! I hadn't noticed until now.

"Just a tiny prick."

"Don't you dare!"

"Surely you've had an injection before."

"I'm not scared of a shot, you lunatic. I'm scared of whatever shit you want to put in me!"

"Hormones, Erin. Simple hormones."

I winced as the needle punctured my skin. "You crazy-assed bitch! The harvest is an egg harvest, isn't it? You're taking my eggs!"

"Oops. I must have hit an artery. Just a few drops of blood." She inhaled, sighing. "You are a decadent treat, Erin. But your blood must be conserved for now, no matter how delicious."

"You bitch. You bitch. You fucking, insane bi—"

My mind went blank again.

DANTE

My body thrummed, and I inhaled.

Erin.

Her blood.

She was calling me again, and I was powerless to resist. My father had disappeared—I still had no idea why—so he couldn't lead me to Erin.

Eventually I would have picked up her scent, but now I didn't have to. She was calling to me with her blood.

Carrying Erin's pack, I stalked through the door, through the hallway, and then into the next wing of the underground hospital. Everything around was nothing more than a blur accompanied by white noise.

I had one objective.

Find Erin.

Take her blood.

Take her.

I finally came to the door that led into the dark part of this compound. The place where I'd found Abe Lincoln and the others.

The place I'd been kept for ten years.

I stalked through each hallway, making turns when my body told me to, each step bringing me closer to Erin.

With every inhalation I throbbed harder.

That dark chocolate. That musky truffle. That lusty red wine crisp with tannins and acidity.

Until—

"Ah, so you penetrated the shield. I can't say I'm surprised. You have abilities I never dreamed of, Dante."

She stood outside one of the doors.

Behind the door was Erin. Her scent was thick.

I had one advantage. *She* didn't know I'd gotten through the shield because of the pin one of her thugs had inadvertently left at Em's apartment.

"You have no idea," I said, baring my fangs on a low rasp. "Move out of my way."

"Of course." She stepped to the side. "I must confess. I was almost sure you'd take longer to get here. I underestimated you. It won't happen again."

She had no idea my father had been spying for me either. She was a woman of science who didn't believe in ghosts.

Good.

She also didn't know I'd sniffed out Erin's blood. What if Erin hadn't spilled her own blood to call for me? What if—

With one hand, I flattened Bonneville against the concrete wall. "If you've harmed one hair on her head."

She bared her teeth. "Kindly let me go if you want to see her."

"Fuck you," I said through clenched teeth, tightening my grip.

"You only think you're in control here, Dante. At this very

moment, one of my servants holds a needle inches from Erin's thigh. It contains an antidote."

"What?"

"You heard me. An antidote. To the poison he administered as soon as I saw you coming."

Rage blew through me like a cyclone. "You what? You poisoned Erin?"

"Your strength has surpassed even what I imagined, Dante. I had to have some leverage, didn't I? Even *you* can't bring someone back from the dead. Trust me on that one."

"You fucking bitch!" I squeezed her neck.

"If he doesn't get a signal from me, he won't administer the antidote. If you want her to live, you *will* let me go."

"No. Not Erin."

"Why not Erin?"

"You know why. If she dies, I die."

"Don't be ridiculous. Your blood bond is nonsense. An old wives' tale. The only person you're bonded to—will *ever* be bonded to—is me, Dante. You're *mine*. You will always be mine!"

How I ached to tighten my grip, to squeeze the life out of this psychopath.

But Erin.

I couldn't take the chance. What if *she* was telling me the truth? What if Erin died because of me?

With reluctance—a lot of it—I let her go.

"Good." She smoothed her white coat. "Now, if you want the antidote administered, here are my terms."

Fight or die in the arena.

I had no choice.

Those were her terms. Get dropped into the fighting pit once more and fight for my life.

My fucking life that wasn't worth a pittance without Erin.

There can only be one who is undefeated.

I was so much more powerful now than I was when last I fought here in this dirt-covered arena. I'd moved things with my mind. I'd healed two people.

I could win this fight with a mere look.

And win I would, quickly, so I could get back to Erin and protect her from this place.

Once I won, I'd get Erin out of here. I'd get her to safety, and then I'd come back for River and my uncle.

I inhaled, gathering every last ounce of rage and letting it pour into my muscles.

Bring. It. On.

Someone dropped onto the ground with a thud.

My opponents had always been masked, but not this time.

"Fuck." He stood and rubbed his behind. "Shit. Dante?"

I jerked. "Riv?"

Oh, hell, no. I would *not* fight my cousin.

"You think I'd pit Erin's life against your cousin's?" Her voice, from above. "I'm smarter than that. It will be two against one this time. And here is your opponent."

Another thud on the ground, and—

I growled as the monstrous being stood, flexing muscles twice as big as mine.

River wasn't ready for this. He was as strong and virile as

any vampire male, but he hadn't been trained for the arena, and certainly not against some kind of monster.

"Easy, Riv. I got this. Stay behind me."

"No, I can help y— Oh my God! What the fuck?"

The monster's gaze met mine.

Eyes I recognized. Eyes that were identical to ones now dead.

My skin chilled. "Oh my God. Uncle Brae."

ZABRINA

You've surprised me, Dante.

I never expected such power.

Even the prophecy doesn't speak of its extent. Perhaps I should have done further research. Perhaps I shouldn't have attempted to find the science behind it and bring it to life.

Bring *you* to life.

You—the chosen one.

But I did.

And you're here. Your strength, your power, your agility—it's all here.

You possess something that I do not, but I still have the upper hand, and I will control you with any means at my disposal.

That includes your little bitch.

And that weapon you don't yet know about.

BLOOD BOND SAGA

PART 15

DANTE

*F*ight or die in the arena.

I had no choice.

Those were her terms. Get dropped into the fighting pit once more and fight for my life.

My fucking life that wasn't worth a pittance without Erin.

There can only be one who is undefeated.

I was so much more powerful now than I was when last I fought here in this dirt-covered arena. I'd moved things with my mind. I'd healed two people.

I could win this fight with a mere look.

And win I would, quickly, so I could get back to Erin and protect her from this place.

Once I won, I'd get Erin out of here. I'd get her to safety, and then I'd come back for River and my uncle.

I inhaled, gathering every last ounce of rage and letting it pour into my muscles.

Bring. It. On.

Someone dropped onto the ground with a thud.

My opponents had always been masked, but not this time. "Fuck." He stood and rubbed his behind. "Shit. Dante?"

I jerked. "Riv?"

Oh, hell, no. I would *not* fight my cousin.

"You think I'd pit Erin's life against your cousin's?" Her voice, from above. "I'm smarter than that. It will be two against one this time. And here is your opponent."

Another thud on the ground, and—

I growled as the monstrous being stood, flexing muscles twice as big as mine.

River wasn't ready for this. He was as strong and virile as any vampire male, but he hadn't been trained for the arena, and certainly not against some kind of monster.

"Easy, Riv. I got this. Stay behind me."

"No, I can help y— Oh my God! What the fuck?"

The monster's gaze met mine.

Eyes I recognized. Eyes that were identical to ones now dead.

My skin chilled. "Oh my God. Uncle Brae."

ONE

Erin

I floated in a cloudy haze. Where was I again? Couldn't see. Couldn't move my arms or legs. A puncturing growl as my insides churned. Hunger. I was hungry. When had I last eaten?

I inhaled and struggled against what bound me as panic churned in my gut. Was it rope? Leather? Not metal. It was pliable. Slightly.

Beef? Something. Some kind of food was in here with me.

I arched my back, stretching my pectorals. Ouch! My breasts. So tender. What the hell?

Then more stomach cramping.

Hunger...and something else.

Hazy memories tried to surface. I licked my parched lips. My mouth was dry. Water. Needed water.

"Hey!" I yelled. "I need water!"

No response. Not that I expected one.

The muscle of my right thigh ached, kind of like the twinge in my arm after a tetanus booster.

A shot.

Someone had given me a shot.

"Damn it! Dante! Dante, get me out of here!"

But nothing. No one came.

A sliver of light poked through as the door opened.

"Erin?"

"Who's there?"

"It's me. Logan."

"Logan! Thank God! Get me out of here!"

He flipped on an overhead light. "I can't. I'm so sorry."

I squinted against the harsh illumination. "What do you mean you can't? Are you crazy?"

A heavy sigh. "I think I am."

"Please, Logan. You're not crazy. Untie me and get me out of here. Dante is in trouble. I know it."

"I wish I could, Erin. I want to. I want to do the right thing. You have no idea."

"Don't let her control you, Logan. *You* are in control. Not her."

"I hate the bitch."

I scoffed. "And you think I don't? All the more reason to let me go."

"I'm here to examine you, Erin, and to take some blood."

"You're not taking any of my blood, Lo—"

"What?"

"Never mind. Sure. Take my blood. In fact, cut me open. I want my blood to spill."

"Are you nuts?"

"I'm as sane as ever." If I could get him to cut me—to open the door—Dante would smell my blood and come to me. Quickly, I hoped.

I gasped as the cool end of a stethoscope touched my chest.

"Any breast tenderness?" Logan asked.

"Yeah. Like two cannonballs."

"Good. That's good. Cramping?"

"From hunger or from gas?"

"Funny, Erin. You know what I'm talking about."

"No, I'm afraid I don't, Logan. I'm on the pill, and I'm not due for a period for—"

A memory speared into me.

The harvest.

Not an autumnal harvest, but a harvest of my eggs. The injection. Dr. Bonneville.

"No. You can't let them do this to me, Logan. You're a doctor, for God's sake. Stop this!"

"I would if I could."

"You can! You're a vampire descendant! Resist the glamour, Logan. You can do it. I've seen you do it!"

"You've...what?"

The memory slammed into me like a ton of concrete blocks.

River and I questioning Logan in the car.

"Exactly. If he was taken by vampires, and it seems likely that he was, given that he has no recollection, and also given that the other patients disappeared without anyone realizing it, we want to know why. Was it to perform surgery? Probably. He thinks he did. Was it because he has B positive blood? Probably. All the rest of the missing people have it. What if there was a third reason? What if—"

Logan turned to me, his pupils dilated.

"What if you're right, Erin? What if you're fucking right?"

What was the third reason I'd been thinking of? I grappled inside my brain, searching, searching...

"She's studying you too, Logan. She could have glamoured any surgeon into coming down here and doing her bidding. But she chose you. Why you?"

"I think..."

"What?"

"I think...I've hurt people, Erin."

"Yes, you told me that. You're a good man, Logan. If you hurt someone, it's not your fault. You were glamoured into doing it."

"I...don't know. I can't think about it. I'm here to examine you. That's what I need to be doing."

The third reason. He'd said I was right.

Logan wasn't clairvoyant. At least I didn't think so. We'd have seen some evidence of that before now if he were.

And I remembered.

I hadn't been thinking of a third reason at all.

Logan had interrupted me just as I was going to say, "What if it's something else?"

I inhaled. Nothing. Of course nothing. I wasn't a vampire. But River had said Logan had a noxious odor. Something had tainted his normal scent, the scent of his heritage.

No. Something had been layered over it. That's what River had perceived.

Something wicked had hold of Logan. Something outside his control.

Goons. Dante had mentioned the goons who tortured him, said they had a horrid smell. A smell that was normal at first, but gradually became...

"Logan, you're a good man. A good doctor. You saved Patty's baby."

"It was a double hernia, Erin. Hardly a life-threatening condition."

"You saved Patty."

"Your boyfriend saved Patty."

"He saved her uterus. But you were going to save *her*. You were going to save her life."

"He managed to save both."

"Dante is special. He has gifts that no other human or vampire possesses, and neither he nor I understand exactly what's going on with him. But don't discount yourself, Logan. Zabrina—"

"You call her Zabrina?"

"Sure. Why not? She no longer deserves any honorific from any of us. Anyway, Zabrina wouldn't have brought you down here as a surgeon if she didn't believe you had the skills. She has the ability to bring only the best down here to do her bidding, and she brought you."

For more reasons than one, though I didn't add those last words. I needed to butter Logan up to get him to release me. Telling him Bonneville had another purpose—which I hadn't quite figured out yet—wouldn't help me.

"Sometimes I hear voices," Logan said.

"I know. But you're medicated. You said they're under control."

"They are. I think. But sometimes..."

"Sometimes...what?"

"Sometimes the voices make me hurt people. I'm a doctor. I don't like hurting people, Erin."

TWO

DANTE

"**D**ad!" River lunged toward the monstrous thing on the other side of the arena.

"Riv, no!" I jumped at him, yanking him backward.

"He's my father, Dante. He'll know me."

"Does he look like he knows anything right now? Look in his eyes."

"I have. That's how I know it's him."

"All right. Forget his eyes. Look at his brute body. Is that him?"

"So he's been working out."

"That's not from working out, Riv. He's pumped up on steroids. She mutilated him, turned him into a beast."

"Fuck you, Dante. You have your father. I want mine. Dad!"

I yanked him back once more. "My father is dead, Riv. And here's the thing. We need to figure out how to get out of this, because the only way we can save Erin right now is if we kill Uncle Brae. I'm not willing to do that. Are you?"

"Of course not!"

"He's a poster boy for 'roid rage. We can't engage him."

"He doesn't seem to know we're here."

"Not yet. Let's try to keep it that way. She's clearly willing to sacrifice him, though I'm not sure why."

"How do you know that? Maybe she's willing to sacrifice us?"

"No. She's—"

I stopped. Was she? One of the rare vampire twins—my father—was already gone. But if she had his sperm, she had no need of him. Perhaps she'd already taken Brae's sperm as well, and if so, maybe he *was* dispensable. Ten years of sperm harvesting would've given her a freezer full.

No. Couldn't be. He was still a rarity, and she wasn't stupid.

I didn't believe for a minute that she was willing to let any one of the three of us go.

Unless...

Unless she'd taken my sperm when I was here previously. Ten years' worth.

In which case...

"Riv, you're the only one who's safe down here."

"What the hell are you talking about?"

"You're new stock. New Gabriel vampire stock. Your dad and I—we're old news."

"I don't get it, Dante."

A theory. Just a theory. Was I willing to stake River's life against my theory? Was River supposed to take both me and his own father out?

He hadn't been trained. Had he? She'd only been holding him for hours, certainly not enough time to get him ready for the fighting pit.

What was she up to?

She definitely had an ulterior motive, though for the life of me, I couldn't figure it out.

Braedon still stood, growling, but making no move against either of us.

Why?

Of course.

He *knew* us. He wouldn't harm his son or his nephew, no matter how full of 'roid rage he was.

"Uncle Brae," I said softly, "what did she do to you?"

He growled, baring his formidable fangs.

"Fuck, Dante, don't rile him up."

"I don't think he wants to hurt us, Riv."

"I never would have believed it of my dad, but he's—"

Braedon's eyes narrowed, and moisture shone within them. Sadness. Whatever he was supposed to do at this moment, he didn't want to do it.

Damn. I was right. He was supposed to kill me or I him. We were both going to protect River. Braedon would protect him because he was his son. I would protect him because he was weaker than I was. Either way, she knew if either Braedon or I had to choose, the choice would be River.

I had to test my theory. It might be the only way to end this.

Forgive me, Riv.

THREE

Erin

"Logan," I said. "You don't have to hurt people. Don't let her control you."

"But she does. I don't mean to, Erin. I don't."

"Did you ever hurt Dante? When he was here before?"

"No. I never saw Dante. But there's someone else."

"Who?"

"I don't know his name. But he's huge. All muscle."

I gulped down nausea. Huge. All muscle. I'd never seen Julian Gabriel as anything but a manifestation, but Levi Gaston had considered him and Braedon to be the ultimate specimens of vampire manhood.

Braedon. It had to be. Logan had tortured Braedon.

"Wh—" I cleared my throat, attempting to force back the nausea. "Wh-What kinds of things did you do to hurt him?"

"Did? Erin, I do it. I'm still *doing* it."

God. Nausea again, this time clawing up my throat with tiny hooks. "Okay." I tried to sound calm. As calm as I could be while tied down and trying to persuade this hurting man to let me go. "What exactly are you doing? And to whom?"

"I told you. This monstrous guy."

"Just him? No one else?"

He shook his head. "No. Not that I can remember."

"And how much *can* you remember about this?"

"It's hard, Erin. It's like it's in another lifetime."

"Like when you're above ground?"

"Yeah. It's like I have three different and distinct lives right now. Two are dream worlds and one is real—whichever one I'm in at the time."

"So you have your life at University, your life down here, and..."

"My other life down here. When I'm not...me."

"Who are you then?"

"I'm not sure. It's like I'm this automaton. This sadistic automaton. And I..."

"What? You what, Logan?"

"I..." He raked his fingers through his hair. "God, Erin. I can't tell you. I can't."

"Logan. Look. I can help you, but not if I'm imprisoned here. She's going to take my eggs, Logan. Without my permission. She's going to fertilize them with vampire semen and implant the embryos into surrogates. I can't let this happen. It's a violation. I'll have children I don't even know about. Please, Logan. Whatever she's doing to you, be stronger. I need you to be stronger." Desperation poured from my voice, poured from every part of me.

"Erin, I want to help you. I really do."

"Then do it. Just do it."

"I...can't."

"You *can*."

"No, you don't understand. She'll... She'll..."

"She'll what?"

"I don't know. I just know it will be bad."

"Look, I can help you, Logan. Dante can protect you. He can get you out of here. He's already gotten Lucy and my brother out. Patty's baby. The other women and some homeless people who were being kept down here. I don't know why."

"I know why," he said darkly.

"Why?" Though I wasn't sure I truly wanted to know.

"Blood."

Abe Lincoln was B positive. Were the others? I had no way of knowing. "She has plenty of blood down here. I saw the blood bank."

"But it's not fresh."

My bowels churned. I didn't like where this was going. "What do you mean, fresh?"

"Fresh. Fresh blood. Fresh human blood."

"And why does she need fresh human blood?" Again, I didn't truly want to know. Yet I had to know.

"I don't know. I really don't. I... Sometimes I see her take people somewhere."

"What? That doesn't help me, Logan."

"She brings people down here, mostly homeless people no one will miss, I think. Then they disappear."

"And she claims she's not a killer."

"What?"

"Nothing. Nothing for you to worry about, anyway."

Of course, in her mind, she wasn't a killer. She probably didn't do the killing herself. And if it was a human life, she didn't care. After all, she was trying to end humanity.

Vampyr omega.

Had she used Logan to kill these innocent victims? Probably not, or he'd feel worse than he already did. He'd have some hazy memory of it, as he did of torturing the monster.

She obviously liked her blood fresh. She'd fed on Dante, but perhaps she required non-vampire blood as well.

Damn! I needed my book. I'd left it in the room where Dante and I had slept for a few hours. I hadn't thought about it when she came in and took me. Dante hadn't woken up, and there was only one explanation for that. She had slipped him something. Otherwise he would have heard me.

"Logan, if you can't release me, you have to at least cut me."

"Cut you? Are you nuts?"

"If you've tortured—"

"I don't like torturing, Erin! For God's sake. I'm not in control of myself when I do it." He raked his fingers through his hair once more. "But I do like it. In some disgusting way."

"It's a glamour, Logan. Somehow she turns you sadistic."

"How? How could she do that?"

"I don't know. I know nothing about vampires."

"How can you know nothing? You're in a relationship with one."

"That doesn't mean I understand everything about them. Logan, there are things that vampires themselves don't even know. Secrets. Mysteries. Things that are kept hidden." I closed my eyes, willing my mind to think. Bonneville had something on Logan, or was able to manipulate his glamour. But how? And why? He'd told me he wasn't schizophrenic, but I'd assumed he was lying. What if he wasn't? What if something else made him prey to Bonneville? "Logan, have you ever been diagnosed with dissociative identity disorder?"

"Multiple personalities? No."

"The voices you hear, you say you know what they are, right? That you can control them?"

"Yeah."

"So you know they come from within you. Not from outside of you, right?"

He nodded. "I'm medicated. I'm... You don't think..."

"Yeah, Logan. I think you've been misdiagnosed. You aren't schizophrenic at all."

"I told you I wasn't. You didn't believe me!"

No, I hadn't, but I did now. "I think you have another personality. One she's taking advantage of."

I expected him to argue the point as he did about the schizophrenia. Instead, he wrinkled his forehead.

"One that's...sadistic?"

"Not necessarily, but one she can exploit. Manipulate. Force to do her bidding no matter how heinous or sadistic. Someone insecure. A child, maybe, or someone with PTSD. Does anything like that sound familiar to you, Logan?"

"I don't know. Maybe."

"It's all right. You're unique, clearly. You are resistant to glamouring to a certain extent, so she's found a chink in your armor. Something she can use to her advantage."

"How could I have missed this? I'm a doctor, for God's sake."

"Were you a doctor when you were diagnosed with mental illness?"

"Well...no."

"Look, Logan. I can help you a lot better if you unbind me. Help me get out of here."

"I can't."

"Yes, you *can*."

He started to speak, but I gestured him to stop.

"If you can't unbind me, at least cut me open. Just a tiny prick will do. Dante will smell my blood, and he'll come for me."

"Erin...Dante won't come for you. Not right now."

"Why not?"

"He's...busy."

FOUR

DANTE

*F*orgive me, Riv.

I growled, my teeth descending. I wasn't angry with my cousin or my uncle. I was angry at *her*. If this was what I had to do to get River out of here, I'd do it.

"Fuck, Dante. What the hell are you doing?"

I stalked toward him, snarling. "Only one of us gets out of here alive."

"Shit. No. It's that dark energy, isn't it? Fight it, cuz. You can fight it. You have to!"

"Fight or die in the arena." The words came out on a snarl.

"Control, Dante. I've heard Uncle Jules say it to you a thousand times. Control, damn it!"

The mention of my father perked my interest. Where was he? His brother was here. He should be here too. I advanced toward River, still slowly, but still surely.

"Dante, you don't want to do this."

He was right. I didn't, but I sure had to make it look like I did. *She* had to know I was serious. Only then would she intervene as I intended.

I curled my hands into fists, tension rising in my body. I might have to actually strike for her to take me seriously, and if so, I'd have to strike hard. She'd know if I didn't.

I didn't want to harm River, but I had no choice.

Quick as a jackrabbit, I lunged onto my cousin and tackled him to the ground. I sat on his chest, pinning his arms to his sides with my strong thighs. A punch to his nose should do it. It would hurt like hell, but it would heal quickly.

I raised my hand and met my cousin's gaze.

Fear shone back at me from his dark eyes.

Good. She'd know I was serious.

I lowered my fist—

"What the—"

In a split second, I was on my back, ten feet away from River.

I'd been tossed. Tossed like a sack of flour in the back of a bakery.

My uncle stood over me, his eyes glaring.

"Uncle Brae? Thank God. I knew you were in there."

"I couldn't let you hurt my son." His voice was gravelly and menacing. It had been altered.

"I didn't want to."

"I know. I know what you're doing. It took me a minute, but I snapped out of...well, whatever was wrong with me."

"She's got you jacked up on something," I said. "And your voice..."

"Dad?" River said weakly. He stood and walked over to us. "Dante, I never in a million years thought—"

"I didn't want to, Riv."

"Then why?"

My uncle cleared his throat and spoke quietly. "He was forcing her to make a choice. He figured she'd choose you over either one of us."

"Me? Why me?"

"You're new meat, for lack of a better word," I said. "Brae and I have been here for a while. It's likely she's already gotten what she wants from us."

"What does she want from you?"

"She's breeding vampires, Riv. She wants our seed."

River held back a retch. "How did you get down here anyway? I've seen you control her."

"She played her trump card."

River swallowed. "Erin."

"Yeah. She poisoned her. Threatened to let her die if I didn't fight once more."

"And you believed her?"

"Of course I did. The bitch is evil."

"But if Erin is..."

"Fuck. You're right." I rubbed my forehead. "How could I have been so obtuse? She wouldn't harm Erin. Not now, after I let all the other women go."

"Don't blame yourself," River said. "She played on your emotions."

"What are you two talking about?" Braedon asked.

"Erin has a genetic marker," I said. "Bonneville—"

"Who is Bonneville?"

"The queen, as she calls herself. She's actually a physician named Zabrina Bonneville."

"Why *does* she call herself the queen?" River asked. "Have either of you ever figured that out?"

I shook my head. "I have no idea. Uncle Brae?"

"I know she's very old."

I jerked. She'd said something like that to me before, but with everything else going on I hadn't ruminated on it. "Then she has a great skincare regimen. I wouldn't put her any older than forty."

"She made a slip once when she was..."

"What?"

"She was feeding from me. Taking my blood."

"I'm sorry," I said. "She did the same to me. For ten fucking years."

"She always fed from me, but recently it's gotten a lot more frequent."

Because I'm no longer here. A sharp pain lanced into my head. I rubbed my forehead.

"You okay, man?" River said.

"Yeah. It's just—" I inhaled. Erin had opened a vein again. She was calling me. Blood to blood.

Bonneville had said our blood bond was an old wives' tale. She was about to be proved wrong. I had to answer the call of the blood.

My body throbbed, warming, rage rising. Only one thought.

Erin.

Get to Erin.

Take Erin's blood.

"The book said female vampire blood can change a male," River was saying. "There's something about male vampire blood, but we couldn't read..."

His words became muffled as a high-pitched noise pierced my ears.

Damn, I could hear her blood flowing from her heart out through her arteries.

She was near.

And she was alive.

Bonneville had administered the antidote. If, that was, Erin had ever been in any danger at all.

Dante?

Cuz?

River's voice.

From somewhere in this dark place.

I looked up. We were dropped in from above. I'd never gotten out of here on my own, not that I recalled anyway.

We were at least fifty feet down.

Had to get to Erin.

Had to get to Erin.

I closed my eyes, opened my mouth, and my teeth descended with a painful snap.

"Auuuggghhhh!" I roared.

My cousin, standing next to his beefed-up father, widened his eyes. "What the hell are you doing?"

My feet left the ground and I rose.

Rose.

Rose until their two heads were specks in the distance and I was standing above the fighting pit on solid ground.

Two icy eyes glared at me.

I roared again, pinning *her* to the wall with the sheer force of my will.

Her blue eyes widened for an instant—only an instant, but I had frightened her. This was the third time I'd moved her telekinetically, something she could not do—or at least had not done—to me.

She hid it well, but this time she'd been frightened.

She, who couldn't be frightened.

I had frightened her.

"Formidable, as I expected," she said, immobile.

"You created me. You love to take credit." I showed off my long and sharp cuspids. "You made me what I am, but only *I* will control it."

I had more to say to her, much more, but something else pulled me away.

I ran.

I ran toward Erin's blood.

I ran toward Erin.

I ran toward life.

FIVE

Erin

"I'm telling you, Erin, it isn't going to work. He's indisposed."

I stared at the river of blood oozing out of my forearm. Logan had unbound my arms so I could sit up. "It will work," I said softly. "I have faith."

"You don't understand her power."

"You don't understand Dante's power, or the power of our bond. Mark my words. He will come, and you might want to not be here when that happens."

"He doesn't scare me."

"He should. If he thinks you had anything to do with imprisoning me, I can't be held responsible for his actions."

"What? He'll kill me?"

I shook my head. "He's not a killer. That doesn't mean he won't pummel the shit out of you."

"Shame," he said grimly.

"What's a shame?"

"That he's not a killer."

"What the hell are you saying, Logan?"

"I'm tired, Erin. So damned tired. It's like I don't sleep anymore. I have these three distinct lives, and I'm no longer in control. Death might be a better alternative."

"Stop saying that! Death is never a better alternative. Humanity needs you, Logan. Now more than ever. You're a good doctor. You just need some psychiatric help. An accurate diagnosis and the right meds and therapy. And you need to get the hell out of *here*."

"I'm not sure any of that is in the cards for me."

"If you help me, I swear I will help you. Dante is in control here, not Zabrina. I'm sure of it."

"Then why isn't he—" Logan stopped with a gasp.

I turned at the cracking sound of metal hinges breaking. The door to my dank cell lay on the floor, the empty doorframe filled with Dante's magnificent form. His eyes glowed, the amber rings around his irises burning hot.

I glanced toward Logan. He cowered.

"Release her," Dante growled.

"I... I can't." Logan stepped backward until his back hit the wall.

"Did you do this?"

"He's only here to examine me, Dante. It was Zabrina who had me imprisoned here."

Dante stalked forward, dropping a pack on the ground, and with brute strength tore the bindings from my feet. He regarded me, zeroing in on the mark on my leg where Bonneville had injected me with hormones. He inhaled. "Why is your scent different? It's...synthetic. I don't like it."

"Hormones. She gave me hormones so I'd release more

eggs. She's preparing to harvest my ova because she no longer has the other VO positive women."

Dante didn't seem to be listening. Instead he stared at Logan. "Get. The fuck. Out."

"Dante, please. We need to help him. She's controlling him, making him—"

"I said *get out!*"

Logan lunged toward the door.

"Dante! I told him—"

"Quiet! You called me with your blood. You know what that means."

I did. And I was ready to take whatever he gave me... although we no longer had a door.

Dante didn't seem bothered in the least. "Where are your leggings?"

"I... I don't know. My legs were bare when I woke up here."

"Damn it!" He spread my legs and inhaled. Then he punctured the inside of my right thigh.

The sharp pain quickly morphed into pleasure as he drew blood from my femoral artery. My arousal was already thick in the air, but Dante was right.

It smelled different.

I smelled different.

Not bad, but different.

When he finished his feeding and licked my wounds closed, he met my gaze. His eyes were still on fire.

"Take off your panties."

"Dante, we don't have a door..."

"Don't care. Take them off now, or I'll rip them right off you."

I couldn't let him do that. I didn't know where my pack

was with my change of underwear. Damn! The book. I'd left the book in my pack.

I quickly wriggled out of my panties, and within seconds, Dante bent me over the table and was inside me, thrusting, thrusting, thrusting.

Taking what I'd offered when I called him to me with my blood.

"Mine," he grunted. "Mine. Mine. Mine."

"Yes, always yours."

I relished the fullness as he pumped into me, and my skin tingled as the climax built. I resisted the urge to cry out as long as I could, but when he pushed into me, nudging my clit against the hardness of the table where I'd been bound, I could no longer hold back.

"Dante! Yes!"

The orgasm shattered me into tiny pieces—each one feeling the intensity of the climax—making it like thousands of releases at once. Shining stars surrounded me, pulsating in time with the contractions gyrating my whole body. The soft melodic jazz wafted around us, enveloping us in a musical bubble.

Still Dante thrust, taking, taking, taking. And I burst into climax once more.

This time he released as well, and so in tune was I with him, that I felt every pulse as he pumped his seed into me.

We stayed joined for a timeless moment, until Dante finally pulled out and released me.

"Erin," he said gruffly.

"I'm okay."

"I know. I'm sorry."

I turned to face him. His eyes held such torment, I

nearly wept. "For what?"

"I'm sorry I didn't come for you sooner."

"It's all right. You came. You always come."

"I shouldn't have let the bitch waylay me. But..."

"What?"

"She said she'd poisoned you, and that if I didn't go back into the fighting pit, she wouldn't administer the antidote."

"I don't remember. She gave me a shot. She said it was hormones."

"It was. I smell them. Are they supposed to make you ovulate? You're not fertile."

"Yeah, but they wouldn't act this quickly, so we're good."

"Did she inject you with something else?"

"Not that I recall, but she could have glamoured me."

"She could easily have been lying to me, Erin, but I couldn't take the chance. I'm sorry."

"For saving my life? Why would you be sorry?"

"Because you were calling to me. Your blood. This is all my fault."

"How exactly is it your fault?"

He pulled a zippered plastic bag out of his pocket. He fingered the fine dust inside. "My father's ashes." He touched his fingers to my forehead. "I should have done this before, and I'm sorry."

"Dante—"

"There's no excuse, Erin. I shielded Abe Lincoln, all the women, Lucy and the baby, Jay, and Emilia. Why didn't I think to shield you?"

SIX

DANTE

Guilt gnawed at me.

Erin.

The most important person in my life, and I hadn't shielded her.

Why?

How could I be so thoughtless?

"Dante, it's okay."

No. It wasn't okay. It wasn't even close to okay. It was so far from okay.

"I love you, Erin."

"I know that. I love you too."

"You should have been my first thought. My first—"

"I am. Just as you're mine. It's normal to take the things we love for granted every once in a while."

I shook my head with a harrumph. "This goes so far beyond taking you for granted."

She smiled. God, she was so beautiful. "Maybe you subconsciously wanted me down here with you."

"That's crazy."

"Is it? If what your grandfather told us about the blood bond is true, you need me and I need you. If we're separated, we both die."

Hmm. Maybe not so crazy after all. But... "Still, I should have shielded you. That will keep Bonneville away from you. Any vampire who intends to harm you. That's what my dad said."

"Any vampire? But not any human?"

"Hell, I don't know. My dad said his ashes are a powerful shield, but that the real power comes from me. *I* am the shield."

She touched her forehead. "Well, you've shielded me now, so we should be good."

I sighed. Would we ever be "good" again? I wasn't so sure.

Then—

"Oh, shit!"

Erin touched my cheek, the warmth in her fingers almost singeing me. I inhaled. She was still the best scent in the universe, but those synthetic hormones. I couldn't wait for her body to metabolize them. They didn't smell right.

"What?" she asked.

"I left River in the pit. With my uncle."

"You found your uncle?"

I nodded. "She threw him in the pit with Riv and me, said it was going to be two against one."

"And they're still there now?"

"I assume so. I...came when you called." I shook my head. "You don't understand, Erin. When your blood calls me, everything else ceases to exist. Only one thing pervades my mind. You. Getting to you."

"You left them in the pit? To fight?"

"They aren't going to fight. Braedon came to his senses. She's got him jacked up on steroids or something. I hardly recognized him. But he won't harm his son. I made sure of that."

"How?"

"I...attacked River myself."

"You *what*?"

"Try to understand. It was the only way. I had to find out if Bonneville was willing to sacrifice River. She's not. I was also hoping to draw Braedon's true personality out. I did."

She sighed. "This is all so screwed up."

"No truer words. Oh!" I dug into her pack, pulled out her book, and handed it to her.

"Thank God! I was afraid it might have fallen into the wrong hands."

"It was on top of your pack when I woke up. I grabbed everything."

She fondled the soft leather cover of the book. "What other secrets do you hold?" she asked softly.

And the book opened.

SEVEN

Erin

The page about vampire blood. I reread the paragraph about female vampire blood to Dante.

"*The blood of a female vampire is a powerful philter. When ingested by a male, it increases muscle mass, strength, and accuracy. All senses become more enhanced, and additional powers emerge. However, it should be used only in the direst circumstances, as the negative side effects outweigh the positive. The male fed on female vampire blood will eventually undergo a metamorphosis—a profound change in form, psyche, and temperament that will eventually end in an inevitable painful death.*

"*The blood of the female vampire, however, pales in comparison to the much more potent blood of the male, especially that from a young vampire on the waning moon of maturity.*"

Then, right before my eyes, the rest of the paragraph came into focus. I read aloud.

"Male vampire blood has unique properties not present in blood from a female vampire. While it will cause changes in psyche and temperament, the effect won't be as pronounced as that from female blood. Its most profound effect, though, is prolonging the aging process. Any vampire who ingests male vampire blood will preserve his youth and vitality for as long as the ingestion continues. He will appear ageless, and indeed will never succumb to normal illness or injury. Any injury, even one seemingly fatal, will heal."

Dante stared at me, his eyes full of introspection. "That means..."

"That means Zabrina could be centuries old. Maybe even older. This must be where the myth that vampires are forever young came from. Maybe there is fact behind the myth."

"We were taught that we ourselves perpetuated the myths to stay under the radar."

"Vampires probably did, but Dante, myths often have their basis in truth."

He appeared thoughtful for a moment. Then, "Does it say anything else?"

The first sentence of the next paragraph then came into focus.

"Heed the warning, though. Male vampire blood has one major drawback, one that can never be reversed."

"Keep going," Dante said. "What's the drawback?"

I shook my head. "The rest is illegible."

"Are you kidding me?" He grabbed the book and scanned the page. "For fuck's sake."

"She has an Achilles' heel," I said.

"But we don't know what it is, so what good does that do us?" Dante raised the book above his head, about to throw it harshly on the ground, when he met my gaze. "Sorry." He handed it back to me.

"It's okay. It's frustrating. More than frustrating." I ran my fingers over the smooth page of the book, and then something hit me. "Man. Oh, man."

"What is it?"

"She's such a narcissistic bitch!"

"Well, yeah."

"I mean a real narcissist. Someone suffering from narcissistic personality disorder. She's so sure she'll never be caught, that she drops hints. She did it when she asked me to do that research, remember?"

"Yeah. What are you getting at?"

"The fingerprints on the little vodka bottle—the ones from a dead woman? They're hers. They're Bonneville's."

He shook his head. "Fucking bitch."

"She was daring us, Dante. Daring us to figure this out, yet never thinking that we would. She considers herself above everyone else. A true narcissist."

"She's pretty smart, if she figured out that drinking my blood would extend her life, basically make her invulnerable. Maybe he's trying to increase the population with the VO positive women and then make us all invulnerable."

"Maybe. We don't know if she's even read the *Texts*. She might have figured all of this out on her own, and if she did, she might not know of the bad effect."

"What does that matter?" he said. "We don't know it either. That damned book!"

"The book must not think we need to know it yet."

"That's just ridiculous. Of course we need to know it. We need to stop her."

"Do we really need to know? We've all but stopped her, Dante. We freed all the women she was holding."

"Not all the women. Patty's still here. And you, Erin. You're still here."

"I'm here only because you're here. You've shielded me, and I could leave if I wanted to. But I don't want to. You and I need each other."

"Still, we need to stop her, Erin. We've freed everyone. What's to stop her from going above ground and finding more vampire descendants who are VO positive?"

"I don't know. I don't know how rare it actually is."

"She's found several right here in New Orleans. Surely there are more."

"Maybe," I said. "Maybe not. This is a new discovery for her, though. I'm pretty sure."

"How are you sure?"

"Because if it weren't, we'd already have seen human women having vampire babies. Your existence would have been outed."

"Maybe," he said. "And maybe not."

"Why do you say that?"

"The council." He raked his fingers through his hair. "The council monitors all vampire activity, which means..."

"They know? You think they know?"

"Damn! I don't know. Bill has been so weird since I returned. And she let me go, Erin. She let me go right when she started bringing women down here. There has to be some connection."

"Yeah, I don't understand that either," I said. "Right when

she finds the women, she lets her male vampire go."

"Except she still had my father and uncle at that point."

"But they're older. You're in the prime of life. A perfect male to father new vampire children."

"Maybe not. Maybe my father and uncle are the true perfect specimens. Being twins and all. That's really rare for us."

"So you've said." I scratched my head. "We'll figure this out, Dante. Trust me. She'll continue to drop clues, thinking we're too stupid to see what she's up to. It's textbook."

"Erin, maybe this is the part of the *Texts* that Bill read. The part about male vampire blood extending life and making us impervious to illness or injury. Maybe the council doesn't know that little tidbit, and it spooked Bill. If vampires knew that, we'd all be feeding on our own males and we'd all be invincible. We could live forever and easily take over humanity."

"Dante, if that were possible, wouldn't Bonneville be doing that instead of trying to breed new vampires? Whatever the Achilles' heel is, it must be huge. Or you're right. That's how she'd be doing it."

"Whatever the Achilles' heel is, it hasn't stopped *her* from drinking male blood."

"True." I looked down. "Where are my pants? We need to get out of here. We need to find Patty and get her out of here. Her recent surgery will prevent Bonneville from impregnating her, but her eggs can still be harvested. As can mine."

"Over my dead body." He inhaled. "Those synthetic hormones. I don't like them."

"Do they smell bad?" I asked.

"No. Not bad. Just not *you*." He pawed through some stuff in one corner of the room. "Here. Found your pants. And your shoes and socks."

"Thanks." I dressed quickly. "Where are we going?"

"I need to see to River and my uncle."

"Then I'm going with you."

"Erin..."

"Dante, where else am I going to go? If I'm with you, you'll be able to protect me, right? You've already shielded me."

"Damn it!"

"You know I'm right."

"I know. But what if she begins controlling me again?"

"She won't. I trust you. I have faith. You need to have faith in yourself."

EIGHT

DANTE

Faith.

Right.

I'd already decided to have faith in myself. But where Erin was concerned, I couldn't take any chances.

"Please, Dante. I know you'll protect me. I *know* you will."

I nodded. She needed me to have faith, and I needed to show her my assurance...even if I didn't feel it one hundred percent. I'd allowed Bonneville to take her from me while we both slept, and I'd allowed her to inject Erin with hormones.

I'd failed Erin.

I would not fail her again. I couldn't. Maybe her faith would be enough for both of us.

"Ready?" she said.

I nodded. "Time to find River and his dad."

"Right." She walked to the doorway and stepped on the wooden door that I'd forced to the ground. "After you."

"No. We go together. Not one before or after the other."

She smiled. "I like the way you think."

I considered Erin my equal, but that wasn't why I suggested walking together. If she was in front of me, anything in our way would get to her first. If she was behind me, I wouldn't be able to see her. Together was the only way.

I took her hand, so warm in mine, and together we ventured into the dark hallway. Were River and Uncle Brae still in the fighting pit? That seemed the logical place to start. I didn't want to take Erin anywhere near that horrible place, but she was determined to stay by my side.

The thought warmed me.

She would always be by my side.

Once bonded, never broken.

Those words no longer angered me. Perhaps I'd heard them first down here, but I didn't know their true meaning until Erin Hamilton had come into my life.

So random, it seemed, that she'd be a nurse on duty the night I broke into the University Hospital blood bank. But was it random at all? Was it fate? Destiny?

A blood bond?

The bond between us was so strong. Why had such bonding between humans and vampires ceased?

Evolution, I guessed. It was no longer needed.

But *I* needed it. Needed it like air. My bond to Erin went beyond love, beyond devotion, beyond anything conceivable in the universe.

It even went beyond the spiritual.

"I love you," I said.

"I love you too, Dante." She squeezed my hand. "Can you get us to the fighting pit?"

I hadn't paid attention when I left the arena. My nose and my instinct had guided me to Erin. But I'd been here before.

I would remember.

"Yes. I can get us there."

"How did you get out?"

I shook my head. "I...rose."

"Huh?"

"We're dropped into the pit. There's no other way out. When your blood called to me, I got out the only way I could."

"You levitated."

"Yeah."

"With River and your uncle just watching you?"

"I guess. I don't think about anything else when you call me with your blood. It's like a blind devotion, you know? I'm acting on pure instinct to get to you."

"I'm sorry, Dante. I didn't mean for you to leave them."

"You needed me. That's where I'm supposed to be. With you. Being there for you when you need me. The book wouldn't have told you how to summon me if it weren't necessary."

"I get that. But still."

"We'll find them, baby, and we'll get them out of here."

She pointed to my pack. "The book still has plenty to tell us. Don't forget that."

"We can't depend on the book," I said. "It's being pretty stingy with its contents."

"It hasn't let us down yet."

I didn't answer. I didn't want to rain on her parade, but if it had told us what Bonneville's weakness was, we'd be in much better shape.

Then something struck me like a lightning bolt.

Her weakness.

She thought she controlled me, but my strength had outgrown hers. I'd controlled her several times now.

Maybe that was her Achilles' heel.

Maybe *I* was her Achilles' heel.

She'd made me by forcing me to drink from her, by training me and strengthening me, by torturing me to bring out my rage and my darkness.

Darkness rising.

But the consequence was that I'd become more powerful than she was.

She'd placed her trust only in the science of vampires, in what the *Texts* told her about consuming vampire blood. But I... I knew there was more to the universe than pure science. Science had its place, but faith...

Faith was more important than science.

Faith and energy and love.

And the blood bond.

Her blind allegiance to science—the science behind the consumption of vampire blood—was a big part of her Achilles' heel. She didn't believe in ghosts. She didn't believe in demons. She believed only what she could see.

And she'd *seen* darkness rising in me.

Indeed, darkness had risen in me, had become part of me. Perhaps it would have controlled me...if not for the blood bond with Erin.

This woman had saved me. Saved me from *her*. Saved me from the darkness.

Saved me from myself.

I didn't for one minute think I'd figured out the secret of the *Texts*, but I knew I'd figured out something important. Something profound.

Something she hadn't considered when formulating her hypothesis.

The blood bond.

It wasn't an old wives' tale, as she thought.

Had she read the *Texts* in their entirety? Did she know their secrets?

Maybe she did, but that didn't matter. As a woman of science, anything she couldn't explain she'd consider pure orthodoxy or dogma.

Now she would pay for her blind allegiance to pure science.

Dante...

I smiled.

Get in my head if you want, my queen. *You no longer control me. I control you now.*

Fine. I surrender to your greatness. I acquiesce. You may control me, but I still have power over you. I still own your uncle and your cousin. You will not find them here.

"You're bluffing," I said aloud.

"What?" Erin asked.

"Sorry, baby. Just talking to myself."

"Oh. Okay."

Maybe I am. Are you willing to take that chance?

I didn't respond in my head or otherwise. I simply wiped her away. I could do that now. I had control.

If she still had power over me, I might be concerned. But I knew now the value that Braedon and River had to her. She wouldn't harm them. Still, I needed to hurry. The thought of River going through even a fraction of what I'd gone through made me sick.

I let my body lead me. We'd been searching for a half hour or more when I finally came to the door I now could recall with certainty.

The door to the arena. This is how I got in. Inside was a

long staircase leading upward, where fighters were dropped down into the arena.

It was locked, of course, but I picked it quickly with a bobby pin from Erin's pack. "Come on." I tugged on Erin's hand and walked through the door.

"Ouch!" She fell back, landing with a thud on her behind.

"What is it baby?"

"I... It shocked me!"

"My father's ashes— Oh." The shield. I could get through with the fleur-de-lis pin tacked to my boxer briefs, but Erin...

"What?"

"The ashes will get you out of here, protect you from vampires meaning to do you harm. They don't let you *in*."

She couldn't get through.

And I couldn't leave her.

Where did that leave us?

"It's okay," she said. "Get in there. Find them and get them out of here."

"I won't leave you."

"Dante, you have to. Nothing will happen to me. I'm too important to her. Well...at least my eggs are. I'm safe until she tries to take them."

"No, absolutely no—"

A roar interrupted me. "Leave my father alone, you fucked-up son of a bitch!"

River.

"Did you hear that?" I asked Erin.

"No. What is it?"

"River. He's yelling. They're not in the pit anymore." I walked back through the door and grabbed her hand. "Come on."

NINE

Erin

D**ante's** hand in mine warmed me and gave me comfort, though my skin was still prickled from the shock—or whatever it had been—that had kept me from entering the door that led to Dante's fighting pit.

"Where are we going? Is River okay?"

He didn't answer, just dragged me along the dark and dank hallways. I listened intently, trying to hear what he heard, but to no avail. I didn't have vampire hearing.

Minutes later, we came to another wooden door. Dante smashed it open.

"You vile piece of garbage! God, your stench is unbearable!"

River's voice. What was going on?

Dante raced into the room, and I tried to follow.

Zap!

Again, I could not. But I couldn't believe what I was seeing. A masked man hovered over a table where a large—*very* large— man was tied down. He was attaching electrical probes to—

I clasped my hand over my mouth.

"Wh..." I cleared my throat, attempting to clear the nausea. *"Wh-What kinds of things did you do to hurt him?"*

"Did? Erin, I do it. I'm still doing it."

"No!" I screamed. "Logan, stop it!"

"I knew I recognized that stench!" River said from somewhere else in the room.

I couldn't see him, but he was obviously incapacitated or he'd be helping his father.

"It's gotten worse since that day in the car," River continued.

Logan was masked, but it was him. His shoulders shuddered slightly when I said his name, but he didn't turn toward me.

Of course he didn't. Because he was *not* Logan. He might share the same body, but this was the second personality, the result of his dissociative identity disorder.

This was a personality that could be manipulated.

So I would manipulate him now.

Dante stalked toward Logan. "You bastard," he growled.

Logan's eyes turned to circles outlined by the black mask.

"Dante, he doesn't know what he's doing," I yelled from the doorway.

"The fuck he doesn't," River said. "He's electrocuting my dad!"

Braedon—I assumed the muscular man on the other table was Braedon—said nothing. Didn't move a muscle. Was he unconscious? Or simply resigned to his fate?

He was muscular and huge, as far as I could see, but Logan had called him a monster. Perhaps that was how this personality perceived him. Or more likely, Bonneville had convinced him Braedon was a monster.

"Logan," I said. "Please. Stop this."

Again he shuddered slightly at the name. Logan was in there somewhere. If only I knew the name of this personality, but I didn't. Logan was my only shot.

First I had to deal with Dante.

"He doesn't know what he's doing," I said again.

"Erin, with all due respect," River said, "fuck off!"

Dante didn't listen to me either. Instead, he bared his fangs, roared, picked Logan up, and tossed him out the doorway. I moved quickly to avoid a collision.

"Uncle Brae, are you all right?" Dante asked.

Braedon grunted.

"He's had God knows how many volts of electricity jolted into him," River said. "Of course he's not okay."

"He'll live," Dante said. "I did."

Since I couldn't get through the door anyway, I turned to Logan, who was crumpled on the hard floor in the hallway. "Hey. Logan." I patted his cheek. "Wake up. It's over."

He shuddered again and then opened his eyes. "Erin?"

"Yeah, it's me."

"Was I..."

"Yeah, unfortunately. You were."

"Shit. I'm sorry."

"You need to stay in your right mind now. Where she can't control you and make you hurt other people."

"I don't know why I do it."

"I know you don't. It's another personality. Something happened in your life, and a certain part of you split off."

"I'm a doctor, Erin. I know how it works."

I resisted the urge to roll my eyes. Logan wasn't the only

physician in the world to think he was above a nurse. This was the first time I'd encountered this side of him down here, though.

I let it go. If my diagnosis was accurate, and this was an additional identity, Logan had most likely suffered a horrible trauma during childhood. Now was certainly not the time to delve into that.

"Easy," I said. "Just breathe. Are you injured?"

"No. I think I'm okay."

"Can you stand?"

"I'll try."

I rose and gave him my hand to help steady him. While I was sorry for any trauma he might have undergone, I found him truly fascinating. If I ever had the chance to go to medical school as I wished, I'd be studying psychiatry for sure.

He stumbled a little but got to his feet. A flash of gold caught my eye. On the inside of Logan's black collar, barely noticeable, was a small lapel pin, identical to the one Dante found in Emilia's apartment.

Before he could stop me, I grabbed him by the collar, took the pin, and attached it to the waistband of my leggings. Then I walked through the doorway into the room where Dante was.

"How is your uncle?" I asked, approaching.

"He's okay. He's been— How did you get in here?"

"Logan had a pin like yours. He's a little out of it, so I took it. I figured I could do more good in here. Let me examine your uncle."

Dante stepped aside. I didn't have a stethoscope or thermometer, so I was limited, but I felt his forehead with my cheek. "He's a little warm for a vampire."

"Of course he is," River said from the other table. "He's just had high voltage pumped into him. Uh...and by the way. Could one of you release me please?"

"Yeah, sorry Riv." Dante walked over to River.

I palpated Braedon's lymph nodes. No swelling. Then his abdomen. He didn't react, so I had to assume I wasn't hurting him. "Can you hear me?"

He nodded slightly. His face was lacerated and his eyes bloodshot. He was indeed muscular. More muscular than Dante even. The muscles looked manufactured. He was definitely on steroids or something else that produced this effect.

"He'll have a hard time talking," Dante said. "Trust me. I know."

I shivered.

Dante had been through this. He'd been subject to this kind of torture. I knew it, but looking at his uncle, tied down in this place, made it really and truly real.

"Let me unbind you." Try as I might, though, I couldn't. "Dante, I need your help when you're done with River."

"Almost there."

I turned. River was rubbing his wrists.

"Did she do anything to you?" Dante asked him.

"No. Well, yeah. She forced me to watch that human stink bomb torture my father. That's something I won't soon forget."

"I know, cuz. I know."

"Ouch! What the hell?"

I turned at the sound of Logan's voice. He was on the ground again.

"What is it?" I asked.

"I can't get back in."

"No, you can't," I said. "Which is just fine."

"But I—"

"No, you don't. It's over, Logan. We're getting you out of here, and you're going to get the help you need."

"She'll kill me."

"She's rapidly losing her power," I said. "Dante can control her."

"Dante won't help me."

I looked to Dante. Indeed, the raging expression on his face didn't indicate he had any interest in helping Logan.

"You're damned lucky you're not one of the goons who tortured *me*," he said, snarling. "You'd be dog shit by now. In fact, you'd be dog shit for torturing my uncle, if not for Erin."

"It's not his fault, Dante. She's exploiting him."

"Yeah...whatever."

I went back to Braedon to continue my examination. He was naked but for a pair of boxer briefs that stretched taut over his muscular glutes and thighs. "Whatever he's on, we need to get him off it. He's probably already infertile."

"Which means she already has enough of his swimmers on ice," River said, glaring. "That bitch is going down."

"She sure as hell is," Dante agreed. "As soon as that book tells us what we need to know." He quickly explained about the male vampire blood.

"She could be centuries old," River said.

"She could be," Dante agreed, "but Erin and I believe she's only about a hundred and fifty. She's the woman whose fingerprints are on the little vodka bottle."

"That explains how she glamoured an entire hospital," River said. "She's a fucking elder."

"Zarah Le Sang. Dr. Blood," I said, more to myself than anyone else. "The woman who could be her twin but is much older. It's *her*. They're one and the same." I tapped my palm on my head. "It's so obvious. Why didn't I see it?"

"You had a few other things on your mind," Dante said.

"Makes perfect sense," River agreed.

"I wonder how many times she's had to change her identity," I said. "And why? Mrs. Moore said Dr. Le Sang saved her son. Plus, I've seen Bonneville save many lives in the ER. How can she be such a good physician yet put so little value on human life?" I shook my head. "I don't understand. I'll never understand."

"She shouldn't have had to change her name at all," River said. "She could have just used her glamour to keep existing with her original name."

"What are you getting at, Riv?" Dante asked.

"I'm saying that, if she changed her identity, she had a reason. We need to figure out what it was. It might be what takes her down."

I continued to examine Braedon. Sure enough, several puncture wounds graced his muscular thighs. "She's been feeding on him."

"Fucking bitch," River growled.

"Easy," I said. "We don't want her running in here."

"Let her," Dante said. "I'll make short work of her."

"Wait." I held up a hand. "We need to keep her out of the way. There's a lot more to do here."

"What is more important than getting rid of her?"

"Finding the cryolab, for one. If she has your sperm or Braedon's, we need to destroy it."

"I don't know," River said. "Isn't that morally wrong or something?"

"Destroying frozen sperm?" I said. "I'd say it's no more morally wrong than you jacking off and letting *that* sperm die."

"Yeah, Riv," Dante said. "Jesus."

"What if..." He swallowed. "What if she's already...fertilized eggs with it? What if there are embryos?"

I sighed. "That would be another issue, but let's not make assumptions. She had VO positive incubators lined up until a day ago. There was no reason for her to harvest eggs or freeze embryos."

"I hope you're right," Dante said.

I sighed again. I hoped I was right too. Another moral dilemma was the last thing we needed.

TEN

DANTE

"One thing I don't get," Erin said. "If she's trying to breed vampires, and Julian and Braedon were the best specimens, why would she put Braedon on steroids that could make him infertile?"

"Because she's nuts?" River said with sarcasm.

Erin shook her head. "Bonneville is a narcissist and a vampire supremacist."

"Like I said. Nuts."

"Yeah, relatively speaking," Erin continued, "but I'm not sure Braedon is on steroids."

"Even a Gabriel vampire can't grow muscles like those naturally," River said.

Erin walked back to my uncle's table. He was resting comfortably after I'd removed the shackles from his wrists and ankles.

"Something's not right," she said, smoothing her hand over his bicep.

"What do you mean?"

"His musculature. At first glance, it looks like he's pumped up, but if you look closer"—she bent down—"it's not right. His musculature has changed somehow."

"Yeah, it's gotten bigger," River said.

"No, I mean it's changed. It's not...normal."

Braedon turned toward Erin, his eyes sunken and fatigued. "No," he said. "it's not normal."

"What happened?" Erin asked. "What did she do to you?"

He coughed. "It's a prophecy or something. She says it to me all the time."

River and I joined Erin at Uncle Brae's side. "What kind of prophecy?"

"I don't know. She hasn't gotten specific."

"A prophecy?" Erin rubbed the side of her head. "Maybe I'm wrong about her being a woman of strict science."

"Not necessarily," Dante said. "If she read about some kind of prophecy in that damned book and figured out a way to make it happen scientifically, she hasn't changed at all."

"Has she injected you with anything?" Erin asked my uncle.

"It's possible." He coughed again. "There's a lot I don't remember. Sometimes it comes back to me."

"I get that," I said. "It's the same for me. The memories came back more easily once I got out of here."

"How long has she been making you drink her blood?" Erin asked.

"Seems like forever," he said.

"As long as you've been here, then. Same as me. Why not my father?"

"I don't know," he said.

"I do," Erin said. "Rather, I have a theory. Julian and

Braedon are identical twins. My guess is she was testing the effect of her blood on Braedon and then recording the differences between the two."

"Why would she do that?"

"Research," Erin said. "Twins are a perfect way to test theories, since they have identical genetic makeup. It's what that freak Dr. Mengele did to twins at Auschwitz during World War Two."

"Fucking bitch," River said. "Whatever she did to you, Dad, we're going to find a way to undo it."

Braedon shook his head. "No. I want you out of here. Just get out of here, all of you. Forget about me."

"Are you kidding?" River said. "No way!"

"It's too late for me, son. Please. Save yourselves. I can't bear the thought of her keeping you here. Of you being subject to—" A hacking cough cut off his words.

"I'm not leaving," River said.

"You are," Braedon said. "I'm still your father, and you'll do as I say. I thanked God when Julian got out, but then I felt him die."

"Uncle Jules died on purpose," River said. "To help us. To help *you*. Don't let his death be in vain."

"On purpose? He took his own life?"

"He did," I said. "And I agree with River. If you don't fight this, Uncle Brae, he'll have died in vain. Where is he, anyway?"

"What do you mean?" Braedon asked. "He's dead."

"Big news, Dad," River said. "Ghosts exist. Uncle Jules is still around."

"Then why..."

"I don't know," I said. "It took me a while to see and hear him at first, though Riv and Em saw him right away. It still sticks in my craw a little."

My father appeared instantly. "Tell him I'm here."

"Uncle Jules is here," River said. "Here, in this room."

"Is he visible?"

"He is. And audible."

"Why can't I see or hear him?"

"Your vision might be compromised," Erin said. "But you should be able to hear him. Just believe. Believe that everything you've been taught about life after death no longer has any meaning. Believe that a person keeps his own unique identity, even in death."

"Not possible."

"That's what we were taught," River said, "but I assure you it *is* possible."

"Dad," I said, "Uncle Brae said something about a prophecy. Do you know what he might be talking about?"

"I'm afraid I don't."

"What about Bill?" Erin asked. "Whatever he saw in the *Texts* spooked him because it had to do with what vampires are capable of. Maybe he saw the prophecy."

"Maybe," I said. "That would make sense. Apparently it's something the council doesn't know about."

"Or maybe they do," River said. "Maybe that's why Levi Gaston didn't want Bill spilling any council secrets."

"Could be either," Erin said. "The council knows something they want to keep mum about, and Bill also knows something that the council doesn't. We don't know which is which, and both could have nothing to do with any prophecy. We just don't know."

I dug in Erin's pack and pulled out the book. No new pages had been revealed. I raised the book. "Damn!"

"Easy, babe." Erin gently took the book from my hands. "We need this."

"It's not moving quickly enough," I roared. "Spill your secrets, you stupid-ass book!"

"Control, son."

Control. Fucking control. "Your twin brother is lying here, his body mutilated by God knows what, and you talk of control?"

"I know. But Braedon is actually doing better. I feared for his life earlier, but seeing his son has had a profound effect on him. I no longer feel that the end is imminent."

"Talking to my brother?" Braedon asked.

"Yeah, Dad. He's here. Open your mind, and you'll be able to hear and see him."

"Jules?" Braedon said. "I'm sorry."

"Tell him he has nothing to be sorry for."

"Uncle Jules says you have nothing to be sorry for," River said.

"If I had more strength right now, I'd get up and force him to reveal himself to me."

"It's not him," I said. "Believe me, I understand your frustration. Everyone here saw him before I did, and he's *my* father."

"He's my brother. My twin brother. We began life as one."

"Give it time. Open your mind," I said. "He'll appear."

"You're weak right now from the electrocution," Erin said. "Try to rest. Rest and believe. When your body isn't so exhausted, it will be easier."

"Yeah, get some sleep, Dad," River agreed.

"Her goon can't come in and torture you anymore," I said. "Erin took his pin."

Erin smiled and tugged on my arm. "Can I talk to you outside for a minute?"

"Yeah. Sure." We walked outside, where Logan was still sitting on the floor. I bared my teeth as a growl rumbled in my chest.

"Easy. He wasn't in control of his actions."

"Don't care."

"I know. But we have more important things to figure out. Like why your uncle's muscles are changing. It's not steroids, or it's steroids plus something else. His structure is changing, maybe from the inside out."

"Why? You dare to ask me why?"

I lay limp, knives of pain lancing through my body, my flesh buzzing from the electricity the goons had sent surging through me.

"Why?" I whispered once more.

Why do you take my blood? Why do you force me to drink yours? Why do you have me tortured? Why do you make me fight? Why do you reward me with human blood that I can't resist? Why, after rewarding me, do you torture me again?

All those questions, but all that came out was another weak, "Why?"

"I don't answer to you, Dante. You answer to me."

Desperate for answers, I did the one thing that made me hate myself, the one thing that her giant ego would respond to.

"Why, my queen?"

"You are meant for far more than a meager vampire existence in the dark, Dante. When I've completed my work with you, you will change the world."

ELEVEN

Erin

"Medically, this shouldn't be possible," I continued, "but granted, I know nothing about vampire physiology."

"Vampire physiology is no different than human physiology," Dante said. "Just our need for the specific nutrients found in blood. At least as far as I know. Since we can interbreed, I assume it's true."

"I wonder why no vampire has ever learned to synthesize blood," I said. "Seems that would have been a priority."

"Why haven't humans learned to synthesize blood?" Dante asked. "Then people wouldn't have to donate."

"Touché. Actually, blood substitutes do exist, but they're only expanders. So far, no suitable oxygen-carrying substitute has been found. Maybe that's part of what vampires require— the oxygen component of blood."

"Could be," Dante said. "I never thought about it."

"Most people don't stop to think about things that are such a basic part of life. How many times does the average person stop to think about the air they're breathing? Or the food they require to sustain their lives? Not many."

Dante didn't respond. In fact, he didn't indicate he'd heard me at all.

"Babe?"

"Sorry. I was just thinking."

"About what?"

"Something Bonneville said to me once. After torture. I was feeling a lot like Uncle Brae must be feeling right now, and I only wanted to know one thing. Why?"

"And?"

"She wouldn't answer me at first, not until I buttered her up by calling her my queen." He frowned, a sound of disgust in his throat.

"Then she answered?"

"Yeah. She said, 'You are meant for far more than a meager vampire existence in the dark, Dante. When I've completed my work with you, you will change the world.'"

I lifted my brow and widened my eyes. "Wow."

"I know."

"Do you remember when she said this?"

He shook his head. "It's no use asking me about timing, baby. When I was here, minutes and hours morphed into months and years. I have no idea of any timeline."

"It's a prophecy."

Logan's voice. I turned to him. He sat on the floor, his knees drawn to his chest.

"Braedon said something about a prophecy. Logan, do you know what he's talking about?"

Logan shook his head. "I don't know any specifics. I've just heard the word a lot."

"You're no fucking help at all," Dante growled.

Dante was understandably upset and angry. Logan had been torturing Dante's uncle in much the same way Dante had been tortured. My heart wept for him, but I also saw the bigger picture—the bigger picture that could help all of us. Logan had information. Or rather, his alternate personality probably had information. If I could figure out how to make Logan Two come out, we could see what he knew. Of course, if Logan Two came out, I had to make sure he didn't go back to torturing people.

I squeezed Dante's arm and then knelt down to face Logan.

"Are you sorry for the evil atrocities you've participated in down here?"

"Of course! I'm a doctor, Erin. I never wanted to harm anyone."

"But you did," Dante growled.

"He didn't," I said. "His body did, but not his mind."

"Doesn't matter. He did it."

I stood and whispered to Dante, "Did you ever do something you wished you hadn't?"

His eyes softened. "Many times. Though I thought I had a reason for it at the time. I did what I had to for survival."

"Maybe Logan only did the same. Look. He has information inside him somewhere. If he knows more about this prophecy that Braedon mentioned, it could help us."

"I'm sorry, baby. I can't get past what he's done, even if he does have some kind of screwy mental disorder."

I couldn't blame Dante for his shortsightedness regarding Logan. I actually felt the same way. I was angry. Logan had tortured someone Dante loved. Dante was my world, and what upset him also upset me. Somehow, though, I had to help Dante see the big picture here.

"Dante, I—"

River ran out the door. "Erin! Something's wrong with my dad!"

I raced back into the room, my heart pounding.

"He's not breathing!" River cried. "I'm going to do CPR. Erin, I need you to do the respiratory breaths."

Quickly I checked his airway. All clear. "Start the compressions."

River locked his fingers together and pressed hard on his father's chest.

One. Two. Three. Four.

Thirty chest compressions, and then I tilted his head and forced two breaths inside him.

Nothing.

"Damn it!"

One. Two. Three. Four. "We need a doctor. Logan!"

He came running, but of course fell backward and yelled when he couldn't get through the door. He couldn't do anything I wasn't already doing anyway. I needed a defibrillator, but this wasn't a hospital room.

Twenty-eight. Twenty-nine. Thirty.

Two more breaths.

"Come on, damn it!"

"Dante," River said while still doing compressions. "You saved Lucy. Please save my dad."

"Riv, I don't know how I did it."

"I don't care! Try!"

Dante pushed me away and laid his hand on his uncle's chest.

Nothing.

"Dante!" River cried.

"I'm trying, Riv. I just don't—"

With a loud whoosh, Braedon drew in a massive breath.

Thank God!

I touched his neck to check his pulse. "It's faint, but it's there. It'll get stronger."

Dante raked his fingers through his hair and then stared at his other hand, the one that had brought his uncle back to life. "It was probably the CPR."

"It could have been," I said. "Or it could have been you."

"Thank you, son." The voice came not from River, but from Julian. "Thank you all for saving my brother. It is not his time to die."

Braedon's eyes opened. "Julian?" His voice was weak and hoarse.

"Yes, Brae. I'm here."

"I can't see you."

"You will. In time."

"I was coming to be with you. To help."

"I know. I felt it. But it's not your time, brother."

"How do you know?"

"I just know. Trust me."

"But—"

"River and Dante need you here. I'm not exactly sure why, but I feel it very strongly."

"I felt it just as strongly that I needed to die, to be with you. To help you. Why is your feeling right and mine wrong?"

"Your feeling isn't wrong, Brae," Julian said. "It's simply misguided. You are still bound by a physical body, a body that's been abused. Right now, you feel like you can't help your son as a living being because of what you've been through. I'm here to tell you that you're wrong. I've seen things on the noncorporeal plane that none of you could comprehend."

"If I died, I could comprehend them."

"Yes, but trust me that it's not your time."

"Why me and not you? Why do I get to live?"

"I don't know yet, Braedon. I don't have all the answers, but they will reveal themselves in time. I'm sure of it."

"I'd gladly take your place, brother."

"Don't mourn me, Brae. I've accepted my fate, and I'm still here for all of you. It is my destiny."

"Sorry to interrupt this brotherly bonding," I said, "but you need to rest."

"You're a nurse, right? My son told me all about you and Dante and your bond."

"Yes, I'm a nurse."

"Then I have you to thank for saving me."

"Actually, it wasn't me. I did what I could, but River did the chest compressions. And then Dante..."

TWELVE

DANTE

My hand still burned from whatever energy I'd expended to bring my uncle back to life. I continued staring at it, mesmerized.

Nothing had happened when I first touched my uncle's chest. Voices were all around me.

Save him! Save him! Save him!

But I don't know how.

Don't know how.

Don't know how.

Only when I'd seen the true horror in River's eyes had the energy risen within me. It traveled like a skittering electric current from deep inside me, my very core, and then through my body and out of my hand.

I had revived him, but had he been without oxygen for much longer, I wouldn't have been able to. I simply performed the role of a defibrillator. This, I knew, was where my power ended.

I could not bring back the dead.

My father's ghost stood at my uncle's side. They were still talking, and I couldn't discern whether Brae could see him yet.

Didn't matter. They needed this time to be brothers.

Erin took my hand. "You're amazing. You know that?"

I shook my head. "I don't know what I did."

"Doesn't matter, cuz," River said. "You did it."

"We need to find your uncle some clothes and get him out of here," Erin said. "Though he might not be in any condition to move right now."

"That bastard did quite a number on him," River said.

Erin stiffened, but I nudged her gently. Now was not the time for her to tell River that it wasn't actually Logan. I wasn't sure I was buying that anyway.

She seemed to understand. "Let's figure—" She jumped when something fell on the floor behind her.

The book.

"How did that—" She stooped to pick it up and checked her pack. "I guess I left the zipper open, but still, how could it just jump out— Oh!" The book fell open, and I read over her shoulder.

When two males grow together in one womb, sired by a descendant in the angel's line, the firstborn will be gifted with all the wisdom of the ancient vampires, while the second will possess immense strength and power never before seen.

More illegible words. Then—

So it is prophesied. So shall it be.

"Was your father the first or second born?" Erin asked.

"First. Brae was born ten minutes later."

"This is the prophecy. It has to be." Erin read it aloud to

River, Julian, and Braedon. "She's trying to turn Braedon into something powerful and then control him."

"Why did she keep me, then? And what are these powers I have?"

"I don't know," Erin said. "Nothing else is legible."

"Of course not." I scoffed.

"Maybe there's something in the illegible part before 'so it is prophesied.'"

"That doesn't do us any good." I shook my head, my fangs snapping down.

"Easy, son. Control."

"I'm fucking sick of control!" Rage consumed me.

"There's something I don't understand," Erin said, her voice soothing me. "It says 'sired by a descendant in the angel's line.' What does 'the angel's line' mean?"

"Who knows?" River said. "Let's just get the hell out of here."

"I need to go." My father disappeared. "It's your sister. She needs me."

"Dad!" I squeezed my hands into fists, ready to punch something. Logan Crown would be a good start. "Now what? What's wrong with Em? She's out of here. She should be safe."

"Your dad will see to her safety," Erin said. "So will Jay."

"Jay can be glamoured," I said.

Erin said no more. What could she say? I was right.

Just one more thing to worry about.

I looked toward the door.

Make that two more things.

Decker and two others stood in the doorway.

"Man, you guys have great timing," River said. "Bring it on."

"Where's your boss lady?" I said. "Still indisposed from the last time I went at her?"

"Get the fuck out of our way," Decker said, ignoring my question. "We're here to take the beast down to the pit."

"Over my dead body," River said.

"Make that two of us," I agreed. "How's the nose feeling?"

Decker scowled, baring his fangs.

I showed him my longer and sharper ones. "You're going to have to do better than that." I pushed him outside the door where Logan still sat huddled.

He was the least of my concerns at the moment.

I pushed Decker against the wall. "Give me one good reason why I shouldn't thrash the hell out of you."

"I can give you three good reasons. Here they come."

I turned. Three more vampires stalked down the hallway. I laughed out loud. "You think they scare me?" With a thought, I pushed energy back at them. They yelled as their bodies flew backward and hit the wall with three thuds.

"Fuck. You," Decker gritted out.

I clocked him up the side of the head, and he fell to the ground.

Back in the room, River was fighting one of the others while the second had Erin smashed against a wall.

He was grinding into her.

My teeth sharpened, and with another thought, I hurled the rogue vamp across the room and outside the door, where he fell against Decker's unconscious body.

"Baby? Are you okay?"

She nodded, biting her lower lip. "He didn't hurt me. But he was definitely glad to see me."

I seethed, while River landed an uppercut to the remaining

vampire's jaw. I grabbed him, tossing him out the door to land on the heap outside.

"Damn, cuz." River wiped the sweat from his brow. "I'm definitely feeling like the weakling here."

"If I knew how I did it, I'd tell you."

Then it dawned on me. I *did* know. This time, I'd known exactly what I needed to do, and I'd channeled the energy into the task.

I was beginning to learn to control the new powers.

As long as I didn't fight the dark energy and kept my own head, I could harness it and produce results.

Again, I stared down at my hand.

Whatever this power was, I didn't have it before. Somehow *she* had brought it out in me. My time here had brought it out in me.

She might have meant it for evil, for her plans to bring vampires back and end humanity, but she didn't control me.

Only *I* controlled me.

The powers she'd given me belonged to me and only me. I would decide how to use them.

I smiled.

I was ready.

❧

"Now, Dante"—she licked the wound on her wrist after forcing me to feed from her—"you are ready."

THIRTEEN

Erin

Dante's eyes shined with new fire. Oh, I'd seen his eyes angry, full of rage, full of passion and desire. I'd seen them filled with sadness, regret, remorse.

What I saw in them now was new—an emotion I couldn't read.

Something in him had changed.

Fear lanced through me. I had to stop him. I didn't know why, or from what, but I felt it as strongly as I'd felt anything in my life.

As strongly as I felt my love for him.

He smiled.

Not at me. Not at River. Not at his uncle.

He smiled at something amorphous, his gorgeous full lips taking on a serpentine quality.

No.

Just no.

I grabbed his hand. "Fight it, Dante?"

He turned to me, stared at me. "I'm going to end this. Now. For all time."

River forced Dante around and met his gaze. "Cuz?"

"I can end their lives. All of them."

"Who?" I said. "The vampires? They're out cold, Dante. You don't need—"

"They don't deserve life. They don't deserve anything."

"Julian!" I yelled.

"He won't come," River said. "Not if Em's in trouble. God. What the fuck? Dante, cuz, you've got to snap out of this."

Braedon sat up on the table. "What's going on?"

"It's Dante, Dad. He's not...himself."

"I'm perfectly fine." His fair skin glowed with rosiness. Rage. "But it's time to end all of this."

I stared into his eyes again. "Dante, *please*. We all need you. *I* need you."

He blinked.

And his eyes changed.

He was back.

"Thank God," I said on a sigh.

"What?" he said.

"You weren't...you for a few minutes there."

"Don't be silly. I was—" He blinked again.

"Dante, you were going to kill the thugs. All of them. We can't let you. We can't let you become a killer."

He widened his eyes. "Shit. I was so convinced I had everything under control. What happened?"

"Easy." I shuddered. "You're back now, but you weren't *you*. I've seen you that way before. At least you snapped out of it quickly this time."

"Cuz, you've got to fight this shit."

"I *have* been fighting it. I'm in control. I was sure I was."

"You are," I said, trying to soothe him. "Everyone has a setback now and then."

"A setback?"

Dr. Bonneville's voice.

I turned and met her cold blue gaze. "Zabrina," I said icily.

"What you experienced wasn't a setback, Dante."

"Get out of my sight," Dante said through clenched teeth.

"I've come to feed," she said, turning toward Braedon. "Your uncle's blood is delicious, but nothing compared to yours. I'll take yours today."

"The hell you will."

I gasped. The words had come not from Dante, but from Braedon. He was standing, his muscular body seeming to take up the full room.

"You think you can stop me? You're forgetting who's in control here, Braedon."

"My nephew released me, bitch. You want to try to take me on?"

"I made you."

"That's right. You did. But if I'm not tied down, just how do you think you're going to control me?"

I gasped as Zabrina yanked me toward her.

"Not a problem," she said. "I'll just feed on Erin. I already know how sweet her blood is. Don't you agree, Dante?"

"I've incapacitated you several times now," Dante said. "Do you really think I'm going to let you take Erin's blood?"

"I think you might."

I gasped as something cool touched my neck and scraped my skin.

A blade.

She held a knife to my neck. I forced my legs to keep from buckling and choked back a cough.

"Even you can't heal a dead person, Dante. I'll have this knife through her more quickly than you can act, and you won't be able to stop her from bleeding out."

Dante's eyes turned fiery. "I'll destroy you," he said through clenched teeth.

In a swift movement, the knife flung away from me of its own accord, hitting the wall and then dropping to the ground. River dashed over and picked it up. Again, I forced my legs to keep standing. An edge of relief simmered in me, but I knew this was far from over.

"What did you do to me?" Dante demanded, walking forward and yanking me away from Bonneville. "Somehow my Rh factor changed. You planted something in me, and now I have these unusual abilities. Tell me. You didn't plan on all of that, did you?"

"The outcome of experimentation doesn't always yield the expected results," she said.

"That's right," River said. "It doesn't. We've figured out your secret."

He was bluffing. We had no idea what Bonneville's weakness was. The *Texts* hadn't shown us yet.

"Then you know I'm perfectly safe here," she said.

I choked back another cough.

Here? She was perfectly safe here? I wanted to explore the thought further, but with the ghostly echo of cool steel pressing into my flesh, I couldn't exactly think straight.

"Logan mentioned a prophecy," Dante said. "The only prophecy in the *Vampyre Texts* involves twin males. My father and uncle. Nothing to do with me. So why did you keep me?

Why do you want River now?"

Zabrina's lips curled into a snakelike grin. "Ask your father."

"My father's dead, as you well know."

I kept quiet. We could ask him, though Bonneville refused to believe in ghosts.

"Then ask your uncle. He and his twin have no secrets."

Dante turned to Braedon, whose look was unreadable. "Uncle Brae?"

"Nothing. There is nothing. I swear it. She's manipulating you, Dante."

"Am I?" Bonneville seethed. "Or do you truly *not* know the precious family secret?"

FOURTEEN

DANTE

Precious family secret? My uncle shook his head, his eyes wide. Whatever secret she was talking about, Uncle Brae didn't know.

Uncle Brae and my father were twins. They did not have secrets from each other.

"There is no secret," I growled. "Now get the fuck out of my sight!" I hurled energy toward her, and she whooshed out the door into the hallway, falling on top of one of the unconscious thugs, her head knocking against the wall. She was out, but she wouldn't remain out. If the *Texts* were accurate, she would recover from any physical blow.

Her power lay in her immortality, her imperviousness to aging and injury. One thing I was sure of now, though. Whatever she was up to went far beyond just forcing a vampire baby from mating a human and a vampire. She'd figured that part out, but that alone wouldn't increase our population exponentially.

No. That was only the beginning.

Something else was the key.

Something that involved my father, my uncle, River...and me.

Especially me.

Erin grabbed the book out of her pack. "Come on. We need information." She opened it. "Oh my God."

"What is it, baby?"

She read aloud.

"When two males grow together in one womb, sired by a descendant in the angel's line, the firstborn will be gifted with all the wisdom of the ancient vampires, while the second will possess immense strength and power never before seen."

"Yeah, we've heard that," I said.

"I know. But there's more now."

"These males will both beget sons of their own bodies, grown in pure vampire women. When the moon wanes and the night turns black, darkness will ascend in one.

"Darkness rising.

"We shall rise again.

"Only the fates can stop the ascension.

"So it is prophesied. So shall it be."

My stomach dropped.

Darkness rising.

We shall rise again.

So many times I'd heard those phrases, only guessing at their meanings.

Now I knew.

She'd fed me her blood to move the darkness along faster. She'd fed on me—and who knew how many other vampire males—to extend her life and make her invincible. Why? So she could continue her work for as long as necessary.

Was this what Bill was trying to keep from us? The fact that he might have inadvertently begotten the end of humanity?

One thing still didn't compute, though. "What does 'the angel's line' mean?" I said. "That doesn't make sense."

"No, it doesn't—" Erin lifted her brows. "Actually, maybe it does."

"What do you mean?" River asked.

"The angel's line. Gabriel. Gabriel is an angel in many religions."

"Then this prophecy could be pure dogma," River said.

"Most prophecies are," Erin said. "Which doesn't explain why a scientist like Bonneville would put any stock in them. But clearly she's got some measure of belief in this one."

"I'm not sure this is what has Bill spooked," River said. "He never put much stock in dogma either. Clearly we're not descended from angels."

"But if he read this, he had to have noticed the parallels," Erin said. "Vampire twins, and then each of them has a son from a vampire mother. Given how difficult pregnancy is for your women and how rare you say identical twins are... It's pretty eerie."

"Plus, if this is truly what he read, then he read it *after* I was taken, and after you and Dad went after me, Uncle Brae. That would have reinforced his belief in the prophecy."

Braedon nodded. "And she's doing her best to turn me into the second twin with immense strength and power. That explains why she fed me her blood but didn't feed it to Jules."

"We need to get you out of here," I said. "If what Erin says is true, and something is happening to your musculature that isn't normal, you're not safe here."

"I'm concerned more with River's and your safety," my uncle said.

"Bull," River chimed in. "You're just as important as we are. We're not going to leave you here and let her turn you into some kind of freakish vampire enforcer."

"That's it!" I said, an image forming in my mind.

"That's what?" Erin said.

"Brae is the enforcer. My father was supposed to be the counsel. And I..." I stopped talking to ease down the bile that rose in my throat. "I'm the one who ascends. Darkness rising. Somehow she thinks I'm the key to bringing vampires back."

"Damn," River said. "Is it weird that I'm feeling a little left out?"

"You're not left out, Riv. If it doesn't work with me, she's coming for you. She's made that clear."

"But why did she choose you in the first place? We both went to Bourbon Street that night."

"Really, Riv?" I shook my head. "Really? You want to trade places for the last ten years? She probably took the one she considered to be easier prey. Maybe it's a compliment to you."

"I'm sorry, man." River rubbed his forehead. "I don't know what got into me."

"So how do we stop this?" Braedon asked. "Dante, you can obviously control her when you need to, but she's already set the prophecy in motion."

"Only the fates can stop the ascension," Erin said softly.

"How do we get fate to intervene?" I asked.

Erin smiled. "I think it already has."

FIFTEEN

Erin

The blood bond.

"How?" River asked.

Dante's eyes brightened, and his smile lit up his whole face. "You're right, baby."

"Would someone please explain what's going on?" River said.

"The blood bond," I said.

"Erin is my control," Dante said. "The few times the dark energy pulled me in, my love for her, my bond with her, is what brought me back." He chuckled. "Maybe the prophecy is true. It was my father who said Bonneville hadn't been counting on the blood bond with Erin. He is very wise."

"Jules was always the philosopher between the two of us," Braedon said. "I was busy getting into fights. Of course, he fought alongside me when I got into it."

"You both fit the prophecy," I said. "No wonder Bill was so freaked out. But why would Bonneville pay any attention to an ancient prophecy?"

It went against everything I knew about her.

Of course, I could probably fill a whole warehouse with things I didn't know about her.

"Let's get out of here," Dante said. "Uncle Brae, are you good to walk?"

"I'll make it," he said.

I followed Dante out of the small room, stepping over the heap of unconscious bodies.

"Logan!"

I'd forgotten about him. Logan still sat in the hallway a few feet from the unconscious vampires, his arms around his knees.

"Leave him," Dante said.

"Leave him to me, you mean." Braedon yanked him to his feet. "Now you answer, asshole. You answer for what you've done to me."

"Braedon, it wasn't him," I said, pleading. "He's got a mental dis—"

Braedon either didn't hear me or wasn't bothering to listen. With vampire hearing, it was most likely the latter.

"Dante," I said, "please stop him."

Dante shook his head. "I'm sorry, baby. My uncle is not a killer. He won't do any lasting harm. But I can't stop this. I owe it to Brae. If I come across the two goons who tortured me, I'll give them the same. It kills me to know that I may have already come across them but didn't do anything because I can no longer scent them."

"That's my fault then. The blood bond."

"God, no! That's not what I mean at all."

"I don't know about the two who tortured you, Dante, but Logan has a psychiatric disorder. He truly couldn't—"

Dante placed two fingers over my lips. "It doesn't matter, love."

342

"But it's not a fair fight!"

"Nor was it fair when I was tortured. I'm sorry. Braedon needs this."

Logan's expression was stoic, and he didn't try to resist. He was willing to take punishment for what he'd done. When Braedon raised his fist, I turned away, burrowing my face into Dante's shoulder.

Thud.

Thud.

Thud.

Fist meeting flesh.

No squeals or yells from Logan. He took it like a man.

"He's had enough, Uncle Brae." Dante's voice was calm but commanding.

I didn't move. Braedon would surely fight Dante on this. Logan couldn't have been pummeled into a pulp yet.

"I'll decide when he's had enough." Braedon's voice was a low growl.

"Don't become what she wants you to be. You're three times his size, and you've punished him. Let it be enough. Please."

Yes, please, I begged silently.

"You sound exactly like your father," Braedon said. "If I didn't know better, I'd think he was speaking through you."

"I assure you it's me," Dante said. "I guess the apple doesn't fall that far from the tree."

"I'll honor your request. It's what Jules would want." Braedon let go of Logan, who fell to the floor.

I raced to him to examine him, nearly tripping over one of the unconscious vampires. "Logan, I'm sorry."

"Don't be. I deserve far more than I got."

I both agreed and disagreed, so I said nothing. "Your nose is broken."

"I'm sure it is," he wheezed. "It hurts like hell."

"Take off your lab coat. I need to make some bandages." Within a few minutes, I'd done the best I could for him.

I turned to Dante. "Can we get him out of here? Please?"

"Erin, he's a doctor. Patty is still down here, and we can't depend on *her*." He nodded toward Bonneville splayed on top of one of her thugs.

"Can we get them both out? Please?"

He sighed. "I don't like to deny you, Erin, but how do you suggest we accomplish that? Didn't Patty just have surgery? And Logan needs some rest after that beating."

The beating you allowed to happen. But I kept that to myself. I didn't blame Braedon. Or Dante, for that matter. Even the Claiborne thugs.

I blamed Zabrina Bonneville.

They were all victims of *her*.

She was the mastermind behind everything that went on down here, and damn it, if it was the last thing I did, I would stop her.

I might be a mere human woman, but I was a woman in love, a woman bonded, and I would help Dante find a way to stop her, once and for all.

SIXTEEN

DANTE

I eyed the unconscious thugs.

Were these the men I'd fought in the arena? Those I'd pummeled and stopped short of killing? It was possible. I was masked, and so were they, so we had no way of knowing.

Or were there more male vampires here? One in particular had been huge and wide. I'd wondered how he could have gotten through the narrow tunnels to this hellish place.

In my life, I'd only seen one male that broad...and he was standing in front of me.

"Uncle Brae, had you ever been in the fighting pit before the last time, with River and me?"

"Maybe. Sometimes I think I was. It's so fuzzy."

I swallowed. "I'm sorry."

"For what?" he asked.

"I think I..." I cleared my throat. "We've fought before, Uncle Brae. I didn't know it was you, and you didn't know it was me, but we've circled each other in that damned place. I'm sorry."

"Are you sure?"

"Unless there's someone else here who's as big and broad as you are, yes, we have."

If what Erin said was true, and Brae was morphing into something not normal, I needed to find out how to stop it. "How long have you been drinking blood from her?"

"I don't know. Seems like forever. Since I've been here."

I nodded. "The prophecy. She fed you the blood but not my dad. You were supposed to be the brawn, and he the brain."

"Lucky him," Braedon said dryly.

"Before we came down here, my dad felt very strongly that your time was running out. Looking at you, I can see he was right. But it wasn't your death he was afraid of. It was some kind of metamorphosis. She's changing you."

"I've felt that for some time. I've been fighting as hard as I can. Seeing you and River has helped a lot. But knowing that Jules..." Braedon shook his head.

"He wouldn't want you to mourn him," I said. Then a horrible thought speared into me. "He left for Em. Dad! Dad, where are you?"

My father appeared this time.

Braedon nearly jumped out of his oversized muscles. "Jules!"

"Hey, Brae. You can see me now, huh?"

"Dad, what about Em? Is she okay?"

He nodded solemnly. "She's going to be fine. Jay is with her, and Jack is taking care of her."

"Thank God." I heaved a sigh of relief. "What happened?"

"She miscarried the child."

An anvil hit my gut. "Oh, no."

"Is Jay all right?" Erin asked.

"He is. They're both saddened by the loss, of course, and they're mourning it. But Emilia is healthy and can have more babies."

"The stress of being kidnapped. Of being here," I said.

"I'm sure that didn't help," Erin said. "There's no way to know. But honestly, miscarriages aren't uncommon. They usually can't be prevented, and most women have no issue conceiving again."

"Most women aren't vampires."

"I know. But she will be fertile again."

"In a year or more."

"Yes, she'll have to wait, but the most important thing is that Emilia is okay."

"Jules, I'm so sorry," Braedon said.

"Em will recover."

"No. I mean, I'm sorry about that, but Erin's right. The most important thing is that she's okay. What I meant was, I'm sorry that you... That you're..."

"Dead? It's okay. I'll explain it all to you soon, but first we need to get all of you out of here. Especially you, Brae. Whatever she has done to you, I'm hoping Jack can reverse it. You don't look...right."

"His musculature is changing," Erin said. "At first we thought she'd been giving him steroids, but now we're not sure."

"It could be steroids plus vampire blood," my father said.

"Wait!" Erin said. "We can find out. Logan has access to the records in the file room. There's a file on each of us. That will tell us what she's done to Braedon."

"Good thinking, baby," I said.

"Of course," Erin continued, "Logan may not be willing to help after—"

Logan stood on wobbly legs. "No. I'll help. What's going on here is wrong. I can get you to the records room."

"We'll hold our noses, Dad," River said with a grimace.

"What about this mess?" River pointed to the unconscious vampires, including Bonneville.

"We could set them on fire," I said.

"Dante..." Erin tugged on my hand.

"I know. We're not killers. But it's tempting. It wouldn't work on Bonneville anyway, if what the *Texts* say is true. She's turned herself into an immortal."

"We still don't know the weakness," River said.

"We know she's safe here," I said. "She said so. Why would she be safe here? And what does here even mean?"

"Underground?" Erin said.

"Maybe. But she goes above ground all the time. At least she did before she went on her pseudo-vacation. She was at the hospital every night for her shift."

"True." Erin pulled the book out of her pack and opened it. "Nothing new. Crap. For a book that's supposed to tell us what we need to know when we need to know it, it sure likes to keep us in suspense."

"At least we figured out the prophecy," I said, quickly relaying the information to my father. "We think that must be what Bill read that got him spooked."

"That would make sense," my dad agreed. "No wonder he was loath to help you when you returned, Dante. He was afraid you were the beginning of some kind of vampire apocalypse."

"Vampyr omega," I said. "That's what it's called. And that's what Bonneville calls the genetic marker that allows a human to give birth to a vampire."

"But if that's the case, the prophecy is something the

council as a whole doesn't know about. Bill read the *Texts* despite the rules of the council not to."

"True," I said. "Which also means they know something else—secrets they want to keep. Something that Bill thought might help us find the missing women. That's why the ghost of Levi Gaston showed up and threatened him when he was about to tell us that night at Napoleon House."

"We still don't know everything," my father said. "But we have a good idea where this is going. Still, Bonneville is a scientist to her core. Why would she put any stock in an ancient prophecy?"

"We've been trying to figure that out," I said.

"And I think I have," Erin piped in. "One thing that's been clear throughout this whole thing is Bonneville's narcissism. She's proved that time and again. She's dropped clues here and there, like asking me to research physical characteristics and blood types, and then leaving the vodka bottle with her fingerprints on it at Emilia's apartment. She was daring us to figure out she was behind all this. That's classic narcissism. To be so sure of yourself that you know no one will figure it out, even when you leave them clues."

"She underestimated you, baby."

"She underestimated all of us," Erin said. "Though she did steal my blood and yours, Dante. She kept you and your father and uncle here for a decade, and she enslaved Logan and others. She kidnapped women. We *will* stop her, but we didn't stop her quickly enough."

"No, we didn't."

I used to dream of severed human heads.

We'd gotten the women out, and we would get Braedon out once we figured out how to reverse whatever she'd done to him. But we hadn't gotten everyone out. Not those sacrificed to feed me. Probably to feed my father and Braedon too.

And we were all still here.

There could easily be a trap we hadn't uncovered yet.

"She clearly found out about the prophecy," Erin continued, "and her narcissism led her to think she could make it come true through science. Everything she did to the three of you had some scientific basis. As a vampire supremacist, she'd be thrilled if the prophecy came true. And if she could be the one to be its genesis..."

"God, she's psycho," River said.

"True enough, cuz." I shook my head and regarded her unconscious body. She looked so innocent right now, a trickle of blood from her lip having dried to brick brown.

But I knew better. She was *not* innocent. Far from it. A narcissist, yes, and also a highly intelligent one.

We'd come far, but the rest of this journey would not simple. Not in the least.

Already I knew.

I'd shown that I could control her, but I hadn't seen the last of her tricks.

Whatever she had in store for me, I was determined to face it, even destroy it if I had to.

But first I had to make sure the others were all safe.

"Logan," I said, "take us to the room where she keeps the records."

SEVENTEEN

Erin

Once Logan had logged in, I clicked on Braedon's name and opened up his file.

"She's been feeding you her blood," I said, scanning as quickly as I could. "But we already knew that. And yes, you're on a high dose of anabolic steroids plus some supplements I don't recognize. She must not have been depending on you as a sperm donor."

"That reminds me," Dante said. "We need to find the cryolab and destroy whatever is in it."

"We will, cuz," River said.

"Or she *was* depending on you," I continued, "but took enough of your sperm before she started this regimen. Remember, you were all here for ten years."

"How can we forget?" Dante said.

"The blood bank is just down the hall from here," River said.

"You want to go?" I said to River. "The freezer will be in

the back. She's probably keeping frozen plasma in there, and if she's taken sperm from Dante, Braedon, and Julian, it will be there, most likely. Unless of course there's another freezer around here. Logan?"

"That's the only one I know of," he said. "But that doesn't mean much. She keeps me in the dark when she wants to."

"I'll go," River said. "Dante, you need to come with me."

"I won't leave Erin."

"You need to come too, Dad," River continued. "I'm not comfortable being the one to destroy all of your...stuff."

"You have my permission, son," Braedon said.

"Mine too," Julian said. "I can come with you, but you'll have to do the destroying."

"Just get it done, Riv," Dante said.

"You can go," I said to Dante. "I'll be fine here. Your uncle is here."

"All right, all right. Stop looking at me like that, Riv. I'll go and help you."

They left, and Julian's ghost disappeared.

I continued scanning Braedon's file. "Here it is!" I pulled up a record. "'The mixture of female vampire blood and the steroid cocktail has resulted in changes in musculature at the cellular level. I'm increasing the dosage of both to see if these changes manifest physiologically.' That's dated six years ago."

I continued scanning. "Here's something else. 'Exposing patient to torture seems to increase muscle mass at a quicker rate.'"

"Bitch," Braedon said.

"I'm so sorry, man," Logan whispered.

Braedon pursed his lips but said nothing.

"It wasn't you, Logan. We all know that."

"*He* doesn't."

"He does. It's just hard for him to separate that out."

Braedon stayed silent, but his giant muscles were tense. I silently begged Logan not to push it.

He didn't, thank God.

"Can we reverse what she did to me?"

"I wish I knew. Maybe your vampire doctor can help you." I scanned through the files, desperately looking for something to indicate how to reverse the effect on Braedon, or whether it could even be reversed. Nothing.

Of course not. She had never planned to reverse it.

"Here's one more thing," I said. "'A megadose of horse steroid makes patient eager to fight. His strength and mass are still no match for the nephew, however.'"

"Dante," he said quietly. "Perhaps the prophecy is true after all."

"Or she forced it," I said.

"I don't know," Braedon said. "Jules and I were told our whole lives how rare we were. Vampire fraternal twins are rare enough, but identical twins? No one knew of any others, not since the fourteenth century. If this prophecy was originally written centuries, even millennia, ago... And our mother had an effortless pregnancy. How often does that happen with twins? Or with a vampire mother?"

I sighed. I didn't know what to say to him.

I was a woman of science as much as Bonneville was.

And I was starting to believe.

EIGHTEEN

DANTE

Nothing.

Just plasma products and blood products in the freezer.

"This is good news, I guess," River said. "She didn't take anything from any of you."

"Or she has another freezer somewhere," I said.

"Think, Dante. While you were here, were you ever forced to...you know."

"Ejaculate, Dad? We're all adults here. And no, not that I recall, but there are a lot of things I don't recall."

"True. I still don't have a full recollection, and I'm no longer bound by the limits of a human brain. Plus, there are other ways she could have gotten what she needed. Surgically."

The thought made my balls hurt.

"How could we have been so wrong?" River asked. "I thought for sure she'd be hoarding your swimmers."

"For breeding, she doesn't necessarily need us," my father said. "Any vampire male will do."

"But why not have the best?" River asked. "Gabriel stock?"

"Unless we're wrong," my father said. "Maybe breeding wasn't her primary purpose. In fact..."

"What, Uncle Jules?"

"If we're right, and my father read the prophecy in the *Texts*, that means the rest of the council doesn't know about the prophecy. But they do know *something*, something that had to do with the women who were taken."

"Yeah," I said. "And Levi Gaston was a genetic researcher."

"Exactly."

"But Bonneville describes Gaston as a hack," I said.

"That doesn't mean she hasn't used his research," my father said. "She considers anyone other than herself a hack. She's that much of a narcissist."

"I don't buy it," River said. "Breeding had to be her primary goal. Why else would she have kidnapped women who can produce vampire babies?"

"Research," my father said. "Pure and simple research. She wanted to see if it could be done. If she wanted a father, she had her thugs."

"So taking us was for an altogether different purpose," I said. "The prophecy."

"Exactly," my father agreed. "But there's one more thing."

"What?" River asked.

"She's over a hundred and fifty years old, and invincible to everyone but you, it seems, Dante. She's been drinking male vampire blood for a long time. She could have just taken all of us as blood slaves for all we know."

"She had her thugs for that," I said.

"True, but they served another purpose. They went above ground a lot to run drugs and blood products for her. Take care of the business she needed."

"How did she bankroll all of this?" River said. Then he laughed. "Stupid question. Drug money."

"Yeah," I agreed. "Plus you can save a lot of money when you work for over a hundred years."

"She even could have stolen money. As old as she is, her glamour is very powerful. Probably more powerful than my father's even."

But not more powerful than mine.

I knew that instinctively.

"I can take her out," I said.

"Are you willing to do that?" my father asked.

"The thought of annihilating another living being doesn't sit well with me. I admit it. But she's evil, Dad. She has to be stopped."

"Agreed," River said.

"What if she has another cryostorage somewhere, though?" I said. "What if—"

"We not only have to destroy her," my father said. "We have to destroy this place."

A horrible thought occurred to me. "Does Bill know? About this place?"

"I have no idea," my father said. "It wouldn't surprise me, though."

"What if the council knows about her breeding research but doesn't know what else she's doing down here? Trying to force the prophecy?"

"Then the council is not who we think they are," my father said. "It's hard to believe my father would turn his back on his beliefs. All he taught us."

"He wasn't a council member when we all disappeared," I reminded him. "Being on the council changed him."

"Or reading about the prophecy did," River said. "Why else would he have thought you and my dad were the primary targets rather than Dante or me?"

"I don't know. I just don't know." My dad let out one of his ghostly sighs.

"I think both changed him. Somehow, the council managed to get him to change some of his long-held beliefs. We just don't know which ones. And then reading the *Texts* really spooked him." I shook my head.

"We'll find out," my father said. "Bill is done lying to us. I'll see to that."

"He's probably recovered from his self-inflicted poisoning by now," I said. "Do you think he knows where we are?"

"I have no idea," my dad said. "I haven't checked in with him. You two, Brae, and Em have been my focus."

River nodded. "He's up to something. He deliberately interfered with Dante's conversation with Lucien Crown, which means he knew Crown was there. He's been tracking him somehow."

"He is his cousin," my father said.

"I know," I said. "But does Bill even know that? Crown himself said that Alex Gabriel no longer exists."

"I have no idea." My dad sighed again. "I will deal with Bill. But not before we end Bonneville. Em is in good hands at the moment. Right now, I'm needed here."

"We have to get Patty and all the others out of here," I said. "Including you and your dad, Riv."

"Hell, no. I'm not leaving."

"Riv..."

"Hey, she might not have held me for ten years, but I'm as in this as the rest of you. I'm seeing this through to the end."

"My brother needs medical attention, River," my father said. "We need to get him to Jack and see if he can reverse whatever Bonneville did to him."

"You mean *I* need to get him to Jack," River said. "Bullshit."

"You're his son," I said. "I'd do the same for my dad."

"I'm not leaving! And I'll bet my dad isn't either."

"He's right, Dante," my father said. "Brae will refuse to leave until this is done. As much as I want to get him to Jack, not one of us can force him."

"I can," I said.

"Probably," River said, "but you won't. Or you'll answer to me."

"I can take all of you out," I said, the dark energy rising within me. "All of you. With a single thought."

"But you *won't*," River said again.

I growled, baring my fangs. "Try to stop me."

"Don't pull that shit on me, cuz. I know who you are and what you're capable of, but I also know deep down that you'll never harm any one of us. I have *faith* in that."

"Control, son," my father said. "You too, River. I want Braedon to get help, but I won't force him or you to leave."

"He'll want to see the end of this," River said. "And so do I."

"Understood. Right, Dante?"

Anger seeped through every cell of my body. I tamped down the darkness that threatened to pull me in, but one thing did not lessen.

This was mine to finish.

Mine.

And I'd be the one.

Because I was the only one who could.

NINETEEN

Erin

I found nothing else in Braedon's file that could help us, but I needed to figure out some way to copy it for the vampire doctor who would be taking care of him from now on.

"Do you have a thumb drive?" I asked Logan.

"Sorry."

I tried accessing my email account so I could attach the records, but the system wouldn't let me. "How do I copy this file, Logan? His doctor will need it."

"Sorry. I don't know."

"Do you have an email address you can log in to and email them to me?"

"No. Not down here. This server isn't connected anywhere else. We have to bring down hard copies of the patients' records."

"You bring them down from University?"

Braedon growled.

"I think so. It's all hazy. Or Bonneville gets them."

"Is there a printer down here? We'll copy them and take them with us."

"Not that I know of."

"Damn!" I wiped my brow. "All right. I'll just memorize the dosages. Or here, I'll write them on my hand. I'll write them on yours too, Braedon. Where's a pen?"

Logan scrambled in a drawer. "Here."

I quickly wrote the steroid and other dosages—man, they were huge—on my forearm and on Braedon's. "There. Memorize them too in case they get rubbed off. I'll do the same."

Dante burst through the door.

"How'd it go?" I asked.

"Negative on sperm. We couldn't find any."

I lifted my brow. "That's good, then."

"She could be storing it somewhere else."

Logan shook his head. "I don't think so. Not that I know of, anyway."

"She obviously doesn't tell you everything," I said. "But if it's not in the freezer, that's a good sign."

"To be on the safe side, we need to destroy this place," Dante said. "And we need to begin by destroying her."

Anger rose within me. "I'd love to have a hand in that."

"Only I can do it, baby. I want the rest of you to get out of here."

"We've been through this, cuz," River said. "We're all invested."

"I know," Dante said, "and I understand. But I'm the only one who can control *her*. In fact, I need to go back into the other wing and figure out what to do with the thugs if they're still unconscious. I'm sure she's awake by now and up to something."

Dante reached into his pack and pulled out the zipped bag of Julian's ashes.

"What's that?" Braedon asked.

"The remains of your twin," River said. "Put that away, Dante."

"Sorry." He dipped his fingers in and then rubbed some ashes on River's forehead.

River flinched. "What the hell?"

"You know it works. Look, Riv, I know you're invested. I get that. I do. But your dad needs medical help if he's going to get back to normal. Hopefully this stuff can be reversed. Honestly, there's nothing any of you can do to help me down here. This is between her and me."

"Fuck no, Dante. Just no."

"Son," Braedon said. "I've seen what Dante can do."

"So have I. That changes nothing."

"No, son, it changes everything. If you can get out, I want you out."

"I'm not leaving without you."

"You're right. You're not. That's why I'm going with you. We'll take garbage man here too."

"The guy who tortured you? You're kidding."

"No, I'm not. We're going to prove what kind of people we are, River. No matter what was done to me, I'm still a Gabriel vampire, and so are you."

River finally backed down. "All right, Dad. I'm just so glad you're alive. Oh. Sorry, Uncle Jules."

"It's okay," Julian said. "I made my own choice, and I have no regrets. You all know why I did it."

"Thank you, Uncle Brae." Dante rubbed some ashes onto the older vampire's forehead. "You'll be shielded."

"We'll get the young lady who had surgery. She'll be glad to be reunited with her baby," Braedon said.

"There are others here in the OR wing," Logan said. "Staff."

"Can you lead us to them?" River said. "We'll get them all out. Dante, I'll need those ashes."

Dante nodded and handed him the bag. "Just a smudge on their foreheads will do it. Use them sparingly. They're more valuable than gold at the moment." He turned to me. "I've already shielded you. I want you to go with them."

"Not likely," I said. "Besides, you need my blood, especially if you're determined to take her down once and for all."

"I agree, Erin," Julian said. "You need to stay."

"Now someone is talking sense," I said. "I'm staying."

Dante bared his teeth on a snarl.

"Don't even with me," I said. "You think those teeth scare me?"

Dante softened, though his teeth didn't retract. "Dad?"

"I'm leaving with the others," Julian said.

"No, Dad. I need you here."

"No, Dante. You don't. This is your fight now. Not mine."

"Dad—"

"I feel strongly about this. This last battle must be between the two of you."

"It will be. But I need your wisdom, your guidance."

"You don't, son. This is all you. Have faith in what you're destined for. Erin will be here to feed you, to give you the strength and control you need. I've taught you all I can for now. You no longer need me. This is something you're destined to accomplish on your own."

"Dad, I do! I do need you. Please stay."

"Faith, son. Have faith." Julian disappeared.

"He's not coming back," Dante said.

"Don't be so sure." I hugged him. "You'll see him again."

"I know. But he won't come back down here. I feel it in my bones."

"He knows you can handle this yourself," I said. "And he's right."

I turned to Logan. "Can you find Patty and the others? Get them out of here?"

He nodded. "I will, Erin. I can. I have to."

"All right. Then go. All of you. Get out of here as quickly as you can. I'll stay with Dante, and we'll be done here soon."

Yes, we'll be done here soon, I repeated to myself.

One way or the other.

TWENTY

DANTE

Erin and I stood alone in the file room.

They had truly left.

Even my father had abandoned me.

But not Erin. Not my sweet, precious Erin.

My teeth descended with a snap, not so painful this time. Hunger surged through me.

I inhaled.

Erin.

Dark chocolate, Bordeaux, truffles, and blackberries.

Erin.

I yanked her to me and crushed my mouth to hers.

Our lips slid together for a few seconds, and then she parted hers, and I dived in, finding her warm tongue and swirling my own around it. I wanted a raw kiss, a kiss that was a prelude of what was to come.

I was going to make passionate love to her, and then I was going to feed.

And feed.

And feed some more, until we were both sated and ready.

I was hungry—oh, so hungry—and we were alone.

Finally alone, even though we were underground in this godforsaken place. How I longed to undress her, to gaze over every contour of her body, glide my fingertips over each inch of her smooth flesh, and then lay her on a soft bed and make love to her with my lips, teeth, tongue, hands, and cock.

But that wasn't going to happen. Not now.

Soon, damn it.

But not now.

She removed her pack from her shoulders and lifted her hoodie over her head. Then the bulletproof vest and the tank and bra underneath. She stood, her bare breasts so enticing, wearing only shoes and leggings.

She quickly discarded her shoes and socks and then rolled the leggings off her smooth legs ever so slowly.

My cock throbbed. So fucking hard for her. A growl left my throat as I parted my lips, exposing my fangs.

She stood before me naked.

Naked and so very innocent.

Except she was not innocent. No. This amazing woman had seen things no one should have to see. Done things no one should have to do. All because of me.

Yet here she was. Still loving me. Still wanting me. Still willing to give me the sustenance from her body that I craved, that I needed.

Once bonded, never broken.

Those words now belonged to Erin and me. Only us.

She slowly cupped her beautiful breasts and then began playing with her hard nipples. The dark skin around them wrinkled.

And my cock grew harder.

"Does it feel good, baby?" I asked. "Does it feel good when you touch yourself like that?"

She closed her eyes on a soft moan and continued to play with her nipples.

I watched, mesmerized. I could look at her forever. Her beauty, her fair skin, her red lips, her pinkish-brown nipples, her slender fingers with nails painted pink as they squeezed and pulled at the hard nubs. Then one hand let a nipple drop and it slid down her beautiful belly, past her black triangle, to her clit. She began gently moving her fingers in a circular motion, closing her eyes, moaning.

Such beauty. Her apple musk arousal—the synthetic hormone scent had lessened, thank God—drifted through the room. I inhaled, letting it warm me, infuse me with all the strong beauty that was Erin.

I could turn her around against the wall, free my aching cock, and thrust into her now.

But it had been far too long since we'd been skin to skin, so I undressed quickly and pulled her to me, kissing her once more with wild abandon. God, the feel of her tongue, the sweet taste of her mouth, the warmth of her lips sliding against mine.

I could kiss her forever, and soon I would.

But now I needed her blood. The kiss had spiked my hunger, and I needed to slake it.

I broke the suction of our mouths with a smack and, for a moment, gazed at her exposed neck, the carotid of her pulse a mesmerizing cadence.

Then I struck, sinking my fangs into her softness.

She moaned, her breath a sweet breeze against my own bare neck. Her red gold flowed quickly from her artery, and

I gulped at it furiously. After a minute, I slowed, letting its sweet, intense flavor trickle over my tongue, all around my mouth and gums, before drizzling down my throat in a warm river.

She fed so much more than my body, even my heart, even my soul.

She fed everything that was me, everything that had been and would ever be me. Time had no meaning anymore. We were united as one in every dimension.

I could stay embedded in her forever, taking only the smallest drop of blood, but my cock had other ideas. Again, I considered turning her around quickly and thrusting into her, but I wanted so much to look at her, see her face, her sparkling green eyes, kiss her swollen red lips.

So I improvised. I pushed the computer monitor out of the way, set Erin on the desk, and spread her legs. Her fragrance wafted up to me once more, and I closed my eyes.

"I smell it too, Dante. It's us. The scent of us."

I groaned and pushed my cock into her wet pussy.

"God," she sighed.

"So good," I said. "Nothing has ever felt so good."

"Mmm, I know."

I kissed her lips as I slid back out and then into her again. Slowly, slowly... No, slow wasn't going to cut it. My need was too great, and from her moans when I quickened the pace, I knew she wanted speed as well.

I thrust into her again, her slick walls perfectly molding to my hard cock.

Again.

Again.

Again.

"Dante, Dante, I'm going to come!"

I clenched my teeth. "Come for me. Now!"

She spasmed against my erection, milking me, until my release shattered me with an intense explosion.

I let out a roar.

Vibrations surrounded us as we both continued our climaxes. The room was shaking, spiraling us out of control as my climax continued longer than it ever had before. With each pulse of her pussy walls, I spasmed again.

Again.

Again.

Again.

The filing cabinets rattled on the other side of the room, and the monitor toppled to the floor.

And still I came.

And still she came.

Until we both reached the pinnacle of our climaxes together.

TWENTY-ONE

Erin

Colors. Pinks, and blues, and bright sunny yellows.

And the music. Always the music. Soft jazz. A piano. A clarinet. Soft drum cadence.

The floating sensation as my climax reached its peak again and then again.

Had we floated again?

No, I was still sitting on the desk. Something was vibrating around us. "Oh my God! Dante!"

I looked down when he moved out of me. His legs were farther apart, and a narrow crack had manifested in the tile floor.

"What? What, baby?"

"Uh...I think you just made the earth move."

Dante's eyes widened. "I don't think it was me."

"It had to be."

"No, baby, it was us. It's always been us. You are part of this power I have. I'm certain of it."

"How can that be? I'm not always with you when it manifests."

"But you are my control. My reason and my control. Without you, the power would be dark. Dark and dangerous."

I smiled. "I think you're exaggerating, but I'm glad you want me to be a part of this."

"We need to finish the job we're doing," he said, his tone serious as he regarded the crack in the floor. "Right now, this underground fortress is collapsing."

I gasped. "Is it going to crumble on top of us?"

"I don't know. But you're shielded. You'll be protected."

"Dante, you told me the shield was against vampires who wished me harm. You didn't say anything about crumbling rock."

His eyes narrowed and shone with fright. "You're right. We need to finish this and get out of here."

"Find Bonneville. Put an end to her."

"How? She's immortal, if what the *Texts* say is true. How do you end an immortal?"

"I don't know." I willed my mind to think. "You've rendered her unconscious a couple times, but that's not enough. A virus, maybe?"

"She'd be immune. A gun won't work, and River and Jay are gone anyway. They were the only ones who carried guns."

"A wooden stake to the heart?"

"Not according to the *Texts*."

"True, but according to the *Texts* she does have one weakness. We just need to figure out what it is." I grabbed the book out of my pack and reread the part about male vampire blood.

"Male vampire blood has unique properties not present in blood from a female vampire. While it will cause changes in psyche and temperament, the effect won't be as pronounced as that from female blood. Its most profound effect, though, is prolonging the aging process. Any vampire who ingests male vampire blood will preserve his youth and vitality for as long as the ingestion continues. He will appear ageless, and indeed will never succumb to normal illness or injury. Any injury, even one seemingly fatal, will heal.

"Heed the warning, though. Male vampire blood has one major drawback, one that can never be reversed."

Then...gibberish.

Damn! I picked up the book, ready to hurl it across the room.

Dante stopped me, grabbing it from my hands. "You didn't let me do that. Remember?"

"But time is running out! This compound has been breached. The roof could cave in. We need answers, Dante!"

"Baby," he said, "you're not going to like this, but you need to leave."

"No."

"I've fed. I'll be okay. I'll take care of her and get out as quickly as I can, but I can't risk you, Erin. I just can't."

"I won't leave you here with her." I'd promised to end her myself for what she did to Dante. But how? I had no power. None whatsoever against an evil and immortal vampire doctor.

I tossed the book on top of my pack.

And it fell open to the same page.

"Dante, look." I picked it up again.

"Heed the warning, though. Male vampire blood has one

major drawback, one that can never be reversed. That which gives life is the one true rival and will bring the ultimate death."

"That which gives life?" Dante shook his head. "God? The universe?"

"Or something a little less intangible."

"Like what?"

"Don't be such a guy, Dante. A woman, of course. A woman gives life."

"I doubt Bonneville's mother is alive, since she herself is nearly two centuries old."

"True. She's probably rolling over in her grave somewhere," I said. "Wait! She'd be a ghost, right? Maybe we can summon her."

"My father said ghosts whose bodies have been gone for over ten years can no longer walk the earthly plane."

"Your mother did, in the graveyard."

"Yeah. That's still inexplicable to me."

"And your mother and my grandmother came to loved ones in dreams."

"Because the need was dire," Dante said thoughtfully.

"I'd say the need is pretty dire at the moment," I said.

"But neither of us are Bonneville's mother's loved ones."

"Maybe a medium could summon her," I said. "What about Bea?"

"Bea doesn't even realize she's a medium," he said. "Plus, ghosts go to her. She doesn't go to them."

"True." I pulled at my hair. "Damn!"

"Maybe it doesn't have to be her mother," Dante said. "Maybe any woman will do. Or any mother, at least."

"She's been around women and mothers many times.

Nothing happened."

"I guess it has to be her mother."

"Who's dead," I added and then jumped.

The door to the records room had opened.

"Get dressed," Bonneville said icily.

We were still naked from our lovemaking.

Dante raised his hand, but she stopped him with a gesture.

"I'm letting Erin go, Dante."

I whipped my hands to my hips, not giving a shit that I wasn't wearing a stitch of clothing. "I'm not going anywhere without him."

"Oh, you are. Isn't she, Dante?"

TWENTY-TWO

DANTE

This was the end.

The end of her.

Or the end of me.

She was willing to let Erin go because her beef was not with Erin.

It was with me.

I hadn't become the dark apocalyptic menace she'd been counting on, and she was immortal. She planned to take her revenge.

I nodded gravely. "Leave, Erin. You're protected."

"Whether she's protected has no bearing," Bonneville said. "I've instructed that she not be harmed. She will have safe passage out of here. On one condition."

"And that is?"

"You will meet *me* in the arena. One final fight. To the death."

Erin gulped audibly next to me. "No. No way. She's im—"

I quieted her with a gesture. "I know what I'm doing."

Though I didn't. I could render her unconscious, immobile, but I had no way of ending her life.

Once Erin was gone, I'd fight her.

"All right," I said. "I have a condition of my own."

"What is that?"

"No weapons. Only our bodies."

"As long as yours is clothed." She looked away. "You're quite a specimen, Dante. We could have done amazing things together. I agree to your terms. You may have unheard-of powers, but I have something you do not."

Immortality. Did she know that I knew? What the *Texts* had revealed to us?

"Dante"—Erin caressed my cheek—"No. Just no."

"It's the only way, baby. This is my fight. Not yours."

"What's yours is mine. That's what you've always told me." Erin turned to Bonneville. "You're a horrid, evil piece of shit! And to think I actually defended you at work. Said what a good physician you were."

"I've been a physician for longer than you know."

"I know that. We figured out your secret. There is no Zabrina Bonneville. No Zarah Le Sang. They're all *you*."

I stalked forward, but Erin grabbed my arm.

"You really expect me to leave Dante here alone? I love him! That's something you'll never understand."

"Dante is mine now. He's always been mine. And since things haven't quite gone as planned, he's now mine to destroy."

"You bitch!"

"Bitch. Queen. Whatever you wish to call me."

"You're no queen," I said quietly. "You were *never* a queen."

"I could have been, once I restored order. Don't underestimate me. My plans may have failed this time, but I will try again. 'Darkness rising. And we shall rise again!'"

Erin met my gaze.

"I love you," I said gravely.

"How touching," Bonneville said. "She leaves now, or I can't guarantee she'll get out of here in one piece."

"I've shield—"

"Your shield means I can't touch her. The Claiborne gang can't touch her. Do you think I don't have others than vampires to do my bidding? Who I can summon with a mere thought? She leaves now, or she stays, and your fate will also be hers."

My fate.

My fate was Erin.

I knew it as much as I knew my own name.

I would find a way to win this battle. I had to.

"Say your goodbyes," Bonneville said, walking out the door. "And for God's sake, get dressed. You have two minutes. I'll be waiting for you in the pit, Dante."

I grabbed Erin, skin to skin, and kissed her harshly.

An untamed kiss, a ferocious kiss.

And I was determined it wasn't a kiss goodbye.

But if it was? I wanted to taste every crevice of her mouth one more time.

One more time.

If only this kiss could last forever.

If only...

Against every instinct, I broke the kiss.

"No!" Erin screamed, tears streaming down her cheeks.

I brushed them away. "It's okay, baby. Have faith."

"But she—"

"Have faith." And maybe she'd have enough for me.

Erin sniffled and nodded, and then got dressed. I did the same.

I kissed her again, this time quickly. "Can you find your way out? I can come with you."

"No. I'll be okay. I'm more concerned about you."

"Have faith," I said again.

She caressed my cheek and ran her thumb over my bottom lip. "I love you so much, Dante. Please come back to me."

"I love you too, baby. Have faith."

She nodded and then walked out the door.

And I walked to the arena.

⚜

I jumped down into the pit, landing on both feet.

"Nicely done, Dante." She sighed. "You are truly magnificent. I feel a little like Pygmalion."

I said nothing.

"You were always undefeated," she said menacingly. "Today, that changes."

"Does it?" I said. "I've already proved I can pin you to a wall, immobilize you, and knock you unconscious."

"You can pin me to a wall now. I assure you that I'll outlast you."

"Eventually you'll need to feed."

"Will I?" She glared, her eyes blue ice.

Ice chilled my veins. Did immortality mean she could beat starvation? I'd eventually succumb to sleep, and she'd take my blood, which would keep her immortal. Was this truly a losing battle?

No. I refused to believe it. I'd come this far. I'd gotten everyone to safety. But how safe would they stay if *she* still existed?

"One way or another, I will end you." I hurled energy toward her and she landed against the wall.

She didn't lose consciousness this time. "Funny thing," she said. "My body tends to get used to things. You've pinned me against a wall, what? Three times now? Head gets harder every time. I won't lose consciousness again."

Red rage heated my blood, until I could almost see my skin burning. My father had taught me never to harm a woman, but this was no woman. This was a monster who had tortured and enslaved me, who threatened everything I believed in. "I. Will. Destroy. You." I raced into her, tackling her to the ground. I landed a punch square to her nose.

"Is that all you've got?" she gasped through the pouring blood. "Your girlfriend did better than that."

Darkness rising.

I summoned every last bit of dark energy, letting it simmer into a boil in my gut, and then I forced it through every cell of my body, pummeling her with my fists, my feet, my knees.

Soon she was a mass of blood and bruises.

But she remained conscious.

"I'll ask again," she rasped. "Is that all you've got?"

Again.

Again.

Again.

My muscles grew weary, but still I pummeled into her.

"I created you," she said with a choke.

"And I cast you out of my head!" I rose. "Stand up. You wanted this fight. Now stand up and take it."

She stood and was surprisingly nimble.

"News for you, Dante." She advanced toward me. "I was never in your head. If you perceived me there, *you* put me there!"

Was she lying? No. Her words rang true. It was always me. The darkness inside me. The darkness that *was* me.

She'd put it there, but I had learned to harness it and now I'd destroy her with it. I imagined a ball of energy in my hand, summoned it, and hurled it at her. She flew against the dirt wall.

But again, she didn't lose consciousness.

"You could have had"—*gasp*—"everything. I gave you"—*gasp*—"everything. I chose"—*gasp*—"you."

I hurled it at her again. Again. Again. "I don't need anything you could give me. Certainly not at the cost of others' lives."

"You're not the man I thought"—she coughed, blood sputtering out of her mouth—"you were. You...can't"—she gasped—"destroy me. You don't have...the power. We can stay down here for a lifetime"—*gasp*—"and I will be the victor. I promise you. As sure as the sun will rise"—*gasp*—"I promise you."

"The sun doesn't rise down here, my *queen*," I said sarcastically. "So maybe you don't—"

I stopped, a thought spearing into my mind.

That which gives life.

Then you know I'm perfectly safe here.

The sun.

Had she been in the sun? She'd gone to Erin's house to tell her about Patty and the baby and that she was going on vacation. All lies. When had that been?

Early in the morning, after Erin's shift. Perhaps the sun hadn't come up yet. Or perhaps it was a cloudy day.

I couldn't know for sure.

I met her icy-blue gaze. "*That which gives life is the one true rival and will bring the ultimate death.*"

Her eyes widened, and despite the darkness, her pupils

turned into pinpoints.

Emotion coiled through me. Could I do it? I'd forced a crack in the floor earlier when Erin and I had made love, but I no longer had her energy to supplement mine.

Plus, it could be nighttime, for all I knew. Daylight had no meaning underground.

Still, River and Uncle Brae had taken everyone out of here, and Erin would be safely above ground by now.

Have faith.

I had to try.

I breathed in, harnessing every bit of light energy, every bit of dark energy, every bit of rage for what she had done to my family and to me.

A fire burned in the pit of my belly, and my muscles tensed and tightened.

I bared my fangs, and they lengthened to their sharpest points ever with a snap no longer painful.

A snap signifying the energy rising within me.

Darkness rising.

And we shall rise again.

Yes, we would rise again.

As fate dictated. Without *her*.

I reached above my head, stretching my arms, and I roared.

A howling roar.

My whole body sizzled with energy. It flowed through me, saturating every cell within me, pinging and ponging until it rose, rose, rose...

Out my fingertips with an explosive blast.

Crack!

The ceiling hundreds of feet above us opened.

Widened.

And the rays of the sun stretched downward.

I shielded my eyes against the light.

A raspy scream gurgled from her throat.

"You brought it on yourself. No strength is without weakness, my *queen*!"

Another roar...

More sunlight...

"No! No! Not like— Aaauuuggghhh!"

Her skin melted on her face as if made of wax. Her screams turned to choking gasps as flames engulfed her.

Though tempted to look away, I watched. Watched without emotion as the self-styled vampire queen turned to ash.

When the last ember flickered out, I inhaled.

"*Vampyr omega*," I said softly.

Not the end of vampires, and not the end of humanity.

The end of *her*.

DANTE

"I can't understand how none of us felt it," Erin said, snuggling into my shoulder after some marathon lovemaking and feeding. "It should have felt like an earthquake. You must have glamoured the whole city into not feeling it."

"I have no idea," I said. "Not a clue. I'm just glad she's toast. Literally."

No truer words. I'd escaped quickly before the underground compound caved in, jumping over the still-unconscious Claiborne vampires. Good riddance. River and I had worked to have it backfilled as soon as I returned, my father and River glamouring anyone who witnessed the opening in the ground. That had taken some effort, but we were pretty sure we'd hit everyone.

I hadn't tried to use my strange powers since then. I wasn't sure I could.

"Seems all those vampire myths had true origins after all," Erin said. "Especially the one about the sun."

I nodded. I was glad it was over. My sister was healing

from her miscarriage. Jay hadn't left her side.

"Patty and her baby are doing well," Erin said. "They're home now."

"The baby won't require blood for a year," I said. "We'll have to tell Patty before then."

"I know." She sighed. "We'll figure something out. But for now, River took care of everyone involved. No one remembers anything. And Logan is getting the help he needs."

I bore no ill will toward Logan, and even River and my uncle were cutting him some slack. We were all just glad it was over.

Except that it wasn't.

We'd gotten rid of Dr. Bonneville and her plan to force the prophecy in the *Vampyre Texts* to life, but the issue of vampire breeding was still paramount.

Dr. Bonneville wasn't the only person interested in that endeavor.

Levi Gaston, another renowned vampire supremacist, had been, and the vampire council had secrets—secrets that Gaston's ghost hadn't wanted Bill divulging to us. The *Texts* were still filled with the unknown. Plus, another secret existed, if Bonneville had been telling the truth—a *family* secret.

I meant to uncover all of it. River and I had talked, and now I had to tell Erin what was coming next.

"Baby, this isn't over."

"I know. We're just beginning. We'll be together forever now."

I smiled. "We will. Once bonded, never broken." I kissed her forehead. "If the prophecy is true, our blood bond saved me. *You* saved me. But that's not what I mean."

"Oh?" She lifted her head.

"River and I have been talking. We're going after the council."

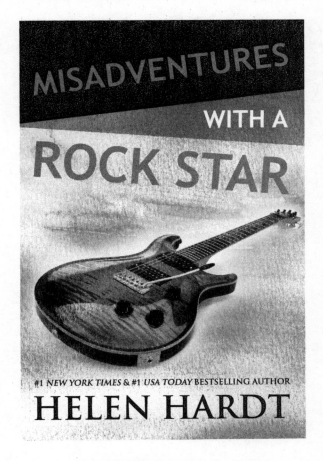

EXCERPT FROM
MISADVENTURES WITH A ROCK STAR

Why was I here again?

I stifled a yawn. Watching a couple of women do each other while others undressed, clamoring for a minute of the band's attention, wasn't my idea of a good time. The two women were gorgeous, of course, with tight bodies and big boobs. The contrasts in their skin and hair color made their show even more exotic. They were interesting to watch, but they didn't do much for me sexually. Maybe if I weren't so exhausted. I'd pulled the morning and noon shifts, and my legs were aching.

Even so, I was glad Susie had dragged me to the concert, if only to see and hear Jett Draconis live. His deep bass-baritone was rich enough to fill an opera house but had just enough of a rasp to make him the ultimate rock vocalist. And when he slid into falsetto and then back down to bass notes? Panty-melting. No other words could describe the effect. Watching him had mesmerized me. He lived his music as he sang and played, not as if it were coming from his mouth but emanating from his entire body and soul. The man had been born to perform.

A true artist.

Which only made me feel like more of a loser.

Jett Draconis was my age, had hit the LA scene around the same time I had, and he'd made it big in no time. Me? I was still a struggling screenwriter working a dead-end job waiting tables at a local diner where B-list actors and directors hung out. Not only was I not an A-lister, I wasn't even serving them. When I couldn't sell a movie to second-rate producer Rod Hanson? I hadn't yet said the words out loud, but the time had come to give up.

"What are you doing hanging out here all by yourself?"

Susie's words knocked me out of my barrage of self-pity. For a minute anyway.

"Just bored. Can we leave soon?"

"Are you kidding me? The party's just getting started." She pointed to the two women on the floor. "That's Janet and Lindy. Works every time. They always go home with someone in the band."

"Only proves that men are pigs."

Susie didn't appear to be listening. Her gaze was glued on Zane, the keyboardist, whose gaze was in turn glued on the two women cavorting in the middle of the floor. She turned to me. "Let's make out."

I squinted at her, as if that might help my ears struggling in the loud din. I couldn't possibly have heard her correctly. "What?"

"You and me. Kiss me." She planted a peck right on my mouth.

I stepped away from her. "Are you kidding me?"

"It works. Look around. All the girls do it."

"I'm not a girl. I'm a thirty-year-old woman."

"Don't you think I'm hot?" she asked.

"Seriously? Of course you are." Indeed, Susie looked great with her dark hair flowing down to her ass and her form-fitting leopard-print tank and leggings. "So is Angelina Jolie, but I sure as heck don't want to make out with her. I don't swing that way." Well, for Angelina Jolie I might. Or Lupita Nyong'o. But that was it.

"Neither do I—at least not long-term. But it'll get us closer to the band."

"Is this what you do at all the after-parties you go to?"

She giggled. "Sometimes. But only if there's someone as hot as you to make out with. I have my standards."

Maybe I should have been flattered. But no way was I swapping spit with my friend to get some guy's attention. They were still just men, after all. Even the gorgeous and velvet-voiced Jett Draconis, who seemed to be watching the floor show.

Susie inched toward me again. I turned my head just in time so her lips and tongue swept across my cheek.

"Sorry, girl. If you want to make out, I'm sure there's someone here who will take you up on your offer. Not me, though. It would be too...weird."

She nodded. "Yeah, it would be a little odd. I mean, we live together and all. But I hate that you're just standing here against the wall not having any fun. And I'm not ready to go home yet."

I sighed. This was Susie's scene, and she enjoyed it. She had come to LA for the rockers and was happy to work as a receptionist at a talent agency as long as she made enough money to keep her wardrobe in shape and made enough contacts to get into all the after-parties she wanted. That was the extent of her aspirations. She was living her dream, and she'd no doubt continue to live it until her looks gave out... which wouldn't happen for a while with all the Botox and plastic surgery available in LA. She was a good soul, but right now her ambition was lacking.

"Tell you what," I said. "Have fun. Do your thing. I'll catch an Uber home."

She frowned. "I wanted to show you a good time. I'm sorry I suggested making out. I get a little crazy at these things."

I chuckled. "It's okay. Don't worry about it."

"Please stay. I'll introduce you to some people."

"Any producers or directors here?" I asked.

"I don't know. Mostly the band and their agents, and of course the sound and tech guys who like to try to get it on with the groupies. I doubt any film people are here."

"Then there isn't anyone I need to meet, but thanks for offering." I pulled my phone out of my clutch to check the time. It was nearing midnight, and this party was only getting started.

"Sure I can't convince you to stay?" Susie asked.

"Afraid not." I pulled up the Uber app and ordered a ride. "But have a great time, okay? And stay safe, please."

"I always do." She gave me a quick hug and then lunged toward a group of girls, most of them still dressed, thank God.

I scanned the large room. Susie and her new gaggle of friends were laughing and drinking cocktails. A couple girls were slobbering over the drummer's dick. The two beautiful women putting on the sex show had abandoned the floor, and the one with dark skin was draped between the legs of Zane Michaels, who was, believe it or not, even prettier than she was. The other sat on Jett Draconis's lap.

Zane Michaels was gorgeous, but Jett Draconis? He made his keyboardist look average in comparison. I couldn't help staring. His hair was the color of strong coffee, and he wore it long, the walnut waves hitting below his shoulders. His eyes shone a soft hazel green. His face boasted high cheekbones and a perfectly formed nose, and those lips... The most amazing lips

I'd ever seen on a man—full and flawless. I'd gawked at photos of him in magazines, not believing it was possible for a man to be quite so perfect-looking—beautiful and rugged handsome at the same time.

Not that I could see any of this at the moment, with the blonde on top of him blocking most of my view.

I looked down at my phone once more. My driver was still fifteen minutes away. Crap.

Then I looked up.

Straight into the piercing eyes of Jett Draconis.

This story continues in
Misadventures with a Rock Star!

MESSAGE FROM HELEN HARDT

Dear Reader,

Thank you for reading *Undefeated*. If you want to find out about my current backlist and future releases, please like my Facebook page and join my mailing list. I often do giveaways. If you're a fan and would like to join my street team to help spread the word about my books. I regularly do awesome giveaways for my street team members.

If you enjoyed the story, please take the time to leave a review on a site like Amazon or Goodreads. I welcome all feedback.

I wish you all the best!
Helen

Facebook
Facebook.com/HelenHardt

Newsletter
HelenHardt.com/Sign-Up

Street Team
Facebook.com/Groups/HardtAndSoul/

ALSO BY HELEN HARDT

Blood Bond Saga:
Unchained: Volume One

Unhinged: Volume Two

Undaunted: Volume Three

Unmasked: Volume Four

Undefeated: Volume Five

The Steel Brothers Saga:
Craving
Obsession
Possession
Melt
Burn
Surrender
Shattered
Twisted
Unraveled
Breathless (June 25, 2019)
Ravenous (Coming Soon)
Insatiable (Coming Soon)

Misadventures Series:
Misadventures with a Rock Star

(with Meredith Wild)
Misadventures of a Good Wife

The Temptation Saga:
Tempting Dusty
Teasing Annie
Taking Catie
Taming Angelina
Treasuring Amber
Trusting Sydney
Tantalizing Maria

The Sex and the Season Series:
Lily and the Duke
Rose in Bloom
Lady Alexandra's Lover
Sophie's Voice

Daughters of the Prairie:
The Outlaw's Angel
Lessons of the Heart
Song of the Raven

ACKNOWLEDGMENTS

Completing a saga is bittersweet for me. I'll miss Dante and Erin, but I'm knee deep into writing Marjorie Steel's story to continue the Steel Brothers Saga, and I'm excited about new projects to come.

Special thanks to the following individuals who helped make this saga happen:

Karen Aguilera, Brian Archer, Jennifer Becker, Haley Byrd, Alma Chapa, Jessica Clements, Jeanne De Vita, Carol Ann Doveatt, Linda Pantlin Dunn, Yvonne Ellis, Martha Frantz, Debbie Gilbert, Amy Grishman, David Grishman, Lia Fairchild, Theresa Finn, Rebecca Jacobs, Tina Jaworski, Jesse Kench, John Lane, Haidée La Pointe, Robyn Lee, Michele Lehman, Jonathan Mac, Amber Maxwell, Dean McConnell, Eric McConnell, Grant McConnell, Dave McInerney, Michele Hamner Moore, Toni Paul, Angel Payne, Lauren Rowe, Krystin Sanchez, Chrissie Saunders, Scott Saunders, J.S. Scott, Wendy Shatwell, Celina Summers, Angela Tyler, Kurt Vachon, Kathy West, and Meredith Wild.

You all rock!

Thank you most of all to everyone who read and loved Dante and Erin. You are why I write.

ABOUT THE AUTHOR

#1 *New York Times*, #1 *USA Today*, and #1 *Wall Street Journal* bestselling author Helen Hardt's passion for the written word began with the books her mother read to her at bedtime. She wrote her first story at age six and hasn't stopped since. In addition to being an award-winning author of contemporary and historical romance and erotica, she's a mother, an attorney, a black belt in Taekwondo, a grammar geek, an appreciator of fine red wine, and a lover of Ben and Jerry's ice cream. She writes from her home in Colorado, where she lives with her family. Helen loves to hear from readers.

Visit her at HelenHardt.com